Cast Away Stones

Cast Away Stones

By Katherine Imogene Youngblood

Lead Editor: Hamishe Randall
Cover Design: Amy Vega
Interior Design: Lisa DeSpain
Cover Photography: Brooke Sexton Photography

Indigo River Publishing
3 West Garden Street Ste. 352
Pensacola, FL 32502
www.indigoriverpublishing.com

Ordering Information:
Quantity sales: Special discounts are available on quantity purchases by corporations, associations, and others. For details, contact the publisher at the address above.

Orders by U.S. trade bookstores and wholesalers: Please contact the publisher at the address above.

Printed in the United States of America

Publisher's Cataloging-in-Publication Data is available upon request.
Library of Congress Control Number: 2017933803

ISBN: 978-0-9972945-7-6
First Edition

With Indigo River Publishing, you can always expect great books, strong voices, and meaningful messages.
Most importantly, you'll always find…words worth reading.

DEDICATION

Dedicated to the memory of my parents,
William and Imogene

"For everything there is a season,
and a time for every matter under the heavens…
a time to cast away stones,
and a time to gather stones together."
Ecclesiastes 3

PROLOGUE
1848

It had been one of those satisfying evening rides, hot, but with a breeze just before the sunset. She had worn her brother's old breeches beneath her skirts, a trick she had discovered that guarded against discomfort, and when she dismounted her horse and entered the barn, her mind was still miles away from the real world.

A muffled cry turned her head toward the corner stall. Bessie! When she saw them in the hay, she felt the blood drain from her face. He had her down in the hay and was violating her. She could see Bessie's panicked wild eyes calling to her from within dark skin beneath his heaving brutality. Dropping her horse's reins, she grabbed the only weapon at hand. A pitchfork.

Then she took aim against him as hard as she could.

Louisiana

Chapter 1

With the earliest whisper of daybreak, the sound of slaves making their way to the cutting fields carried across the meadow. In the outer paddock, the young woman stood next to a large nut-brown horse, adjusting his bridle, and for a moment she took a deep nervous breath as he stood alert, his velvety ears turned forward, waiting to be mounted.

Catarine Dupre then lifted her flounced cotton skirts, placed her booted left foot in the dangling stirrup, and mounted the horse like a man. The horse, spry in the morning coolness, immediately began a fast walk as she took her seat, wetting its hooves in the dewy grasses as they walked along the fence line of the property.

Across the wide lawn, she could see that her home was still silent. Just beyond its porches, the wooden-framed slave houses already stirred with their morning issue of smoke as they sat surrounding the big house like a crescent moon. Noting the purple sky had given way to the urgency of orange daybreak, Catarine, aware that all things living and breathing that worked together for the production of sugarcane would soon begin, knew she must make her escape at once.

Catarine's heart hammered in her ears as she cantered in wide circles, building courage to jump the pasture fence. It had been a desire of hers to ride Atlas but she never thought she would, much less steal him. She swallowed hard, adjusted her seat, and gave him the neck reins he needed to clear the fence.

This was it. She kicked him into a fast pace straight for the fence which would take them onto the path and through the woods beyond. Sailing over the fixed wooden barrier was the easy part. He went airborne effortlessly, touching nothing, the sound of him catching his breath echoing in the breeze. They came down with a hard landing but Catarine maintained her balance.

Atlas knew what to do. Perhaps he'd been this way before, for he never slowed his pace. His rhythmic equine puffs, along with the triad hoof strokes against the supple earth were the first harmonious peals of freedom to Catarine. Atlas dodged the low branches of the magnolia trees and maneuvered swiftly through the gnarled root system that the occasional oak spilled into the well-worn path. He ran as though being pursued, and as if, he too, had been longing for an escape, his black mane flying behind him freely. Catarine had cantered her own horse down this familiar path, ducking under the low-lying branches many times before. These were her woods.

She urged him on until they'd cleared the woods that separated private acreage from the wild. A sharp pang of sadness stung her heart as they crossed the meadow and into the next thicket. In Catarine's mind, an image flashed of her mother awakening, believing it to be a day as any other. Her mother would presently find the note she'd left in her own room; the note Catarine had carefully written in her best hand on the rosebud note paper. Yet, her mother would not find it strange to know of Catarine's plans, for it was a lie her mother would not disbelieve. The fabrication was, after all, a necessary one. She'd lied to her mother before and felt no guilt, although perhaps she should have, but this requisite deception, curiously, made her heart burn with aching remorse.

Catarine envisioned her mother wearing one of her silken robes, easing into her morning, and sipping tea left for her by Bessie. Poor Bessie! Last night, Bessie had come to her room and pleaded with her not to go. She'd asked her if there was another way, but Catarine had already hatched this plan of escape. And because of the horrific event that had occurred only hours before, well beyond their control, she and Bessie were now both free of their foe.

Catarine rode on through mid-morning and saw no one, heading southward towards the city of New Orleans. She entered a cool thicket that was overshadowed by oaks draped with moss that made a canopy with fine shade. Catarine stopped Atlas, dismounted, and while allowing him to eat the woodland greenery, she fetched her leather water bottle from the saddle bag. And as she leaned against the trunk of a gnarled oak, she appraised her situation.

Adjusting her corset, she felt the cash within that she'd layered just so to take on her journey. Feeling the thickness of currency gave her relief, assurance that she was prepared. However, time was of the essence, and she must be moving on.

The rhythmic buzzing of tree locusts commenced their droning and would continue until nightfall. The humid air moistened her skin and clothes so that her underclothes clung to her. She knew that prolonged hours in the saddle would tax her and she was anxious to shed her garments. As they moved through the last area of woods next to the Mississippi River, Catarine decided it was time to carry out a crucial part of her plan.

She found a thick area of woods to make her transformation. She tied Atlas to a small tree to graze while she quickly made her switch. She opened her saddlebag and withdrew her items. On top, wrapped carefully in two handkerchiefs, was the doll Bessie had given her years ago. They'd traded doll babies as little girls playing behind the smokehouse, their favorite place to pretend. Then she readied her brother's old clothes that she had brought with her. Despite the fact that they were contained in leather, Andre's clothes still held a vestige of his own scent, a combination of musk and coffee.

Being only a year apart, the two of them had been very close. Catarine was the eldest sibling and the strongest as it turned out. Andre hadn't been excessively weak, not like the rest of them, the babies their mother lost shortly after birth. His weakness came later in life. With a perpetually mourning mother, she and her brother were left to amuse themselves or, after the cane was seen to, at their Daddy's feet.

Smiling, she lifted her skirts and removed all her undergarments, then placed the breeches on her bottom and fastened the waist band. She then removed the damp dress over her head, and keeping her corset in place, donned both undershirt and shirt. She ended with a twist of her hair, pinned up with fasteners, then sat the cap over all her locks, hoping she looked convincingly boyish. As much as she loathed the idea, she kept her dress, stuffing it in the saddlebag. It would most likely be needed where she was going. And, she feared it wouldn't be in her favor if found discarded.

The ride to New Orleans promised to be long so her intention was to keep Atlas at a walk most of the way and attempt to stay on dry land. With the Mississippi to the south of her, she followed its meandering shores a stone's throw away remaining just next to the bushes and on top of the levee.

It was Atlas' ears turned forward and his sudden tension that warned her that someone or something was nearby. He startled at what sounded like the shuffle of leaves at the same time a flock of birds took their flight towards the river, and then stood stock still listening. When nothing was heard in the next few seconds, Catarine wondered if they'd caught the sound of a squirrel or some such feral creature when Atlas' nose quivered and, with the toss of his head, urged her to proceed. They went on a few paces, Atlas pulling at the reins to go faster. She allowed him to go into a trot, but held him off from an all-out run in the unfamiliar area.

That's when the piercing staccato yap broke into the stagnant air. The barking stretched into a howl that poured across the midday sky. A bloodhound had come between them and the Mississippi River.

She turned Atlas in a northeast direction, away from the levee. The bloodhound caught sight of them and gave chase. As Atlas leaped over a log and cantered into the brush field, Catarine felt herself nearly slip off the saddle, but she quickly righted herself as they bolted toward a level expanse. Human voices drifted in pieces to her ears, confirming that the hound wasn't alone. The voices were not familiar which gave Catarine hope that last night's deed hadn't been discovered. She allowed Atlas to open into a full gallop, leaving the dog farther behind.

She then pressed him into a more wooded area as soon as she found a grove of trees sufficient to hide them. She knew swamp was somewhere north of them and she didn't want to get drawn too far off from the Mississippi. All sounds of her pursuers eventually ceased and the only noise she heard was the whirr of insects around her head.

She used this time to adjust herself in the saddle and shorten her stirrups a notch to prepare for any other unexpected jump. Her forearms were starting to ache as she realized she'd been clenching the reins like a vice. She tried to relax and lean back, dangling her long legs as her horse meandered along, grazing on the occasional fern.

She led Atlas to a creek where he pawed the water, splashing them both, and then settled on sucking as much as possible through his bit. Hovering insects inspected the both of them, while Atlas swatted wildly with his tail, swinging the black coarse strands from side to side, whipping Catarine's legs in the process, but when Catarine received a painful sting from the newly arriving yellow flies, she backed both of them away from the bog and withdrew to a grassy area.

They walked for several miles and had seen no life except a large gator they'd frightened away from its repose. Although they were a good distance away, Catarine spotted the shacks of the impoverished souls who made their living in the swamp. She stopped her horse and looked from afar through the trees at these dwellings, built of mud and moss, and knew with consternation that they had entered the area in Louisiana most feared by passersby.

These were the Acadian folk who trapped and fished the land and waters along the river, selling crawfish nearby, who eked out a living purely by their grit and mettle. She remembered seeing them for the first time when she was around five years old. They had come to her plantation, a caravan of them, selling their freshly gathered mudbugs and yards of boudin. They jostled up through the trees and stopped in the carriage path where she'd been playing alone. An older man had addressed her. She knew he'd spoken French but still she couldn't understand his speech. She ran inside for her Papa. While they transacted, she'd listened carefully, fascinated, her Papa understanding the strange dialect.

She'd also noticed the children all looking out at her, equally absorbed in watching her and listening. She waved to them but they made no response, as if the gesture was foreign or misunderstood. One of the boys, she remembered, had scooped out the live crawfish from a box in the back of their wagon with his bare hands and placed them in a cloth sack for them. They'd crawled up his arm and some scattered on the ground as he worked. She was astonished at his disregard and learned later that these bugs lived in the soil near her very home. These people, her father told her, lived completely off the land and he respected them. As she passed near them she was reminded that they knew every inch of this swamp near the Mississippi and she didn't. Nonetheless, she intended to proceed unnoticed.

They inched along silently on damp grasses, managing to choose steps that kept them away from the bog. Warm moss flourished on each tree and the thick air blew over and around them. Catarine was astonished when they came upon a young boy, not more than six or seven years old, squatting on one of the grassy patches like a frog, holding an oyster knife, opening and scooping out his lunch from shellfish he took one by one from his waist bag. He was shirtless and his feet were bare. Catarine silently watched as he worked the shells open expertly with the enormous knife, then using the shell as a cup, held his head high and tipped the mollusk contents into his mouth with a sucking sound. He did this over and over. He must have eaten ten or twelve of them before looking straight up into Catarine's eyes impassively, which took her by surprise.

He then looked straight back to his work as if she was of no account, an insect or wild animal that he wasn't troubled about in the least. As she turned to go, thinking it the best action, she heard him speak in Acadian French, "Trespassers not 'llowed on our land, or you find yourself en difficulté." She turned back around in the saddle and saw that he was still about his knife work hunched down. Straightaway, she turned Atlas aside from the Acadian dwellings and picked up his gait.

Only a few paces away the ground grew wetter and spongier. Every turn they took seemed to be the wrong choice. Atlas grew reluctant and wanted to turn back but she pressed him on in the one direction she thought correct. He took a step on a green grassy area that looked promising but instead of grass they found muck that grabbed his hooves and aimed to not let go.

Catarine knew not to dismount in this mess. She let him have full control of his situation with all the reins he needed and lifted her feet up off his sides. It was a struggle as he used his powerful neck for leverage, but one by one, he managed to release his limbs from the filth, throwing his massive head backwards several times until they were out. After that, Catarine rubbed and patted his mud-flecked, vein-swollen neck and then let Atlas take his own course. He headed swiftly towards the lightest part of the woods where the afternoon sun was streaming in with promise.

As Catarine came to the north side of New Orleans, she was faced with the thing she'd most dreaded so far; she let Atlas go. She knew she had to do it and had utmost confidence in his ability to find his way home.

Speaking gently to him and giving him unhurried caresses, she said a grateful good-bye. Catarine then broke off his reins but left his bridle and saddle in place, then shoed him on back in the direction from which they came. She then started her walk towards New Orleans, looking quite like a boy, saddlebag slung across her shoulder.

By dusk, she found herself approaching the busy city at the corner of Esplanade and Broad Streets. She could see the street grooms preparing for night by lighting the torches along the north side of the street. The city had the magical glow of merriment, the lights bright and dancing. The Dupres had frequently, along with many other plantation families, visited New Orleans during holiday seasons, staying in downtown apartments, many riding back and forth in the new steamboats that arrived near their front doors along the levees of the great river.

Catarine knew to stay clear of the area where family friends might be, but the season was right for her to get lost in the city. It was cane cutting season and hot summer at that. The only visitors from the plantations might be a few bored women shopping for the latest French fashion, as the note to her mother had indicated she would be doing. The odds were on her side to simply disappear, especially dressed as a boy.

She knew that Hotel Bourbon was a favorable place to stay and she hoped it would be the place for her to hide out incognito. Her mother had warned her against the seedy parts of the city that bred the yellow fever everyone was in fear of contracting. So, she pulled her cap down over her eyes and headed for Orleans Street.

She spent the next few hours at the window of her rented room. She never saw anyone she knew beneath her on the street below. She collected her wits, renewed her plans as well as her determination and she reminded herself that she was safe. They wouldn't be looking for her anyway. Not yet. Her mother would tell everyone of the note that she'd found, telling her Catarine had gone to New Orleans to shop for several days. This wouldn't be suspicious. But they would look for her stepbrother, Mason, when they noticed he was missing. And they'd be even more alarmed if his horse Atlas made it back to the plantation. The frantic search for Mason would begin, but they wouldn't find him. No one would ever find Mason because he was buried beneath the grain barrels in the barn.

Chapter 2

Simply going down to the lobby to snatch a few morsels of food became quite an adventure. Arriving there, Catarine heard divine music coming from the floor above, an exquisite minuet she'd remembered from sometime before. A spiral staircase ushered her to the foyer of the second floor but when she entered the ballroom through the side doors, she felt like she had ascended into another kingdom. The grand ballroom was filled with the most beautiful women that she had ever seen, each covered in exotic colored satins that were an exhibition of splendor before her. She realized that this was one of the famed quadroon balls!

The boldest and most captivating commodities in the entire ballroom were these women's bosoms, which were gloriously powdered and presented framed in lace, their only competition being the owners' equally alluring faces trimmed with flowers and feathers of every color and style. Each young woman was a genuine charm, exquisitely fashioned to accentuate their beauty as the men circulated them. The silver and crystal clinked and danced around them as well, but each woman, whether they were dancing, sitting, or laughing still seemed to take center focus of their given area as the room floated and spun about them and their bosoms.

Catarine, thinking of her own small mounds, bound and invisible under her white baggy shirt, paused to admire the sensational display. The loveliest woman in the entire ball-room, dressed in a pale peach evening dress of silk and rich lace, had been laughing and inspiring a crowd, which had gathered on all sides about her as she told a tale. A green, heart shaped medallion strung on a black velvet ribbon lay upon her ravishing chest, and matching ear medallions swayed back and forth by her face as she laughed. Abruptly, the beautiful woman stopped laughing and looked directly at Catarine with interest, which made Catarine turn away with her cheeks aglow.

Trying to find her way back to the door proved difficult. She'd only wandered away a bit but throngs of people had been pouring in and against her which made movement nearly impossible. What's more, she was not dressed properly, and it was obvious to all that she was in the wrong location. Indeed, dressed as a young man, Catarine looked as if she should be attending the arriving guests' horses or perhaps washing up out back. There were so many people crammed in, and with sweat and drunkenness ensuing, if the butler had allowed another ten inside, the walls would have certainly collapsed.

A nearby garçon yelled at her, "Boy, get back to the kitchen!"

"Wait! He's with me!" the peach beauty yelled, lurched herself in Catarine's direction and grabbed her arm.

"All right, my apologies, Mademoiselle," he replied to her.

"So, what's your name, *girl?*" the silk-clad quadroon whispered to Catarine.

When she came near her ear, Catarine could smell brandy and sweet gardenia. Catarine expelled the breath she was holding and nearly collapsed as she stood eye-to-eye with the stunning young woman. The woman held her steady by the shoulders with strong arms, her bejeweled clutch and fan both swinging unobtrusively from her left arm.

"I, I, my name is Catarine."

"Don't worry, I'm not going to tell anyone you aren't a boy," she reassured her, leaning in with a grin. "But you must tell me your tale! You must have something most interesting to say about yourself, going about in breeches."

"How did you know?"

"Your eyes. They are most lovely!"

Catarine's breath grew rapid and labored and she tried to pass beyond the beautiful young woman to escape the crowd as well as the interrogation.

"Quick, let's get out of here now while my mother isn't looking," the beauty spoke again, grabbing Catarine's hand and pulling her along towards the rear door as a few men were beginning to head their way. Behind them couples lined up to dance to a new waltz that was starting. It was Strauss' Viennese Carnival. Catarine recognized the opening measures.

They retreated through curtains and a small door, taking the staircase to the ground floor and into a quiet back hallway, and turning, came upon one of the young women and a gentleman engaged in what Catarine instantly knew was meant by a word her mother had used: Cuckoldry. The woman appeared bored by the situation, which was remarkable due to its personal and sultry nature. The older gentleman was kissing and licking the woman's neck and was pulling at the décolletage edge of the poor woman's dress, attempting to dislodge her breasts, or so Catarine feared. Catarine quite forgot her manners and stood stock still to watch them, having never seen or even heard of such hedonistic behavior. The peach-dressed quadroon pulled her along again.

"What were they doing?" Catarine exclaimed.

"Une aventure passionnée! I don't think it requires an explanation."

They entered a small sitting room and sat down together on a settee, or rather Catarine was forced down. Then the young woman extended her hand properly and said, "I'm Daria Morinay. Don't you have breasts?" She peered into the loose white shirt that Catarine was wearing.

"Yes. Just barely. But, I'd be much obliged if you didn't look at them now." Catarine's eyes returned to the large breasts of Daria Morinay, which were directly before her.

"All right, tell me why you are dressed like a boy." Daria scooted closer to Catarine on the settee and peered intently into her eyes with a look of delight, as if expecting a long, interesting story.

"I ran away from home," Catarine shrugged and averted her eyes, afraid to look into Daria's inquisitive face.

"Is that all?" Daria's lovely eyes narrowed. Catarine noticed them to be a slightly greenish, hazel color, nevertheless, very large and expressive.

"Yes, that's all," said Catarine, looking away. She couldn't tell a fib and look anyone squarely in the eyes. "And I'm afraid my stepfather will fetch me back." There was enough truth in that statement to suffice.

Daria began stroking her hand and then gently turned Catarine's head back to face her, examining her eyes as if she were a physician.

"Pardon me for saying so, but there's more to your story. I'm no fool. In fact, I can always tell if someone is lying to me. What else are you hiding?"

Daria spoke the words pleasant enough; she wasn't being rude, rather, she was almost giddy with excitement. Catarine played with the seams of her breeches after she'd retrieved her hands from Daria's clutches. Her new friend's eyes danced with humor and expectation, which disarmed Catarine in spite of her loathing to confide in anyone.

"Nothing! Nothing at all!" Catarine whined, sounding like a small girl, meeting Daria's gaze for a moment before averting her eyes again.

"That's not true. But I'll make a deal with you. If you want to stay hidden, you should come with me tonight, away from this crowded hotel in the center of town. I'm going to my grandmother's house."

Catarine considered this proposition. She certainly liked this Daria Morinay!

"All right. I'll go with you."

"Come along now and you can tell me your story later. At least you look enough like a boy to fool anyone!" Daria exclaimed dramatically, standing up, clapping and twirling her skirt around in a circle a couple of times as she moved across the room.

"I didn't fool you at all!"

"That's different. I'm not just anyone." She laughed. "I notice people. Especially if they are…uncommon."

Catarine noticed that Daria alternated between grand hand gestures including using her fan, and kind, personable ones that were almost too friendly for someone whom one just met.

"Well…thank you…I suppose."

"Come on, let's hurry. I'm afraid my mother'll be coming."

Daria gathered Catarine up, whose hair had started coming unpinned and falling down from under her cap, making her disguise perilously absurd, and walked her out the door and along dark Orleans Street. They passed revelers and couples, but due to the hour, all were engaged in their own affairs and not heeding the "young man" and the quadroon and they walked along arm in arm.

"Where are we going?" Catarine asked.

"Pauger Street."

The two women shuffled along, each with their own new curiosities and doubts of each other. Catarine was too tired to argue but happy to have a friend. Daria was full of energy and also rapturous at the thought, not only of having a new friend, but a French runaway. And she also longed for a diversion from her mother's ongoing expectation of a marriage de la main gauche.

"She is my grandmother but everyone calls her Auntie Rose," Daria whispered as her manner changed suddenly. They entered the house quietly and crept into the parlor on tiptoes. "Shhh! I think she is asleep already. Let's just go on upstairs."

Catarine nodded her head in agreement and followed Daria up to a charming little room that contained, to Catarine's dismay, too many mirrors. There, she helped Daria take off her ball gown which Daria surprisingly just threw on the chaise lounge with disgust.

"Let me find you something comfortable," Daria said as she rummaged through her drawers for undergarments and lacy slips. "You are smaller than I but this should do. Would you like a bath?"

"Won't we wake your grandmother, er, Auntie?"

"I suppose so."

To Catarine's surprise, Daria helped her undress also. Then moments later, they lay face to face on the iron bed like old friends. Catarine didn't know what to say and she was the worst for making small talk.

"This is a lovely house," was all she could think of saying.

"Yes, Auntie's rich. Are you surprised?"

"No, I guess not."

"Where are you from?"

"I lived on a plantation on the River. But I've been here before. I know about, er, things in New Orleans." Catarine stumbled.

"You mean the ball where we were earlier? Or my colored grandmother being rich?"

"Both, I guess." Catarine said and laughed. "Yes, I know about les gen de couleur libres. Tell me about the quadroon balls."

"I'd rather talk about slavery."

"Really? You seemed to be having a grand time at the ball."

"I think the entire practice should go away. Our mothers take us to show us off with the hopes we can catch a rich husband." Daria spit the words out as if they tasted bitter. "That's the last thing I want!"

"Hmmm. What do you want?" Catarine asked.

"To travel. Or go to university like a man." Daria answered wearily. "That won't happen in this country. I studied for a short while in France. My father sent me. But it only made me want more. Here we are all expected to either run a business or be a second wife to a white man."

They both were quiet for a while looking up at the wooden ceiling slats and feeling the night breeze blow over them.

"I've been doing all the talking. Now I want to hear about you."

Catarine felt suddenly tired. Part of her wanted to share about her hopes and dreams, as Daria had done freely, but she held back. Disclosing her personal thoughts was not her forte. Still, she found her new friend to be extraordinarily disarming. So she took a deep breath and plunged into what proved to be, from Daria's rapt interest, an absorbing description of her childhood, which including being tutored at home mostly by her father, riding horses daily, and running the grounds with the slave children. They talked until the sky was beginning to lighten into a new day.

Catarine opened her eyes to find that it was not just a lovely dream. She was actually in New Orleans, in a new and very interesting place. She loosened herself from the tangled quilt, arose from the bed slowly and left the sleeping Daria. She crept down the stairs where she smelled coffee stronger with each step. Stopping on the bottom steps, and from around the corner she viewed the woman who must have been Auntie Rose. She sat at a little table that was draped with lace on which sat a flowered tea set. The woman sat stirring her tea with one hand and reading what looked like a Bible.

"I see you there lookin' at me," the woman said without looking up. "Come on down and get you some breakfast."

Catarine eased around the corner and crept into the room where the old lady sat, the daylight streaming in behind her tapestry padded chair giving her a queenly glow that settled around her like a shawl draped over her shoulders. Her golden skin was both wrinkled and healthy, her black hair looped in a plaited knot behind her with only an inkling of grey at her temples. Buoyant, green eyes finally looked up from their reading to appraise her visitor.

"And who might you be?" she spoke again, amused, this time leaning back and taking in the full view of Catarine standing in Daria's pantaloons just inside the doorway.

"I'm Daria's new friend," Catarine said as she suddenly began hearing her heartbeat in her ears.

"Don't you got a name?" Auntie's voice rose at least an octave. Catarine considered lying for half a second.

"My name is Catarine."

"And your last name is?" Catarine groaned at this, and licked her dry lips. Auntie must have noticed her reluctance because she said, "Girl, you tell the truth and all of it in this house. But it stay here with me. Ya hear?"

"Catarine Dupre," Catarine said with a frown on her face.

Auntie started shaking her head from side to side and began the process of standing. Once on her feet she was quick to walk to the kitchen and Catarine followed her, surprised at the height and strength of the old woman.

"If your name is all you can tell me, so be it. Get you some food. Maggie, feed this girl."

She spoke to the black woman who Catarine hadn't seen yet. Then Auntie disappeared. Maggie was a very dark black woman, dressed in a striped gray maid's frock, who came to Catarine, and without speaking or looking directly at her, took her by the arms and sat her down at the kitchen table. She then proceeded to bring her an abundance of food and coffee. While Catarine was eating and Maggie was shuffling back and forth in the kitchen, Daria entered looking for her.

"Oh, here you are!"

"Mmm, yes, this is really good!"

"Why are you eating in here?"

"Your Auntie asked Maggie to get me breakfast."

"In here?" Daria exclaimed. "You've met Auntie Rose? I guess it didn't go well."

"I didn't think it went badly," Catarine said after a gulp of sweetened coffee.

"I'll fix it; don't worry. I see you have a great appetite. She will like that!"

"Oh, not really. I just didn't eat anything last night. What do you mean 'fix it'?"

"Nothing…"

Daria sat with Catarine as she finished her large breakfast. Maggie set tea in a china cup down before Daria who thanked her warmly and caressed Maggie's arm for a moment. Maggie smiled but remained silent.

"I'll see to it that you can stay as long as you like, Catarine. But we will have to talk to Auntie Rose. You will have to talk to her."

"I appreciate everything, truly I do," Catarine began her explanation. "But I do not want to impose. I have means to stay elsewhere. And speaking of that, I must to go back to my room in Hotel Bourbon. I have possessions there."

"If you are hiding, that is not the place to be," Daria warned. "Take my advice. You'll be spotted if you stay in the center of town. Of course, it depends on how badly you wish to remain free. You were, after all, dressed up like a boy."

"I really don't need my stepfather finding me."

"Won't your mother miss you?" Daria asked with concern in her eyes. She reached out to touch Catarine's arm when she didn't answer directly.

"Yes," Catarine finally said with eyes downcast.

A few moments later she looked up into Daria's eyes and neither could smile. Catarine had tears in her eyes and the grim look of tragedy. As if to change the mood, Daria rose and twirled as she had done the night before, only this time she had no full skirt to flare about her.

"That settles it. We can fetch your stuff and you'll stay with me for now," Daria said decidedly, although Catarine wasn't sure this was the best course of action. "I have work to do in town anyway. You shall come along." She smiled back at Catarine with a mischievous twinkle in her eye.

They went back to Daria's room to dress, Daria in a lovely blue frock that made her look like a milk maid, her hair done up in a white tignon. Catarine dressed herself in the old boy breeches and white shirt and began the job of pinning up her locks as she stood looking out the back window. Daria produced a mirror for her.

"No, please take that thing away," Catarine complained, holding up her hand against it. "I can do this without a looking glass."

"How can you do up your hair without it? Besides, you look so lovely."

"I hate those things."

"Well, let me at least help you. You need to make sure you can look like a boy in the day light. A harder task than last night when no one was looking at stable boys," Daria giggled.

They set out back to town with Daria walking along properly holding a portfolio of papers to deliver for her grandmother's business affairs. Catarine played her part well, shuffling along and taking large strides, and spinning around the gas lampposts. They laughed at the foolishness of it all although no passerby knew why.

"Slow down!" Daria exclaimed. "I can hardly keep up with you! Have you done this before?"

"Not really, although I've dressed up as a boy before."

"Well, then you have!"

"I meant I've never been on the run; I've never run away before."

"You must be in the habit of running though, because you are quite spirited."

When they reached the downtown area, they decided to split up, Catarine going into her room to fetch her stuff and Daria to do her first business errand at the bank nearby. Catarine walked down Orleans Street to the hotel thinking that she wasn't quite sure what she wanted to do. She was quite taken with Daria. And she needed a friend, especially one who knew the area. Catarina reached the hotel and just as she was entering the lift, a man in a brown suit came out of the one adjacent to hers that made her gasp and sent her heart racing. Her stepfather's solicitor!

She wondered if he was in New Orleans looking for her or her stepbrother or on some other business matter. But either way, she must not be spotted by him. She made the decision then and there to gather all her belongings, which consisted mainly of her money, and to get out without being seen. She was so thankful she had possessed the presence of mind to check in under the false name, Andre Monroe. She got safely out the side entrance, saddlebag in hand, and as she was forced to view herself in the mirror, found she still looked quite boyish. Outside in an adjacent alley, she took the opportunity to smudge a little dirt on her hands and face to add a finishing touch.

"Have you been in a fight?" Daria exclaimed when she saw Catarine's smutty face, finding her leaning in a derelict manner against the brick wall, legs wide open and hands pocketed.

"No, I saw someone I know. I hope to not be spotted."

"And how can you stand like that? If I hadn't seen you clothe yourself, I'd swear you *are* a boy!"

"Can we get back soon?"

"I guess you've made up your mind then." Daria was openly delighted.

"Yes, but I'm really worried."

Catarine became somewhat irritated that Daria was finding this situation so amusing but, to be reasonable, she didn't know the half of it.

"What's the worst that could happen? They really can't make you come home. You're of age, right?"

"Yes, but…"

"Well, then cheer up! And let's have some fun!" Catarine forced a smile on her face as they went along again. This time she wasn't running along and swinging around lamp poles. She merely walked along beside Daria, listening to her talk. The rest of Daria's business went along well with her delivering rental agreements to tenants and getting signatures and payments from various people. Catarine was surprised at the extent of her grandmother's holdings but it wasn't discussed.

When they returned home, Daria told her to go upstairs and change her clothes and return back to the parlor. There, she would present her properly to Auntie Rose. Catarine's dirty, wrinkled frock was not a garment in which to impress one's potential landlord but it was all she had at the moment. Catarine hoped that Daria would explain. As she mounted the stairs she began dreading the whole evening ahead. She hoped Daria would explain much and that she would only have to confirm the story when she was summoned to the room. When she turned the doorknob and entered, she was astonished to find a new dress, pressed and hanging against the chiffonier in Daria's room.

Clean undergarments had been draped across the bed that looked to be meant for her as well. Maggie must have done this for her. This cheered Catarine and made her wonder if Auntie had asked her to make it or she had just done it of her own accord. Catarine washed her dirty face and smoothed the newly starched dress and began to prepare for the evening.

Sitting on the edge of Daria's bed, she counted the five mirrors in the room, which were a curiosity to her. One large standing mirror to view one's entire being. One large wall mounted mirror. Three hand held mirrors, all lovely and ornate. Daria was indeed a lovely creature and perhaps this led to the desire to see one's self frequently in the glass. Or perhaps one's beauty was enhanced by excessive viewing and self-knowledge.

Whichever it was, Catarine was repelled by her own reflection because her hair had always been habitually awry from activity and her face flushed with heat. Ordinarily, she spent many of her days outdoors and upon entering her home, would glance in the hall mirror. For years, the glances were paired with the exact moment her mother would scold her for becoming "so filthy out riding those horses". This had fixed an abhorrence in her for seeing mirrors, and gave her a sense that she'd made a mess of things. Ignoring one's appearance seemed, at times, medicinal to her.

"Aren't you coming down?" Daria asked breathlessly as she entered the room. "Auntie is waiting in the parlor."

"Auntie, this is my new friend, Catarine Dupre. I know you met her this morning, but this is a proper introduction,"

Daria looked from Catarine to her grandmother with a forged smile pressed across her face and her eyes held a speck of tension. "She's come from her home. It's a plantation north of Baton Rouge."

"Glad to meet you, Mademoiselle Dupre. How you get on?"

"Glad to meet you too, Ma'am."

"Un, uh, now," Auntie Rose interrupted. "You call me Auntie Rose like everybody else. Now tell me what brings you to New Orleans."

"Er, well, I had to leave. I am an adult, you know. I left because I couldn't abide my stepfather any longer. He's not a very nice man."

"Daria say you run away. But you say you can't *abide* the man. That make much more sense than you run away." She glared at Daria. "Good for you, Mademoiselle Dupre!"

"Thank you, Auntie."

"Auntie Rose," she said leaning forward to make herself clear. "You say my whole name. Because I ain't your real auntie, see?"

"Yes, ma'am. Yes, Auntie Rose."

"Now," Auntie Rose said, getting down to business. Catarine looked at Daria, who remained surprisingly silent. "You ain't gonna stay here for free. Nobody stay here for free. Not even Dar."

"Oh no! I don't want to," Catarine exclaimed. "I can pay you whatever you want."

"I doubt that but we square up soon enough. Let's figure out where you gonna stay. You gonna work? Or just sit around on your fanny."

"Auntie!" Daria interrupted at this. "Catarine is used to being busy. She almost ran down the streets today. I couldn't keep up. I'm sure she can do anything you ask her."

"Hush up, Dar! Let her speak for herself. She ain't mute."

"No, I don't like sitting around or staying indoors for that matter, except to read or at night. What do you need me to do?"

"Let me think on it for a while," Auntie cut her eyes narrowly at Catarine and turning her head slightly away, appraising her as if she wasn't quite sure Catarine could do anything at all. "Just what can you do?"

"I'm well-schooled in everything. I'm good with figures, arithmetic. I can write. But I'm best at horsemanship and grooming, although I don't suppose that you'll need me for that skill."

"You don't suppose that?"

"I reckon I really don't know." Catarine started feeling uncomfortable in her seat and Daria's expression changed from forbearance to slightly cautionary.

"You girls run along now. You two are making me tired." And they were suddenly dismissed from the parlor.

The next few days were a bustle of activity, although nothing seemed to get accomplished. Daria explained to Catarine that Auntie would be thinking for a while and that they best not ask her any questions directly until she called them back into the parlor to discuss what to do about Catarine. Each day they set out into the city on errands of various kinds, which was apparently Daria's current means of employment. Daria dressed in something new and attractive each day and Catarine dressed in her brother's clothes, which she washed out and hung dry each night. The city was crammed with lively residents going about engaged in what appeared to be single-minded, thriving enterprises. Daria never disclosed the nature of any of Auntie's business dealings and Catarine thought it rude to ask. So, when Daria would enter into a professional discussion of any sort, Catarine would mill about nearby and play the part of the lazy street boy until Daria was done. The two young women went from stem to stern doing Auntie's bidding and meeting all sorts of people. While this was exciting, it made Catarine a little nervous. She regretted that she couldn't enjoy it completely, as she would have done so if events had not transpired as they had.

One errand took them to another hotel, the St. Louis, during which a slave auction was being held. This was a location that Catarine had visited with her father just before he took ill, except that it was for an extravagant dinner and concert by the

French Opera. During the slave auction, Catarine noticed that the people being sold were in fancy dress, men in top hats and ladies in ball gowns, to facilitate the sale. She knew of the auction but had never been. Trade of that sort had been handled by the men, either her father many years ago or her stepfather. It was considered to be a place to which ladies didn't come.

Catarine was well aware the plight these pitiful human beings faced. Her father, stirred to action by the mourning of a young woman he had bought, worked to find her husband who had been sold away earlier and reunited them. He had shared many a story of their troubles and was against splitting up the families, as was the practice of some of the other slave owners. Catarine knew of the movement against slavery, and people with notions to grant freedoms to their slaves were in the minority, as she had found out herself most personally when her mother remarried.

Jacob Koch had shocked them all with his vehemence regarding the marriage of a young slave couple. Catarine had planned a simple ceremony for them, which was to take place under the trees one Saturday evening. The slave women had woven flowers together as a decoration. Koch exploded in anger, forbade the ceremony, then a week later, sold the poor young man to a planter upriver. He never gave Catarine or his wife an explanation for his mean-spirited behavior.

Catarine couldn't help being appalled at how vastly unkind he was compared to her dear father. Abraham Dupre had not called himself an abolitionist. In fact, Catarine would not even consider her father that progressive a man, although he had an honorable and compassionate soul, and he considered it his righteous duty under God to care for those in his household as a good shepherd would care for the sheep of his flock. To him, the flock included the slave families who lived and partook of life along the Mississippi River, just as his own flesh and blood lived and breathed and drew life from the earth.

He would have never dreamed of treating man or beast any different from his own children. But Catarine was not sure if the granting of freedom to the slaves was something her father even considered. He existed in the world of his own kingdom, his present doings. Although he could teach her about lands far away, places recounted in books and found on maps, he still would return to matters at hand and generously manage and sustain his realm with a watchful eye. To set the captives free might topple the balance of things, Catarine reasoned her Papa would say. Yes, Catarine imagined that she and her Papa would disagree about the circumstances now, indeed.

At the auction block, when she looked into the eyes of the poor souls they brought out to display, and finding only blank stares, she assumed they'd been beaten or were simply resigned to their situation. It was an enormous crowd and the auction-eer bellowed his proclamations in both French and English, striving for the rapt attention of the multitude.

Catarine spotted one young slave boy who looked para-lyzed with fear. He must have been around ten years old and wore a suit that was too big for him. He came up on the auction stage with wide glaring eyes, red and swollen. He looked out on the crowd with such terror, it looked like he feared he was about to be shot. Catarine's heart felt as if it could break and she hoped to stay around and see who purchased him, praying it would be a kind gentleman. In fact, she noticed several of her father's old friends who lived in nearby plantations in the crowd making bids.

She should have been afraid of being noticed herself but she wasn't, for all eyes were on the auction block and she cared more for the action at hand than her own safety. During the bidding on this child, the last shout being for two hundred dollars, Daria appeared and fetched her to come along.

"No, let's wait and see what happens to this little boy."

"He'll be fine, I'm sure," Daria assured her.

"What do you mean?" Catarine was incredulous. "How do you know that?"

"Most of the men here are probably kind to their slaves."

"No, they aren't!" Catarine exclaimed. "I can assure you of that!"

"What can we do anyway?"

"Nothing, I suppose."

"Let's go then."

"No, I'm not leaving until I see who buys him. You go on if you must." Catarine's face flushed with emotion.

"All right, I'll stay with you." Daria's focus remained on Catarine as she watched the auction. Daria had seen the show before and felt assured that most of the people sold went to fair owners. Daria noticed how Catarine's eyes were intense, and seemed to grow greener as they watched.

The young boy was disrobed to his skivvies, as requested by a potential buyer, which produced wailing from him and disquieted many in the crowd. Catarine turned and grabbed Daria by the hand with a look of panic in her eyes. The crowd had grown even larger at that point and they were pressed in the middle. Finally, a top price was called by the sugar cane king, who Catarine knew of as her family's main competitor, and someone she believed might be a fair owner for this howling, pitiful boy. Catarine exhaled a long sigh of relief when it was over, even though they were leading the poor son away kicking and screaming.

"Heavens! What a show. I never meant us to be here at auction time, my dear," Daria exclaimed kindly as they began an attempt to wedge themselves through the crowd.

"I think we both could use a green fairy. Especially you. Have you ever had one of those?" Daria asked when they made it to the edge of the throng and out the hotel entrance.

"What is a green fairy? I've had enough distress for one day. I do not wish to partake in anything else disturbing." This made Daria dissolve into laughter which only produced a flush of anger across Catarine's cheeks.

"I'm not being flippant. I'm sorry. It was upsetting, I know. Come with me."

Again Daria took Catarine by her arm and propelled her along the streets. Catarine was suddenly tired and compliant. They turned several corners heading down Bienville Street to Bourbon Street. On the corner they entered the Absinthe House. Catarine stopped cold at the door and Daria went straight to a barstool.

"Come on," Daria motioned to Catarine who stood stock still gazing around the room with a wary look. She viewed a beamed ceiling and large wooden bar that stretched out in front of her behind which were multiple bottles of whiskey from which to choose. A few patrons stood around ignoring the young man who seemed afraid to enter.

"Who's your young friend?" the bartender asked Daria as he prepared her drink. Daria turned around to face Catarine, and leaning her back and elbows upon the bar, with wide signaling eyes indicated the chair next to her.

"Come introduce yourself, my love," she said to Catarine.

"Andre," Catarine said adopting a slightly lowered register. She extended her hand to the bartender, "Andre Monroe."

"Let's drink together," Daria suggested as she sipped the green liquid, which drew her lips together in a pinch and produced tears in her eyes. "Aghh."

"I'll have a brandy," Catarine requested of the bartender, still in a lower voice. Daria looked at her quizzically as if she'd made a grave mistake.

After the brandy was given and the bartender had moved on, Daria scolded her softly, "You should have ordered the absinthe. Brandy's a woman's drink. But at least your voice sounds real enough."

"I don't think I could stomach that. Brandy's the strongest I've ever had." Catarine whispered in her own voice to Daria. "My Papa drank brandy."

They drank for a while in silence before Catarine spoke.

"They looked so forlorn."

"Poor little boy," Daria agreed.

"They come to us in droves. Why do we need more of them?"

"It's a big business."

"It's got to stop. Many…most are not treated fairly."

"Around here things are better than in the other states."

"In New Orleans things are different. It's not so favorable on the farms."

They sat for a while in silence. It was Daria who finally spoke. "I must tell you about an auction I saw a long time ago. After that, I made sure never to see one again. It was a poor mother, probably around our age, with three of her children. They had to push them onto the block. She was already crying so hard! I don't know if her husband had just been sold, I'm not sure, but she knew what was coming. They sold the oldest away first. He was around six or seven. I don't know. But they all wept bitter tears and were forced to say goodbye in front of us all. It was horrible! Then someone bought her. And they left the two smallest ones sobbing and clinging to one another. The stupid owner just kept telling them to be silent the entire time. I had to walk away. I just couldn't stay and watch those poor children. I had to listen to the mother's cries as I was walking away. It took a while for me to forget it."

"I don't know what to say," Catarine said quietly, staring into her drink. "It's a sad world in which we live. I was hoping New Orleans would get my mind off such injustice."

"Speaking of the city, I still haven't shown you everything."

"I've been here before," Catarine spoke quietly, looking into her brandy, still despondent, the slave auction remaining in her thoughts.

"I'll wager you haven't seen the most interesting parts. I bet your visits were, let's say, chaperoned with the intention of… um, concealing the most entertaining areas of New Orleans."

When Catarine looked up, she could see that Daria had a mischievous smile across her face. After each polished off their drink, they paid and left with good-byes to the bartender and headed down to the French Market. Daria wanted to spend the rest of the day shopping. This suited Catarine just fine because she needed more clothing, and the women had worked out a plan for how to accomplish this.

The march farther downtown was as captivating as the slave auction and far more genial. They sampled an eclair at Vincent's, a scrumptious tasty treat they discovered to be a favorite they both shared in common. Daria entered a French boutique on the corner of Royal and Conti to purchase imported calico to have done up for Catarine and undergarments while Catarine waited at the open market near the Mississippi River. It seemed to Catarine that all races and creeds were there either bunched up together with their merchandise spread out on the ground, hung from baskets against the side of iron fences, or in between the free standing booths.

From a distance, it had the look of a chessboard. Gaslights were strung across the path on each side up and down the street, lacing up the whole affair, the needlepoint holding it all together. She recognized the thin natives on the end, spread out on the ground, quietly selling the same herbs and homemade bowls that they'd marketed to her plantation.

Stout German women were set up in the booth next to the Indians with their array of vegetables, clad with pocketed aprons, sitting back watching over their wares with a parental protective eye, lest a careless hand bruise or mishandle their colorful display. As Catarine walked along, the voices mixed and blended into a harmony of vocal texture that made her smile. She could only understand the French, English and bits of the Choctaw but listening to the Italian, Portuguese, and German made her long for far-away lands.

What's more, Catarine noticed that being among the foreigners calmed her and that anonymity was soothing, for she felt virtually unnoticed as a boy surrounded by curious humanity, a vast difference from walking about in the more customary places. She took to leaning against lamp posts with her leg cocked up, and aimed to enjoy the smell of the coffee and pralines while waiting for Daria.

When Daria came along, holding several boxes that she promptly handed off to Catarine, she pushed up her sleeves and headed straight for the Gascon butchers. Surprising Catarine, Daria spoke their dialect fluently and ordered two chickens which were then taken from their cages squawking. The birds, with tiny feathers in a cloud about them, were placed on the block only moments before having their heads hacked off and then raked into a bucket. Daria paid the wife of the butcher, then donned thick gauntlets that she withdrew from her sack before handling the birds.

"That's it then," Daria said. They walked on. Heading through the vendors near St. Louis' entrance, they passed the Moroccan ladies who approached them holding rosary beads up with smiling faces. Turning away from them, Daria looked at Catarine with a serious look. "Did you hear the Gascon lady?"

"No, what do you mean?" Catarine asked.

"She said you are hemna, a woman," Daria explained.

Chapter 3

A few days later, when the late summer rains poured in and deep puddles formed, the women sat looking through windows pondering the best course of action for Catarine. From the upstairs window of her bedroom, Daria gazed out at the dogwood tree being pelted by the showers. She knew her new friend didn't want to be found, so much so that she went about dressed as a boy. Something about that delighted Daria immensely, so she intended to give it her best to both protect her new friend and play along with the peculiar game.

Auntie Rose, with pursed lips, stood at her parlor window frowning and gazing at the deep muddy trenches made by carriages in the heavy rainfall, and thought of the fact that she now harbored a white runaway mistress from a nearby planta-tion. Not good business for someone in her shoes. Catarine sat mesmerized in a window seat she'd found in the back of the house and watched the yard filling up with water as the drops splashed down with a rhythmic force that showed no sign of retreat. She felt enormous comfort in this home, a reprieve from her growing fear of being in the open. With each passing day, she wondered what was happening at home. Did they think she just ran away? Or did they suspect she left because she had something to with Mason's disappearance? Or perhaps they thought something had happened to both of them. Surely they hadn't found his body.

That night Auntie Rose gathered them in her parlor and set forth a plan.

"Girl, I guess you better stay here with me. I don't want anybody see'n you 'round here and I 'spect you don't either. You can tend the garden starting tomorrow morning. If it a raining still, you helping Maggie. And wear them boy clothes," Auntie ended her speech by picking up her Bible and donning her spectacles.

"Yes, Auntie Rose," Catarine knew it was the only appropriate response.

Auntie appeared unwilling to take questions, and when Catarine looked over at Daria, she merely smiled back and remained silent, something she seemed to only do in her grandmother's presence. The women sat listening to the sound of the clock ticking and the gentle steady rain. After sitting for several minutes, Catarine began wishing for a book to read and ventured a more detailed look around the room. She spotted a small shelf in the far corner that contained a few books and also a globe upon a table nearby. While pondering whether it would be rude to simply get up and survey them, Auntie startled her by speaking again.

"I s'pose it'd do you two some good to hear some of God's word," Auntie said in a loud voice. She then cleared her throat of any residual phlegm that might impede the reading and proceeded to orate a passage.

"The rod of reproof giveth wisdom:
But a child left to himself bringeth his mother to shame.
When the wicked are multiplied, transgression increaseth:
But the righteous shall see their fall.
Where there is no vision, the people perish:
But he that keepeth the law, happy is he."

"Mademoiselle Dupre, you a Catholic girl?" was how she ended the passage after a pause.

"Yes, Auntie Rose, I am," Catarine answered and could see Daria smiling in the background.

"That's good, because in this house, we go to mass and we also read God's word," Auntie said. "God didn't give us eyes to read and a Bible if we not s'pose to use 'em. I got schooled like all the rest of the French girls, just like you and Dar. So I can read and write and do arithmetic. I'm gonna use my head till the day I die. I 'spect you two to do the same, now. Both of yous!" Auntie turned her gaze to Daria with the last phrase.

Then looking at Catarine she added, "So you get you some books and keep your mind sharp. Don't just be out tending plants. I 'spect to see you reading, ya hear?"

"Oh, yes, ma'am, I love to read," Catarine was thrilled with this suggestion but she noticed Daria rolling her eyes.

"All right then, get you a book over there or from the upstairs room. Dar, you best be doing something useful too."

When the rain subsided and the soaked ground had absorbed all of God's watering, Catarine was given the task of weeding the large vegetable garden on the sunny side of Auntie Rose's house. She found it to be an easier task to accomplish with breeches on than cumbersome skirts, as she had tended flowers from time to time for her mother at home. And her cap held back most of her hair effectively rather than the useless bonnet that she was accustomed to using, even though the cap didn't provide as much shading from the sun.

She'd spent most of the morning making her way through okra and tomato plants, and lifted squash and cucumber leaves to get to the weeds, making piles as she went on her hands and knees. Her mother had always told her it wasn't good for a woman to sweat, but Catarine thought maybe she had been wrong. It felt good, even if it soaked through her shirt. Her mother always insisted on her riding in the early mornings or late evenings in the summer months due to this, her only request, as Catarine had been trained and allowed to ride by her father.

As Catarine approached womanhood, requests by her mother had altered many of her girlish practices. She'd been, no doubt, attempting to keep her lady-like as much as possible. The dirt on her hands made Catarine look less like a girl than ever, as even her finger nails held black stains beneath them.

As Catarine sat back to survey the end of the weeding enterprise, she heard the distant sound of women screaming coming from the avenue along with the sound of galloping horses against the cobblestones. She sprang up and ran into the street as Daria and Auntie Rose also exited the front door just in time to see a runaway carriage drawn by two horses turn the corner at a speed that nearly toppled the thing. There was no driver and the reins flared behind the horses freely. Catarine instinctively ran straight into the middle of the street, blocking the way, with her arms outstretched to both sides.

"Move! You'll be killed!" Daria yelled at Catarine. But as soon as she had spoken, the horses stopped just short of Catarine and she swiftly grabbed their bridles and spoke to them. They pawed the cobblestones a few times then became calmer. As the ladies' screams turned into mere crying, a tall man dressed in a bottle green suit covered in mud came running around the corner.

"Oh my, heavens," he cried, waving his hands up in the air in desperation.

"You are drunk! You imbecile!" one of the ladies in the carriage, the older of the two, composed herself enough to yell at him upon his arrival. "You could have killed us both."

By then Daria had run out to the street's edge to join the scene. Catarine remained with the horses, and appeared to be breathing into one's nose and whispering to both of them.

"If it wasn't for this boy here, we'd have toppled over," the older lady spoke again looking at Catarine.

"Is a accident," the man said.

"You fell off drunk, you idiot," she told him again. "And you will not be driving us home." And turning to Catarine, she said, "Boy, will you drive us? I'll give you two dollars to drive us home." Catarine looked back toward the house at Auntie Rose. It was Daria who spoke up.

"He is working here. No, he cannot go with you. Your regular driver will have to take you."

"Well, I'll be," she said in a sarcastic tone to Daria. "What's your name? Maybe we can hire you? Are you a slave?"

"Her name is Mademoiselle Morinay," Catarine spoke up. "And no, if you had good eyes, you could see she isn't a slave!"

The horses both nuzzled her as she stroked them while the drunk man made several efforts to climb into the driver's seat, finally seating himself and belching at the same time. Catarine gathered up the reins and handed them to him.

"Momma, I'm scared," the young woman finally spoke.

"We are not going to ride with you!" the older lady said to the driver. "Do not let him go." She pleaded with Catarine not to let go of the horses. The ladies stepped down out of the carriage as the man cleared his throat.

"Hmmph," he said and put his nose in the air. "I'll go on without ye, then."

"We will walk the rest of the way rather than risking our lives. Carry on," the older lady said with a swing of her arm as they stepped to the side of the road.

Catarine released the horses and got out of the way. The man reined the horses on and the ladies walked on down the avenue without a further word with their heads held high.

After the ladies turned the corner and were out of sight, Auntie Rose, who had remained on her front porch the entire time viewing the episode, withdrew inside shaking her head and mumbling to herself. Catarine and Daria glanced at each other and then were overcome with laughter.

"You were amazing!" Daria exclaimed after regaining her voice. "I can hardly believe how skilled you are with horses. I was so afraid at first that you would be trampled. But obviously you knew exactly what you were doing!"

"They were just afraid and needed someone to tell them to stop and settle down." Catarine explained. "But yes, I do understand horses."

"And those ladies didn't think you were anything but a boy."

Several days after the carriage incident, an older gentleman came by unannounced to Auntie Rose's house. He wore a grey suit and pants and carried a top hat and cane. His grizzled hair revealed his age and his ocher skin tone, his creole heritage.

"Mademoiselle," he said with a deep bow when Auntie Rose received him into her parlor. His voice had a smooth melodious quality about it. "I'm Xavier LaCoste and I have been sent here by my employer, the Monsieur Villemont, you may have heard of him? He is interested in the young man who is in your employ. It has come to his attention that this young man is talented with horses."

"Monsieur LaCoste," Auntie began. "I'm pleased to make your acquaintance but our young man is not interested in employment beyond that which he finds in my residence."

"My employer is willing to pay handsomely since he is in dire need of a stable manager. Is your boy a slave?"

"Heavens no!" Auntie exclaimed, threw back her head and laughed, and just as she did, an idea came to her. "He a light creole, as white as they come, but free."

"Pardon, Mademoiselle!" Monsieur LaCoste said with flushed cheeks. "I never saw the boy, I just, I just am, Oh dear…"

"It's quite all right, a common mistake," Auntie turned to lead the man outside. He followed her bustling skirts to the front door with Maggie looking on.

"I'll let Monsieur Villemont know your reply. Please accept his apologies, Mademoiselle." With that he departed, placing his hat snugly on his head and using his cane to steady his stride down the path to the street.

As soon as the man had left, Auntie Rose called for Daria and Catarine. Catarine was washing up from the garden and donning her new dress for the quiet evening inside but Daria wasn't back yet from her business errands. Catarine presented herself in the parlor and was alone with Auntie for the first time since they'd met several weeks before.

"It's just as good Dar ain't here. Give us a time to talk," Auntie began. "Mademoiselle Dupre, you told us very little 'bout yourself and I'd like 't know more. Just why did you run away? I need to know if they are gone come looking for ya."

"Yes, ma'am, yes Auntie Rose, I understand."

Catarine started her story with hands folded in her lap, but her eyes were darting around the room. She did her best to lay out the truth. She told her that she was born in the plantation house to parents who were originally from France but settled in New Orleans, buying land with family money to start a sugar cane business. Her father had been a fine man, intellectual, a good businessman, kind-hearted and also an accomplished horseman. Her mother, never much interested in traditional studies, didn't take part in the business side of things but spent time painting on canvases and china. Catarine was the oldest and had a younger brother. The plan had been to train Catarine to take over the business since she was most interested and also most like her father.

Her brother, Andre, was more delicate and preferred his mother's company and painting to the business, horses or the outdoors. They decided to educate Catarine at home but allow Andre to go away to Paris for his artistic training. Tragically, Andre contracted yellow fever and died during his second year at school. It had been a huge blow, since her parents had hoped keeping their children away from New Orleans insured immunity from the dreaded fever.

They all grieved immensely for him. Her father, who was becoming weak and sick with what the doctors said was heart disease, laid plans to turn over the business to Catarine rather quickly. He taught her everything else she didn't already know about running the plantation and gave her a secret cache of money they hid in the wine cellar. After her father's premature death, her mother, being both fragile in mind and body, lay about grieving the death of her son and husband and was troubled and anxious for quite a while. Catarine managed her inexpressible grief by spending even more hours in the saddle but also rallied to run the business, doing things exactly as her father would have done, which served her well.

Her mother, finally coming out in public and being the lovely woman she was, fell prey to a trickster. Jacob Koch, a German man who'd sold a business up north and moved to

New Orleans, and rather than simply purchasing a place that was up for sale, wined and dined her mother, convincing her that she needed a man to run their plantation. He had a grown son named Mason, who managed to act civil for the time being, which aided in the deception, leading her mother to believe the two were replacing what she'd recently lost.

Despite Catarine's begging and her dislike of the Koch's, for she had an ill feeling about them and also felt she could run the business alone, her mother married Mr. Koch. He quickly took over the sugar cane business along with his son and they ruled with an iron hand. The slaves all hated them and started rebelling. They'd been accustomed to Catarine and her father and had been treated well, but with the new owners, a different atmosphere of oppression became the norm. What's more was that Mason was a terrible young man who demanded sexual favors from the slave girls whenever the mood came over him, even behaving indecently towards Catarine with sly looks and even grabbing her whenever he caught her alone. A few times, he kissed her forcefully, which she rebuffed and reported to her mother.

Unfortunately, her mother, having come to the slow realization that she had made a grave mistake, only became more depressed than ever and took to staying in bed for days at a time. Catarine was virtually on her own in her plight, her only ally being her life-long friend, Bessie, the slave girl. She concocted a scheme to run away with the money that her father had hidden away for her.

"What I really want to do is to enroll in school abroad, or perhaps up North," she said rapidly turning to Auntie Rose. "I hear some of the universities are now accepting women."

"That's quite a story," Auntie said. "So you just up and left one day?"

"I, er, yes. I needed to get away from Mason and my stepfather. Er, it seemed like the right time." Catarine fiddled with her skirt and looked out the window for Daria to return.

"But it's the start of cutting season. Surely he would leave you alone now more than before. Why didn't you leave in the spring?"

"I was just too afraid to, I guess. I should have. Also, they will be too busy to come looking for me during cutting season," Catarine was able to look right into Auntie's green eyes with her lie, but her heart pounded loudly in her ears.

"Well, I guess that's true enough," Auntie squinted her eyes at Catarine, just as Daria had done the night they met, only Auntie didn't possess the girlish delight. They held each other's gaze for a few seconds until Auntie spoke again. "All right, sugar, I just wanted to know your story. You can stay here awhile. But you be thinking 'bout that schooling. And ask Dar 'bout that too. She thinking of schooling again too."

Daria returned just in time for supper, which they all took together in the dining room. Catarine talked gaily for the first time while they ate, about the food, her new dress, how she was enjoying New Orleans, but when she asked Daria a question, the only response she got was a half-hearted shrug of Daria's shoulders. Auntie discussed the pleasant weather and had a few business questions for Daria herself, which she answered with a few words, her eyes directed at her food. When her grandmother asked if anything was wrong, Daria said she had a headache from the day.

Later that evening, when Daria and Catarine were in their room dressing for bed, Catarine removed her lovely new gown, placing it carefully away. Daria finally broke her silence.

"You might as well throw that thing away," Daria said, spitting the words out but not looking at Catarine.

"Why?"

"You need to wear boy clothes and stay in disguise. All the time. From now on. And stay inside as much as possible. You hear?" The two women stared at each for a few minutes before Catarine spoke.

"Why are you saying this?" Catarine said slowly, standing eye to eye in front of Daria, nearly naked in her pantaloons. With a wary look in her eyes, Daria grabbed Catarine by the shoulders and shook her.

"Because you are wanted for murder, that's why!" Daria yelled into her face as she clenched Catarine's arms. "The law wants you for killing someone named Mason Koch!"

Catarine gasped and covered her mouth with both hands, sitting down hard on the bed behind her. She then stared expressionless as Daria fished something out of her bag.

"I saw this in the *Le Courrier* today," she said as she threw the newspaper down on the bed next to Catarine.

"Oh my God," Catarine said in a hushed voice as she saw her name in print alongside the word *murderer*. She suddenly felt ill and incredibly despairing. She lay down on the pillow as her eyes became misty and unfocused. Daria remained fixed, standing in her spot and gazing down upon Catarine.

"I'm so sorry. I haven't told you everything," Catarine finally said in a whisper.

"No, no you haven't," Daria said in a quiet voice.

"You must hate me," Catarine said as her tears began. "I'm so sorry. I'll tell you everything."

"Hate you?" Daria said as she sat down next to Catarine on the bed. "I don't hate you. I love you. And I don't care what you've done."

"I'll do anything to protect you, Cat," Daria spoke as Catarine wept into the pillow, her voice as soft and soothing as a warm embrace. "I'll run away with you. You know I loathe my life here. Just tell me what you want me to do." Sitting up, Catarine sniffed and wiped her nose with the handkerchief Daria had given her, and began to tell her the entire story. She started with the same story that she told Auntie Rose, only she didn't finish with the little white lie at the end.

"You see, what happened to make me leave wasn't cutting season. That's what I told Auntie. It was this. The night before I left something awful happened. Bessie, the house maid who attends my mother. You see, she has always been a great friend to me growing up. She has a special love for the horses. So after her work is done, on the way home at night to her quarters, she usually stops by the barn and feeds the horses leftover figs and strokes them.

Mason watches her and plagues her. That night, I'd been out on a late ride. When I came back, I entered the barn with my horse and discovered Mason on top of Bessie in my horse's stall, defiling her. I saw that her skirts were up and he was in the very act! I yelled at him to stop, but he just told me to go on and mind my own business. I couldn't just turn away! I had to stop him! So I put my horse in the cross ties, grabbed the only weapon at hand, a pitchfork, and went back to the stall to defend poor Bessie. I banged him on the head with the back of the pitchfork but he only rose up to attack me! He stumbled at first as he came toward me with his pants down. This frightened me and I almost dropped the pitchfork. I didn't realize it had shifted in my hand! The original blow hadn't rattled him much. So I decided to take one big hard swing again to perhaps knock him out so we could get away. Horribly, I was successful with the hard blow but, unfortunately the outside tine of the pitchfork went directly into Mason's eye socket and into his brain, dislodging his eye. I tried to forcefully withdraw the pitchfork from his eye, thinking it would help but instead he dropped to the ground and died instantly.

Bessie and I were horrified and couldn't speak for what seemed like several minutes. In fact, I must have been in shock for a while because I don't remember what happened after that. I only know because she told me later. Bessie ran to get Moses, her oldest brother, to dig a hole to bury him. They decided the best place would be under the grain barrels in the barn. There had been surprisingly little blood. I do, however, remember fetching my money from the wine cellar in the middle of the night and slipping it into my double-layered bodice, slits I'd cut and stitched back. I barely slept that night but Bessie came to my room before sunrise to see if I was all right and to say goodbye. Bessie implored me not to leave as she felt no one could find out about Mason anyway. But I'd decided to take Mason's horse and make it look like he left. I thought that would make the most sense…for a while. I also reminded Bessie how I had wanted to go to university since I wouldn't be supervising the plantation. Things had just changed too much. Perhaps I could be a lawyer or doctor, or maybe a teacher. Who knows? But now…"

"You still can," Daria reassured her. "We just need to get out of town. Go away up north."

"I wonder if they found his body," said Catarine, staring bleary-eyed into the flickering lighted lamp.

After Catarine's confession, the two women each felt an alliance between them, an endearment to one another, for both felt they each had only the other on which to rely. Daria, although she hadn't Catarine's circumstances, had spent count-less nights longing for an escape from her well-devised life's choices. A woman of color in New Orleans was only granted a very limited quantity of options. And they involved marriage of some fashion, unless one inherited a large sum of money. In Daria's mind, marriage produced feelings of trepidation. Like-wise, the acquisition of large sums of money likely involved male companionship of some kind, therefore, the thought of which brought dread and disgust to her mind.

Although she'd been schooled for a time in Paris, she knew she couldn't return without funding. But she'd fallen in love with the world at large through her one travel adventure and also through the books she used to love. The lovely books! They now just made the longing worse. But with the beautiful and brave Catarine at her side, Daria could finally live out her dreams and be brave enough to escape along with her.

Catarine, feeling sheltered from the consequences that awaited her, rested safely next to Daria. In Catarine's mind, Daria had become her strength, the confident free woman of color who knew both classes in New Orleans, the high society and the street folks. Catarine felt sure that with Daria by her side, she'd be protected. Surely, Daria could hide her from danger until they could get away.

"Cat, my grandmother wants you to take that stable work," Daria said when Catarine came down for breakfast. Daria had arisen early. When Auntie Rose saw her descend, she inadvertently mentioned that a man came by wanting Catarine to work.

"What?" Catarine said. "I'm not sure that's best."

"One good thing is that you'd be tucked away on the outskirts of town. And they believe you to be a boy. That's in your favor."

"Yes, but the moment they don't…"

"Let's cut your hair."

"I was already thinking about that," Catarine said. "If I must…"

"I know, darling," Daria said. "Your hair is so lovely but it is necessary."

"Whatever you think, Dar. I'm just not sure I should take that post."

"Auntie wants you to do something. She's questioning me. She senses there is something we aren't telling her. Thankfully, she hasn't seen the newspaper!"

"What do we tell her?"

"I'll think of something," Daria assured her.

But only moments later Catarine received another shock. As soon as they descended the stairs and entered the parlor, Auntie Rose made an announcement with obvious irritation.

"A man who say he your daddy's lawyer came here today, Mademoiselle Dupre," said Auntie.

Catarine, who was about to be seated on the settee anyway, collapsed instead as her legs gave way. "He say his name is Fuhrmann. A German. That ring a bell?"

"Oh no!" Catarine gasped with wide eyes, her hands covering her mouth tightly as if to safeguard herself from undue confession. Had Fuhrmann spotted her?

"Do it?" Auntie asked again, this time her voice rising. Catarine could nod her head up and down but nothing more. Daria, although numb beside her, reached out and placed a soothing hand on Catarine's back. "Well, if so, we got big problems, because he told me more than I wanna know, that's for sure."

Auntie stood up slowly from her place at the window, her comfortable chair, and made her way across the parlor to stand in front of the settee. She held her cane, balancing on it perilously, as she spoke sternly to the girls.

"I know both ya been hiding something from me! And I don't like it. Not one bit." At this she started walking around the room, a little too fast for her age and ability, shaky on the cane, and when she stopped in front the girls again, she tried to balance herself and wave the cane in the air to better express her frustration.

"Y'all just rile me up!"

"Auntie, be careful!"

"Dar, you best hush up right now! I'm not done talking! I told you, Mademoiselle Dupre, that I require the truth in this house, did I not?"

"Yes, ma'am."

"Well, you commence on telling it now or you out the door."

With this command and her severe wobbling, Auntie made her way across the room and slowly lowered her weight onto her favorite chair preparing to concentrate. And tapping on the chair just next to hers, said, "And you come over here, Mademoiselle Dupre."

Catarine, a bit distracted by Auntie's display of rage and elderly infirmity, pulled herself together, walked to the appointed seat and cleared her throat. She looked from Auntie's scowling eyes to Daria's, which had the look of feeble longing in them, before she began. She didn't mean to cry telling the story but she did. Perhaps it was because she felt caught.

"I didn't mean to lie, I really didn't," she began, tears running down her cheeks. "I know all about the tangled web."

Daria looked over at Auntie and could detect a slight smile, but they both remained silent and let Catarine continue. She told about her last night at home, about Bessie and Mason and the accident.

When Catarine became weepy, Auntie stopped her and called for Maggie to bring brandy. After the brandy arrived, Maggie remained in the room which confused Catarine.

"Should I proceed?" Catarine asked after a few sips had cleared her throat, noting that Auntie and Daria were looking at one another in an odd way. "Pardon me, but will Maggie be silent about this? I'm just concerned…about my safety… I just don't know who to trust." And with that, her voice quivered and she sipped her brandy again.

"Cat, Maggie is a mute. She cannot tell anyone even if she wanted to," Daria explained.

"Oh," Catarine said, sitting back surprised. She took another sip, and wiping her tears away briskly, prepared to go on when Auntie interrupted her.

"So, if you telling the truth, and it looks like you are now, you ain't no murderer, you a savior."

"I don't think I killed him on purpose, but perhaps I did."

"Ahh, now, and if you did, it was to save another, and in my book, that's justified."

"I suppose so. I was trying to save Bessie."

"Well, this calls for two things," Auntie proclaimed. "One is you're a coming to mass at St. Augustine's in the morning. You do your confessing. Make things right between you and God. And two is you going to work at that stable outside a town. Get you away from the glaring eye of New Orleans."

"Grammy, how is that going to help?" Daria shot up from her seat as Catarine started tearing up again.

"Daria Morinay! I decide the best course of action! Now hush up!" Catarine and Daria could only look at each other with dread in their eyes.

Within the stingy hours of darkness, Catarine woke with a start, her brow beaded with sweat and the gown she was wearing twisted and up around her midsection.

It had been that dream again. The one in which Bella, the old mare her mother used to ride, was tied to the beating tree, old Mr. Koch lifting his wicked hand against her. In her dream, she was back in her old bedroom and Bella's high-pitched neighs, cries they had been, had awakened her and in the next instant she had been down outside watching the horrific scene. As she had felt her gown billowing violently around her, she saw the sky above, with fingers of white anger splayed across the heavens, and Mr. Koch beating the mare across her hindquarters and the poor horse prancing and kicking, pulling against the tie that held her fast. After he drew blood, with Catarine's yells of protest being squelched dumb in her throat, he let the wild-eyed mare go, not to freedom, but back to the pasture where she was kept.

Catarine sat up in bed. She sat a long while, shaking. Then she heard the soft rains begin again. As the steady rainfall began its washing, Catarine's breathing eased and slowed and she put her head back upon the pillow and fell asleep.

Chapter 4

At St. Augustine's the three women all entered the church in somber moods. Seating was split up by whites and blacks but, as Auntie Rose said, "Sit where you like, because some free folk be so light, you fit right in". So Catarine sat with her new family in the "colored" pews.

The free colored people had the most in attendance by far, as they owned the most pews. The slaves in the back pews sang the loudest and worshipped with gusto, drowning out the larger crowd of dignified whites. Rhythmic stomping and clapping was felt throughout the building and Catarine delighted in the steady vibrations as she stood reading the songbook.

A small pianoforte, played by a bonneted white lady in a cotton day dress that had fitted, bodice puckers fastened down her back, aided the voices with her playing but only secondarily. Balmy, smooth hymns were sung forth in a kind of lyrical, unseen dance. Catarine noticed proudly that the group she was with was dressed as elegantly as they were the night of the quadroon ball only more discreetly for a Sunday morning.

They were a beautiful congregation, mankind, all of them gathered in the church building together for the same purpose. Attendance that day lifted her mood even if she didn't know what was to become of her. And coincidentally, the reading was about peace. "My peace I give you…"

Later that afternoon, Daria and Catarine began to say their goodbyes.

"I'm so mad at my grandmother, I could bite a bullet in two—she must be losing her mind," Daria said as she flopped down on the bed after folding up items for Catarine and enclosing trinkets into a hatbox for her.

"I'm not going to Paris. I cannot take these," Catarine said holding up the dangling earrings Daria had given her. "What will I do with these in a stable?"

"But I want you to have them," Daria exclaimed. "And I really don't want you to go at all!"

"I know, but listen," Catarine sat down on the bed next to Daria. "I've been thinking. Let's run away. Will you go with me?"

"Where?" Daria said sitting up straight.

"Where do you want to go? I'll go anywhere you want, just away from here."

"When? Now?"

"I don't know. Soon. We must plan it. I can go to work at the stable first, then we will leave when we have everything planned."

Daria, who had only been out of New Orleans once, to her schooling in Paris, longed to go other places, other cities.

The books she read growing up had made her hunger to see something different. She was expected to become a placée if she stayed in New Orleans, a second wife of a rich French man, like her mother before her. Although she didn't dislike her father, she saw very little of him. It wasn't a life she cared to embrace.

"Yes! I'll go. Let's run away!" Daria said rather loudly then cupped her hands over her mouth quickly.

"Shhh!" Both girls giggled and began discussing possibilities into the night.

"Dar, are you awake? Daria." Cat whispered. Catarine hadn't slept and it was in the middle of the night. "Dar! Wake up!"

"What is it?"

"I can't go to that man's place. They will know I'm a girl. I just know it. Let's leave now."

"Are you sure?" Daria's voice rose to a higher pitch.

"Yes, I'm sure. I'd have to dress with other boys. That's what the hired help does. I'd have to sleep in the barn and surely I'd be with other boys. Men."

"Oh, I see."

"Ok, but listen to me," Daria sat up in bed and took Catarine by both hands. "We can reason with my grandmother in the morning. She will listen to me; I know she will. I can't just leave her without any explanation."

"Like I did my mother."

"You had to."

"I'd planned to leave like that anyway."

"It's no matter. You were there with that horrid stepfather! Don't forget that!"

"I haven't."

"So, let's do this. Let's pack up our belongings and talk to her in the morning. We can plan our trip and leave in a few days. I've been thinking about going to either New York or Boston. Do you have enough money for that?"

"Yes," said Catarine smiling. "That's one good thing in all of this. My dear father left me plenty of money. We can take a ship. How would you like that?"

"I think a ship would do nicely. And once we are away and in another place. You'll be perfectly safe."

"That sounds so very wonderful."

When Catarine opened her eyes and noticed the brightness around her, she realized instantly that the day had progressed further along than she'd expected. She jumped out of bed and when she did, she saw two tapestry bags on the floor in front of Daria's open armoire that had been cleaned out. Dread filled her throat and gave her a queasy feeling as she made her way downstairs barefoot against the wooden floors.

She found Daria and Aunt Rose having tea in the dining room. They smiled when they saw her standing at the door with big solemn eyes. It was Daria who spoke.

"Catarine, come in and have tea. And Maggie made us some lovely blueberry scones." Catarine slipped into the chair next to Daria and dared to glance up at Auntie Rose. Auntie Rose wore a slight smile on her face but was stirring her tea with an absent gaze.

"Grandma, you don't mind if Catarine takes her breakfast here in her nightgown do you? She had a bad night and didn't sleep much."

"No, my dear, not at all," Auntie said still looking down.

Catarine licked her dry lips and looked at Daria who also continued to smile. All three of them hovered over their tea, sweetening and sipping for what seemed like forever. Maggie brought in scones and they gave their full attention to the buttering and nibbling of warm sweetness. Beams of sunlight cut through the drapery and left dappled spots on the carpet next to the table where they sat in silence, the palpable sounds of silver and china working in concert with the distant ticking clock.

"I guess I'll get use to it," Auntie announced as if to herself. Catarine looked up at Daria but both her and her grandmother kept their eyes on their plates.

"You'll be fine." Daria said.

Maggie came in, poured out more tea, left again and still they sat in the hush of the late morning. Catarine bunched up the fabric of her gown and twisted it since she'd run out of things to do with her hands. Daria began staring at the sunbeams.

"I'll miss you so much," Auntie's voice was shaky and her hand flew up to her mouth, dropping the silver spoon hard on the china saucer. Although she immediately regretted it, Catarine exhaled deeply when she heard this but the other two women ignored her.

"Oh, Grandma!" Daria got up and came around to Auntie Rose and embraced her. They rocked back and forth until Daria slipped down on the floor at Auntie's feet then rested her head on Auntie's knees.

"I'll miss you, but you gotta go," Auntie said. "You go on with your friend. Go to your dreams. But I do got some advice for you. You better say you her slave. Go as a rich white woman and her slave. That whatcha do."

"Why, by God, should we do that?" Daria exclaimed sitting back on the floor, her bare legs protruding from under her skirts.

"Things are different up north. They not all free up there. You know that. If you think you gonna be a free person of color anywheres but Louisiana, you wrong. Just saying."

"I was worried," Catarine said while folding gowns and pantaloons in the tapestry bags a few hours later. Daria stood holding out her hats, trying to decide which to bring, as she only had three hat boxes.

"I know you were. She wants me to go but not thrilled about the reason. What do you think about what she said?"

"About you being my slave?" Catarine laughed and shook her head. "I'm not sure. I suppose if someone asks us."

"The problem is that sometimes you must show proof."

"Should I bring these?" Catarine held up her boy clothes.

"Maybe, but I can't imagine that you'd need them again, *Andre*."

"The first thing is to decide where to go. I say New York, you say Boston."

"I know you are probably right about us getting more opportunities in New York. And less chances of being caught. But Boston is where so many of the abolitionists live. Emerson gives lectures there."

"Want to flip a coin?"

"For our future?" Daria, eyes aglow, turned to look at Catarine who had donned one of her discarded hats, the one with the purple feather in it. Daria placed the orange one on the side of her head, the one she had on the night they met.

"Absolutely!" Catarine laughed. Daria then produced a silver dollar from her jewelry box and handed it to Catarine. "You do it, *Monsieur!*"

"Heads we go to New York. Tails we go to Boston." Catarine jostled the coin around in her cupped hands, and kissed her hands, then with that, Daria grabbed her hands and kissed her hands also. Catarine threw the coin up in the air and it spun around a few times and glimmered in the light of the afternoon sun that was streaming in the window, then bounced on the plush rug under their feet. They stared down at the silver coin resting flat on the floor between them then looked up at each other, both smiling broadly.

"That settles it!" Daria exclaimed.

Daria was able to purchase their tickets at the shipping office the next day. They were to sail three days after that. After much packing and exchanging of clothes, Daria began her many goodbyes. Catarine packed and repacked books. Daria packed and repacked clothes, deciding to include the drab dresses Maggie made up for her quickly in case she must pass as Catarine's slave on occasion.

On the day before they were to set sail, another knock came on the door. Mr. Fuhrmann presented himself again to Auntie, who quickly scooted him away, yelling in anger.

"You get own out of here!" she cried shaking her fist as he retreated off her porch. After that he took to strolling up and down their street, then leaning against the nearby lamppost, near enough to spy their front door. There he stayed for most of the day, smoking cigarettes and tipping his hat to passersby.

That night the women all hatched a plan to guarantee their safe escape. They furtively moved Catarine out the back door, dressed as Andre, only this time wearing a dark cloak, and instructed her to check in to the colored hotel on Julia St. where only musicians, sailors, and whores visited.

"It's wild and rambunctious, but no one will spot you there," Daria said. Auntie and Maggie would keep close tabs on Mr. Fuhrmann, the latter following him in the shadows if necessary to make sure he was unaware of Catarine's movements. Maggie saw Fuhrmann safely checked into a downtown hotel, many blocks away from where Catarine was staying.

The next morning, Daria made a huge show of her departure with all their bags, taking a hired buggy to the departure site. When leaving they made sure to declare their goodbyes loudly on Auntie's front porch.

"Have a lovely time in Savannah, darling," Auntie said loudly, giving a long hug to her granddaughter.

Catarine awoke before dawn after a tumultuous night of sleep. Twice the crowd below at the dance hall had been loud and ebullient enough to wake her, and her bed hideously uncomfortable, but her main struggle was the growing concern about being found out for her crime and the need to keep herself hidden until they could get safely away. She dressed quickly, making her toilette.

As she headed out the door, she glanced up and down the street, checking for her enemy, Mr. Fuhrmann. Their plan had been to have Maggie stationed at Catarine's hotel at daybreak, and to alert her if Mr. Fuhrmann was spotted nearby. As she was surveying the streets, she saw neither of them.

The day was young and the early morning mist hung in the air about her. A fog engulfed the dock area, much to her relief, for it would be difficult to recognize anyone farther than a few feet away. Catarine arrived first to board the ship and, not seeing Fuhrmann anywhere, squatted down beside two barrels where she could watch the others arriving. Shortly, she saw Daria being unloaded from her carriage along with all their baggage. Catarine strolled up to her and Daria breathed a huge sigh of relief.

"It looks like we are not being followed so make your change quickly, dear," Daria said, handing her a dress bag. Catarine then walked to the nearby trader's shop, a close friend of Auntie's, and disappeared inside. She reappeared only a few minutes later looking quite the young lady, ready for her voyage, and joined Daria near the ship.

The captain himself was greeting the passengers at the gang plank. He gave a short courteous bow to the women, introduced himself and declared to be at their service. His navy uniform was similar to the French captains in picture books Catarine had seen at home. Both had the same long overcoat, gold buttons, and a magnificent gold-handled sword at their side. Only the hats were different.

"Ah, Mademoiselle, so pleased to have you and the other distinguished passengers on the steamer bound for Havana then on to New York. I'll introduce you to your sailing companions when it pleases you," he said, directing his comments to Catarine.

Catarine noticed the handsome young purser as he was escorting the ladies to their cabins individually. He wore tan knee breeches, a white linen shirt and a short navy jacket. His face was handsome and tanned, his dark brown hair curling out from beneath his large tricorne hat. The women both had a moment to view the docks from the port side of the ship before the purser came for them. They were relieved to see only strangers, passengers and the workers, no doubt, all about their tasks of seeing the ship safely and timely off. The morning sun had just broken through the gray horizon with a placid orange greeting, its warmth pouring yellow rays through the cloud's edges that reflected against the glassy sea.

"I'll be happy to escort you to your cabin," the elegant purser said to Catarine as he offered her his arm. "Would you be Catarine Dupre?"

"Yes, I am."

"And you have your slave, er, a servant with you?"

"I have a friend with me. She is right here," Catarine said with a frown on her face, indicating Daria who was fanning herself and watching the morning birds with a pained look.

"Her name is Daria Morinay and she's a femme de couleur libres, a free woman. She should be on your list as well."

"I see, Mademoiselles, I apologize," the purser bowed and flushed. "Both of you, please come with me and may you both have a wonderful voyage."

"How nice," Daria spoke with an air of disdain.

"Anything M'lady, you so desire, please, make it known to me. I'll dedicate myself to your comfort on this journey," he promised.

Once in their room, Catarine began to feel out of harm's way and they both began to unpack their things. Catarine was careful to hide her money that Daria had so carefully saved for her in a small but sturdy wooden chest, under the bottom bunk and hidden within the tapestry bag. Catarine felt a wave of relief wash over her, as she felt the ship begin to move. She collapsed happily on her bed and laughed quietly to herself.

The first day passed pleasurably. The weather was good, seas were calm, and the bright blue skies poured forth hope and peace all around. Catarine and Daria enjoyed making a few introductions as they cautiously explored a bit of the ship. The deck was clean and wide and the passengers were walking about aimlessly, chatting in a friendly manner. They lounged in the canvas chairs and enjoyed the sun's rays on their faces and the cool breezes that gently caressed them.

"I'm headed back to my family in Manhattan," Elizabeth, a young girl who had been visiting relatives, confided in Catarine. "I've just enjoyed the spring with my aunt and uncle in New Orleans. My mother is French. My grandfather's a milliner there. My father wanted us to settle in a more hospitable place, er, a bigger city in the North. We'd heard so many stories of the savages, you know. But New Orleans is much larger than I imagined."

"Oh yes, the savages," Catarine laughed. "But they are really harmless. I think they are afraid of us more. I've only seen a few, the ones who trade in Baton Rouge."

"Baton Rouge, that's a funny name. Why name a town 'Red Stick'? Are the trees there red?" Elizabeth asked.

"Oh no, it's just a town on the river. A trading post at one time. Its name is taken from the large red pole on which the natives mounted their sacrifices. The blood dripped down and made the pole red. Isn't it horrible? But they don't sacrifice anymore."

"Where exactly are you from?" the woman named Magdalene asked Catarine. She had been vague about her background, unlike Daria who had told them about where she had lived and gone to school.

"I'm exhausted!" Daria declared, trying to change the subject. "The sunbathing makes one so…relaxed." She then yawned and looked away, feigning boredom.

"I grew up in the country but I'd like to forget about those days," Catarine laughed. She was grateful the others laughed with her, and then she was quick to move the conversation along. "I've been living in New Orleans, of late, but I'm ready to see bigger things still. New York is our destination."

"Wonderful!" Elizabeth exclaimed as the bell sounded for afternoon tea. Catarine and Daria exchanged looks and excused themselves.

"Well done," Daria said as they left. "I'm glad you didn't tell them anything personal."

"I almost did but thought I'd start talking like you," she laughed. "You've got a knack for talking to people."

"You mean, rattling on and on about useless subjects? I hope this won't be too difficult for you. We are supposed to have adventures, remember?"

"Yes, although talking socially over tea isn't my kind of adventure."

"Just what *is* your kind of adventure?"

"I have all sorts in mind."

Dinner that evening was in an elegant room with lovely tablecloths and exquisite furnishings. The first class passengers sat together and conversed over the meal they were being served by candlelight. The servers were careful to keep their wine glasses from becoming empty.

The two women, being caught up in their thoughts and relaxed with the free flow of wine, dined in virtual silence, only politely acknowledging greetings spoken to them with a slight smile and a nod or two. Daria was content and sat daydreaming about what might be ahead in New York and meeting the famous people who were now setting forth new ideas in the world. Catarine sat hoping she was finally away from the danger of discovery and away to a new place, unknown and unread.

It felt fitting, almost celebratory, that they were dining with sterling silver and quality dishes. Although the ambience was an unexpected surprise, Catarine was mesmerized by the flickering candle lights against the delicate pattern of her lovely plate. She gently sipped her tea from the beautiful Havilland china cup and took a small bite of sponge cake as she absently stared into the dancing flames of the half-burnt candles before her. Out of the corner of her eye, she did, in fact, see a man sit down to her left across the table, but she continued with her thoughts until she felt him staring at her.

Annoyingly, she glanced over at him, and then dropped her silver dessert fork onto her plate so hard that all the guests at the table looked up suddenly.

"Hello, Catarine," said the man with a sickening sweet smile, amused at her reaction. "Such a coincidence, is it not, that we are both sailing on the same ship?"

He toasted her with his wine glass and brought it up slowly to his simpering mouth. As he took a long luxurious gulp of wine, Catarine just continued to stare back at the face of Mr. Frederick Fuhrmann.

When I was just a little thing, I starting wishing I was white. I knew the Lord make me this way, this black, and he musta had good reason but I still wished it. If my momma had known it, she'd have sorrowed to her grave. The way it was, she did anyway but my wishing woulda added to it. If she'd a known…

At night, I'd lay on my bed, on the side facing the moon and the field where the horses ran free, and I'd see my black arms laying there 'gainst the sheets. I'd squint my eyes up so tight to shut out my blackness and peek over to the outside world. Sometimes I'd play the game of look, see. But I always lost. I'd shut my eyes closed all the way and think about being white. Creamy white, like Catarine. Being white, you could go ride them horses anytime you want. You could climb up in your daddy's lap and read. Black folks don't have time for that. I'd shut up my eyes and think. Pretending is what Catarine called it when we use to play. I'd pretend to be white. Then I'd peek and see if I was white. I'd peek out of my squinted eyes and see if I had white arms laying there. But I'd always see my own skinny black arms, dark against the sheets. Arms that lifted loads no white girls were asked to bear. Then I'd shut my eyes again and dream of what it must be like to be Catarine. She a sweet nice girl, my best friend in all the world.

I wished she didn't leave. I cried for her for days on end. For days, nobody knew she was gone forever but me. That morning, watching her jump the fence and leave this place for good, I was wishing it was me leaving. She was always so brave. When she was out of sight and the last leaf was stilled in them woods across that fence, I fell down on my bed and cried myself sick. Luckily, nobody else was around. They all gone to their chores. When I went to Madam Marie's room, I told her I'd been sick all night. I was sick all right and was for days to come I didn't care an ounce about that wicked Koch boy dying. I was glad to be rid of him. He was as evil as his father, or soon would be if he didn't get himself killed by somebody. He'd bothered me one time too many, that's for sure. He thought he could come along and grab any one of us he wanted. And call hisself a Christian man too. I caint never understand that. They don't follow the Lord's ways, that's for sure.

I probably should have been nervous about what happened. But all I could think of was the fact that Catarine was gone. And that grieved me to no end.

It was later that week that everyone realized something bad had happened. The first thing was old man Koch looking for his boy. First he asked the cutters, because they came home talking about it. How Mason had gone off and didn't come back. When our people laughed about it quietly with each other in the quarters, Moses and I exchanged glances. Then later in the week, Koch came by yelling to us all, swearing that if any of us knew where to find his boy, we'd be sorry for not saying so. No one spoke. He'd gone away mumbling about trying to find Mason in the city and teaching him the lesson of his life.

Then his horse came back, sweaty and covered with mud and still wearing its saddle. I was inside with Madam tending to her clothes when all the commotion started outside. Everyone was astonished. Koch had doubled over and he started wailing instantly. I didn't expect him to react that way. It was strange to me for an evil person having such deep feelings of loss. After that he organized men to search everywhere for Mason. They scoured the countryside for weeks.

The day that horse came back, when I was with Catarine's mama, she and I had just turned and looked at each other, both of us unconcerned. She didn't look grieved at all. And I'm sure she noticed that I didn't care either. Truthfully, Koch was the only one who'd cared.

So for a time, while the search for Mason was under-way, life on the farm resumed. With Koch away searching, the production was managed by Demetrius, the senior field hand. He was the one who had been trained by Monsieur Dupre and knew cutting, purification and the delivery routes like the back of his hand. He stepped up and took Koch's place, even though he wasn't asked, for Koch and his son had ruled like they was Pharaoh and king of Egypt. But somebody had to do it. So he just did it and everything just fell in place. Like he the boss. Moses say he was a right smart one too because he talk to everyone like Monsieur Dupre done when he alive. Commanding like, but agree-able. He was good to everyone. He cared.

I remember Monsieur fondly. Catarine had herself a good daddy. And he was good to me too. Very good. My momma told me he thought of me as a special girl. A special black girl. I never like to hear that because I didn't want to hear about being black so I dismiss the rest of what she say to me when she talk like that. But, Monsieur Dupre, he did treat me real good. He let me pet the horses anytime I want. In fact, he let me ride them horses too.

When they done that, he and Catarine, when they teach me to ride, it was a big "to do" on the plantation. Because he wasn't just letting me on the horse in any ol' way. He was teaching me how to ride like he done his own daughter. Like the French do, all fancy. And he taught us both to ride like we was boys. They all be talking about that. They tease me about it, my folks. Her own momma wasn't happy about it either but when it's the master of the plantation doing it, ain't nobody gonna tell him to stop. My own people, they raised their eyebrows at it too. A girl riding like that caused many to shake their heads. And one of their own being taught anything from the master was surprising, even if it was the good Monsieur Dupre.

There was much high spirits and gaiety between us, Catarine and me. We played as little girls, even though she was four years my elder. And we kept being bona fide best friends; right up until the day she left. It didn't matter to either one of us that she was free and I was not. Not for a long while. Until I realized what that meant. Then it only mattered to me and I kept it secret in my heart.

At Sea

Chapter 5

Despite her extreme shock, Catarine regained her composure and finished her meal with grace and poise. Her mind had frozen shut but she managed to smile and swallow her food, each bite feeling huge and tasteless. She and Daria exchanged looks of alarm across the table. Somehow Catarine mustered enough courage to dismiss herself to her cabin, signaling Daria not to follow with a shake of her head. Thank God Mr. Fuhrmann didn't follow as he would have likely either thrown her overboard or robbed her on the spot. The money! How long had he known she was on board? He had followed her, of course. He must have. She quickly locked the door behind her and ran madly to the locked chest under her bed. To her relief, it was all there, every bit of it.

Her mind swam and churned as she tortured herself over the next hour, pacing the floors and reviewing her rehearsed plan, which now seemed excessively juvenile. If Mr. Fuhrmann meant to do her harm, she must know right away! But why had he been following her? Her head pounded and throbbed, finally gaining her complete attention, and leading her to an immediate decision. She needed a drink, and a strong one.

She rang for the purser, requested brandy, and turned down his generous offer of assistance. Maybe tomorrow she could explain to him her need of protection from Fuhrmann. But she'd have to contrive a suitable story. Her head was pounding even harder when Daria slipped in the room.

"I spoke with him at length," Daria informed Catarine as a knock came upon the door. They looked at each other in fear.

"I have your brandy, Mademoiselle," the purser said, muffled through the door, to Catarine who stood braced against the other side. She moved the bolt back and opened the door, allowing him in with the silver tray containing a small corked bottle and a brandy snifter.

Each sip of brandy warmed Catarine's throat and dulled her worry as she listened to Daria recount what happened at the dinner table following her departure.

"He acted so blasé" Daria explained. "He didn't seem concerned at all that you'd left the table. He started by introducing himself to me as Frederick, as though I'd never met him. Then told me he was only concerned for your welfare. I scarcely believe that! And he also declared to be traveling due to business unrelated to your family. Ha! What do you think of that?"

"Frederick Fuhrmann is a liar," Catarine said shaking her head, still holding her brandy and as she reclined against the wall next to her bed, Daria sitting in the solitary chair next to her in their compact quarters.

"That seems to be likely," Daria continued. "Nevertheless, I conversed with him as if I gave credence to his story. And I came up with a story for him to explain our presence here. I talked of us attempting to enter university in the North, as we have discussed anyway. I'm not sure he bought it."

"That is a plausible story, well done," Catarine said, sitting up and refilling her brandy glass. "After all, what can he do to me on this ship? He can't have me arrested here, if that's his aim, can he?"

"I'm sure not. It would be at our arrival in New York. We must mind our "p's" and "q's" on this voyage, then be off the ship and on our way quickly when we arrive."

The two women settled in for the night quickly. Daria was off to sleep by the time the moon could be seen from their porthole, high in the sky. And as the waves lapped against the wooden berth way below her, Catarine drifted into a dizzy dream where the sky was red and dazzling, the color of brandy.

It must have been the brandy. This time she cried in her sleep but couldn't wake up. For some reason, her sobs failed to wake Daria. Bella, dear Bella, beaten again. Her hindquarters bloodied by Koch. He was a relentless fool! His whip had chards of broken glass tied in bits of leather. Who would ever do this to a lovely horse such as Bella? She was good. Who would do this anyway? Such cruelty. Catarine tossed and turned and finally woke herself up to escape the horror.

The next morning Catarine dressed and slipped out without Daria. She settled on a dress that was a calming green everyday frock, her bonnet large and protective.

Walking down the port side of the ship that led to the dining room, she spotted Mr. Fuhrmann's brown coat around the mid ship mast as he stood talking to an officer she didn't know. She automatically ducked into a doorway for a second, then shaking off her fear, walked right up to him.

"Excuse me, Mr. Fuhrmann, but I'd like to speak to you privately," she said. Once again she could detect the amused look on his face as he touched the back of her arm, leading her to the side railing of the ship.

"You wish to know the purpose of my voyage, no doubt, Mademoiselle, but I also wish to know yours," he spoke directly, watching her eyes closely.

"I want to know why you've been following me," she said returning his steady gaze.

"Oh, Catarine," he chuckled. "You flatter yourself. I am not following you, another man's fiancé. I scheduled this trip months ago."

"I don't believe you!" she snapped. "Mason told me you were going to New York in December, not now."

"It's obvious that you were misinformed, is it not?" He smiled smugly. "Now, tell me, why are *you* traveling? I think it is rather unwise for two young women without a male chaperone to be away from home and so far. Just think of all the dangers."

She fought away tears of panic that she felt coming to the surface.

"And to tell no one your plans?" he questioned. "That is foolishness, Catarine."

"Please just leave me alone," her voice rose in frustration as she backed away.

"So sorry to have disturbed you, Mademoiselle," he said pleasantly as Mr. Crosse, the purser and a ship's hand approached them, concerned.

"Is there a problem here?" Mr. Crosse asked Catarine quickly.

"Something I said must have disturbed Mademoiselle Dupre, Mr. Crosse. But I meant no harm whatsoever," he explained. "You see, I am her solicitor."

"No, he isn't. Not mine, at least. He is trying to thwart my plans," she began explaining to the confused Mr. Crosse, who looked back and forth between them. "I wish for him to leave me alone while on this ship."

"Of course, M'lady," the purser said. "Mr. Fuhrmann, I'll ask you to not approach this lady again during our voyage."

"Absolutely not, my dear Mr. Crosse. I am a gentleman," he stated calmly, then walked away with confidence.

"Once again, I offer you any assistance at all, M'lady," Mr. Crosse said warmly as he looped Catarine's arm under his and began walking her in the opposite direction.

"I might concede to it this time," she said, feeling the comfort of his strong arm.

"Pardon?" he said, turning a quizzical look at her.

"I just don't trust him. And, yes, could you please look out for me and my companion while on this ship?"

"Oh yes, Mademoiselle, it's quite my responsibility. I could post a guard at your door, if you wish. I would be honored to help," he said warmly, his blue eyes sparkling.

"Oh, could you? That would be wonderful, and a great comfort to us," she said.

"Certainly. And here we are. I'm sure you will be safe here. I'll be back to fetch you shortly." He led her to the dining room that contained many of the passengers enjoying breakfast.

In a short while, Daria joined Catarine for a meal displayed on a sideboard loaded with pastries, tarts, biscuits, jams and cheeses of various kinds.

"I do wish Fuhrmann hadn't shown up. I'm not quite sure what to do about him," Catarine said applying butter to an apple tart. She kept her head down and contemplated her new problem.

"He might not be as bad as we originally thought," Daria answered. "Let's try to enjoy ourselves."

"I'm going to ignore him for now," Catarine answered as they made their way to a table with their morning meal.

"For now we should just enjoy the moment. Like this scrumptious strawberry tart. It's heavenly."

The women enjoyed their breakfast in silence, drinking Cuban coffee with their pastries while conversation ensued around them. Catarine found it interesting to hear the businessmen nearest them discussing the transatlantic mail.

"Collins, it is a surprise finding you on this line. Are you spying out the competition?"

"The government's paying both New York and Havre lines a pretty penny to carry mail each fortnight."

"So I hear. What's that got to do with your line?"

"I've been talking to the folks in New York. My line is faster than the Cunards. You'll soon have your mail carried by my line."

Catarine watched the men huff and guffaw over their coffee then rise to have their morning smoke in the fiddley. She thought they both must have been vastly rich especially the one named Collins, and wondered at how much they traveled. She longed to question people such as them about the world they'd seen.

"Are you worried?"

"No, just thinking," Catarine replied, still pondering the gentlemen.

"You seem a thousand miles away."

"I am, so to speak. Did you hear those men?"

"Talking about mail and money?"

"Yes."

"Not very interesting to me."

"It was what they weren't saying. They've been everywhere in the world and seen a good deal of things, no doubt. I wish I could ask them about it. About the world," Catarine said with a sigh.

"At least we are here. We made it this far. Now, let's go exploring!"

After breakfast they arose and went outside to explore the promenade deck. After a pleasant stroll in the sunshine, Mr. Crosse joined them.

"Ladies! I've been looking for you. Let me take you on a tour of the ship."

"Oh, yes," Catarine answered, her voice uplifted for the first time that morning.

"We do not need any assistance," was Daria's simultaneous reply.

"Oh, my goodness, what to do," he laughed out boldly but offered Catarine his arm, which she gladly took. He proceeded to guide them along. "The *New Amsterdam*," he went on to say, "is the largest ship upon which I've been privileged to serve. It's nearly 150 feet long."

The substantial steel barricade encasing them gave Catarine a settled feeling as well as the purser's muscular arm, which held her fast. The ship certainly was impressive, as they had already seen. They had both been amazed by the exquisitely carved wood in the dining area. As they entered room after room, Catarine listened to Mr. Crosse speak on and on about the ship's fascinating qualities while Daria, settling into her easy charm, either attended with rapt appreciation or asked further questions about the steamer itself or glories of his own life at sea.

It was Daria who tried to draw Catarine into the conversation. "I don't know which is more fascinating, Mr. Crosse, this steamship or the life you must lead on the sea. Can you imagine, Catarine, what Mr. Crosse must see on his voyages?"

"No, it must be wonderful. And the people you meet as well."

Catarine began imagining at that moment the purser's attention on pretty girls with each voyage. She surmised that she and Daria were his pick on this particular voyage. The thought was a little disconcerting since, having been so close to Mr. Crosse during their walk, she had become aware of his desirability. He was strong and sure of himself, but kindness itself. He smelled of something pleasant she could not identify, perhaps a foreign spice. And his eyes danced with excitement when he talked, disarming anyone who looked into them.

As it happened, the purser, in his charming way, managed to both delight them with his knowledge of the industries of the new steamship and impress them with his brute strength by lifting several large metal items along the tour. He then expertly maneuvered Catarine into a corner alone long enough for a kiss just before the end of their walk. He achieved this by suggesting that Daria, because she admired floral arrangements so, should enter the ship's galley and request a special bouquet for their room. He then turned a quick corner nearby and caught Catarine close to him by her waist. With his handsome face near hers and his crimson smiling lips, she didn't mind the kiss he gave her on her lips. Catarine, in fact, liked it quite a bit and being caught like this by Mr. Crosse was a much more pleasant experience than overtures she'd received from Mason.

Over the next several days, Catarine and Daria spent their time relaxing in the sun as their ship headed for Havana, "…a boisterous place," as Mr. Crosse had informed them. It was a lovely time of year to be approaching the Island of Cuba, another piece of information gleaned from the purser, which made the women even more excited as they would presently be able to view it for themselves. As the days grew warmer and the air balmy, flocks of birds thickened the sky. Having just arrived for winter the gulls followed the stern of the ship, hoping for bits of chum. Other passengers told them this was a sign that land couldn't be far off and that they would be in Cuba shortly. Their itinerary stated they would be arriving at the port of Havana by sundown and they'd set sail again the next night.

"Do you think we should leave the ship?" Catarine asked.

"I do so want to, but I'm a bit afraid."

"Let's be brave!" was Catarine's reply. Daria clapped her hands and threw her arms around her neck.

"Yes, we are off to see the world! Why should we be cowardly?" Daria exclaimed.

Catarine, looking at her friend sitting on deck in the afternoon sun, as giddy as a young girl, was suddenly confident that they were both going to be all right, not just in Havana, but always, if they stayed together.

As the ship approached in the morning sun, the port of Havana looked sultry and exotic. The stewards and stewardesses had made their rounds early that morning, making sure all were prepared for a day in Havana. Catarine and Daria dressed with excitement, preparing for every eventuality. Orders were finally given that passengers could disembark. The queue was long to leave the ship but they waited patiently.

At the wharf, large banded wooden barrels lined the dock that made it hard to see the downtown area as they were going ashore. The barrels smelled of whiskey, and each one was taller than a man. After walking the gangplank and through row upon row of barrels, the crowd of passengers spilled out into a muddy street lined with palm trees and shops. The merchants, dark skinned and Spanish-speaking, bid them to come inside but most of the passengers took a casual approach and walked around shopping leisurely. Catarine and Daria followed the main group as they meandered through the boutiques and walkways, which were lush with vegetation. Leaves as big as floor rugs hung about with enormous flowers of every color and shape. Daria scurried over to stand under a huge crimson blossom that towered above her head, and waving her arms up high, still could not reach its velvet pedals. Most of the men were setting out to buy cigars as the women began to be drawn into shops that sold silks and trinkets. Tours were being taken by carriages in groups of four, departing from beneath the shade of the most immense lavender blossoms Catarine had ever seen.

Catarine, fishing coins from her bag for their fare said, "Look, they're going 'round by the Imperial del Paseo."

So they, along with two young women they'd met aboard the ship, stepped into the creaking carriage. It rocked and squeaked as each new passenger stepped up and took their seat.

"Ready?" said the ebony driver in Spanish as he flicked his solitary horse with the whip. The carriage responded to the pull reluctantly but once the big wheels began to roll, the mechanism settled into a routine. The horse knew the way to go without direction from the driver for he kept his eyes mostly on the ladies behind him, one of which who spoke fluent Spanish.

They proceeded down a lane that took them to a very long grassy area lined on both sides with towering palm trees. On one end of the lawn, as they turned into the del Paseo, was a fountain topped with a statue of a man on horseback. In the distance they could see the grand estate to which the carriage was heading, the trees at military attention.

After a round through the splendid estate, they continued the tour while the driver talked of the great Havana hurricane a few years back. The interpretation continued with the help of their Spanish-speaking passenger, although it was mostly unnecessary, because it was obvious what he was expressing. They clearly noticed the damage that the hurricane had rendered. He stopped the carriage before an enormous oak that had been toppled by the storm, its roots exposed to them, standing taller than the building next to it. He pointed out vast damage to houses and buildings that they passed, nature having nearly pounded them to pieces. They then proceeded onward to their ultimate goal, the exquisite Cathedral of Havana, or La Catedral de La Virgen, as the driver said.

Entering the glorious cathedral, the women covered their heads then began to look above and about them with a reverential silence. Having been in her own St. Louis' Cathedral many times, Daria was struck by the immense size difference, the pillars alone being massive by comparison. The atmosphere was set apart, divine, and time stopped as they wandered through the pews speechless and unrushed.

When the women felt they had completed their tour, they each stepped into the courtyard to the side of the Cathedral and the triumphant afternoon sun welcomed them. Others were strolling about and relaxing, talking and laughter could be heard. The four of them gathered and waited, refreshed and unhurried, until their driver fetched them for their ride back.

Following the tour all four ladies dined at a villa cafe near the dock. As they sat dining, they could view whiskey barrels, held fast by large straps to a wood arm, being hoisted into the hold of their ship. Daria whispered to Catarine that she thought it was unusual that they hadn't seen Mr. Crosse anywhere. Catarine had been disappointed in this but kept it to herself.

"I'm not sure I care for this Spanish wine," Daria made a face as she put down her glass with disgust.

"I suppose we shall all be drinking whiskey now," Catarine mused looking beyond Daria at their ship.

"We are always needing good wine, locally. The imports are so unpredictable," Magdalene added to the conversation. "We have a family vineyard in France, but none here. Unless you count La Freme Plantation, that's where I grew up."

"I've heard of it." Catarine said noticing Daria's look of warning. "How wonderful it would be to own your own land."

"You've heard of it?"

"Oh, er, I suppose..." Catarine stammered and flushed, looking down at her dessert.

When she looked up, she saw Fuhrmann sit down at a table across the cafe.

"Sounds lovely, dear," Elizabeth spoke. "I'm from Toulouse myself. We left in 1826. I was only a baby."

Daria sighed longingly, with a distant look on her face. "I was born in New Orleans and have been there most of my life. I've always wished to travel, and now, thanks to dear Catarine, I'm able to make this journey with her."

As they were leaving, Fuhrmann asked to have a private word with Catarine. At first she said no but then acquiesced and asked Daria to wait for her. As Catarine feared, the discussion centered around Mason and she had no time to prepare her answers.

"Are you responsible for Mason's death," Fuhrmann boldly asked, leaning forward and looking deep into Catarine's eyes.

She turned away quickly, catching her breath. She was aware that all the blood had just drained out of her face.

"All right, your reaction tells me you know all about it. Let's do this. Don't answer just yet. But listen to my proposal."

Catarine nodded and looked up at him as he sat back and continued. "I am aware that you hated him. Am I correct?" Catarine nodded again. "I am also aware that Mr. Koch was arranging this farce of a marriage for his son to insure the estate would stay in their hands. I'd been asked to draw up the agreement. What I'm sure you don't know is that I never cared for the man or his son."

Catarine was surprised to hear this piece of information indeed. Fuhrmann had always appeared polished in his capacity as the Koch family solicitor, the front man on all legal matters. In her mind he had been guilty of all kinds of sins himself.

"As a lawyer, I'd like to remain in the dark about what happened the night of Mason Koch's death. You are wanted by the law for his murder because of evidence found at the scene and because of the fact that you fled the same time Mason went missing, which could possibly be argued as circumstantial. Remember that in the future if necessary. I'm willing to overlook the fact that we are on this ship together. It is coincidence. I didn't follow you. In fact, if you are ever caught and if anyone gets their hands on this ship's manifest, it could look like I'm in league with you in this."

Catarine finally summoned her pluck and stated, "Pardon me, but that sounds like an extraordinary coincidence if I've ever heard one!"

"I suppose you'll just have to take my word for it, dear. But the main point I have for you is this: I'm willing to help you stay hidden and shall we say, informed, and in exchange you can help me out with a few matters."

"In what way can I possibly help *you*?" Catarine's curiosity was piqued by Fuhrmann's statement but she didn't get an answer to her question at all.

Instead of answering her, Fuhrmann's gaze was taken elsewhere, up and beyond Catarine and his face turned instantly sour. Catarine turned to see Mr. Crosse, dressed in civilian attire, approaching them.

"I see you two are getting on better," Mr. Crosse said to both of them but looked into Catarine's face with an expression she couldn't decipher.

"He is helping me with a private matter," Catarine said looking at Fuhrmann who sat unmoved with an irritated countenance looking up at Mr. Crosse.

"Shall I leave you to it then? I had hoped to escort you back on board, Catarine."

"Why board the ship just yet? We don't sail for another hour or so, right Mr. Crosse?" Mr. Fuhrmann said looking at the purser.

"True, we do have some time," said Mr. Crosse, looking a little embarrassed as he fished for his pocket watch from his trousers and cleared his throat. And starting to ask Catarine a question, "What would you…"

"Well, then, you two young lovers go on without me," Fuhrmann interrupted, rising up from his chair and touching Catarine on the arm as if they were old friends. "Go for a nice stroll, why not? It's a lovely evening." And he bowed slightly to Catarine, gathered his hat and departed, walking toward the ship.

By the end of the discourse between the two men, Catarine couldn't find Daria anywhere so she took the stroll with Mr. Crosse as Fuhrmann had suggested. She was beginning to feel controlled again, a familiar feeling from her days with Mason Koch. As they strolled along Mr. Crosse, suddenly a fount of pleasantries as before, gave a narrative about Havana. She kept her eye out for Daria and grew worried as the sun inched downward toward the horizon. He talked about a Conquistador, Spanish ships and pirates but Catarine couldn't follow his history lesson although she knew it was most likely fascinating. Her distraction was multifaceted and beginning to give her a headache as he droned on. At least he didn't seem to be expecting a reply.

Finally, she broke into his lecture about a fatal epidemic, and said, "I must find Daria. I don't see her anywhere. I wonder if she went aboard? I can't imagine that she'd board without me, but I can't think of anywhere else she'd be."

"All right, let's look for her," Mr. Crosse said. "We can check with Mosley. He is purser today and would have seen her board." They made inquiries with the staff on the steamship but didn't find Daria. By then, Catarine was supremely nervous as they were all to be on board in a quarter hour and set sail after that. They began questioning Magdalene, Elizabeth and anyone Catarine could find who knew Daria by sight.

Finally, as Catarine was about to cry she spotted Fuhrmann with Daria approaching the ship, having just turned from a small avenida and strolling together toward the dock area in a hurry. She was so relieved to see her that she broke free from Mr. Crosse's arm and ran back down the gang plank to Daria, embracing her neck, Mr. Crosse following at her heels.

"Where have you been? I was so worried," Catarine said with noticeable emotion.

"Oh dear, I'm so very sorry," Daria said kissing Catarine on the cheek sweetly. "It couldn't be helped. I wondered if you were already aboard." And they embraced again leaving the two men, Fuhrmann and Crosse standing there glaring at each other awkwardly.

Mr. Crosse broke up the reunion by stating, "It's time we all boarded now or we shall all be left behind in Havana."

The next day's weather brought a raw and primeval outlook so thick that Daria's late morning stroll about the deck made her feel that she needed a second wash as soon as possible. The steamy air swirled into her face the moment she went outside, and though she was familiar with it in many ways, this was a new depth of humidity that left salt deposits on her skin. She carried handkerchiefs with her on days like this in New Orleans. She had slept late again which was her usual practice. After all, she was a city girl. They'd all been raised to attend parties until the wee hours of the morning, beauty sleep it was, giving regard to one's toilette in leisure.

As early as she could remember, she knew of the balls and galas in New Orleans. Her Mama attended these as well as her aunts and occasionally her Grammy. Mostly, as a young girl, she and her cousins stayed with her Grammy on the nights of the balls. That's when her Mama and aunties attended, entertaining the white French men. After that she was whisked away for a couple of years in Paris to attend school, along with the other children of her father. Those were the best years of her life so far. She felt included. Loved. And what's more, she was away from New Orleans to somewhere different. That was all that mattered to her, to be loved and to see the world. And now she and Catarine were going somewhere new. And, what's more, out of this heat!

"I cannot believe it is this hot in October. There's no wind!"

Daria heard Magdalene talking about the weather as she approached the women lounging on deck. Daria sat with Magdalene and Elizabeth who were just feet away from the ship's railing where Catarine stood next to Mr. Crosse. Daria hoped to position herself close enough to hear their conversation.

"We are sailing northward, toward Florida. You'll notice, the sea is dead calm today, unfortunately very typical for this location. We can only go so fast under steam power alone and must air our sails until the wind picks up."

Daria watched as Mr. Crosse took Catarine's arm in his and walked her down the side of the ship away from the women. Then they paused to have a look overboard. She thought she heard him say, "See how the sea is like glass? If you look about in the water on days like today, you might see a porpoise."

He smiled at her sweetly, drawing her in front of him, and encircled her by her waist as they looked out at the water together. Daria thought that Catarine knew her geography well enough and didn't need a lesson from Mr. Crosse. And besides, why was she being taken in by him so? It was obvious to her that she didn't really trust him. He was a cad. He must think, with his clever talk on every matter under the sun, coupled with the fact that he was indeed handsome, that he could woo any woman he wanted who boarded his ship.

Mr. Crosse, dressed in his purser uniform, had Catarine so close, as to be nearly embracing her in front of him. Daria noticed that both his arms were around her waist and their heads next to each other close enough to be touching.

Daria leapt up and interrupted them with a warning. "Excuse me, but this seems highly inappropriate for an officer in uniform."

"To tell the truth, I do have duties to tend to, as much as I regret it," was the reply from Mr. Crosse as he unwrapped himself from Catarine. "Until the evening comes," he said, kissing Catarine's hand softly as they parted, giving her a mischievous smile that Catarine returned.

"I thought you were vexed by him," Daria stated. "You said as much last night."

"Yes, I did say that," Catarine confessed wistfully looking toward the departing purser. Then turning to Daria said, "But he's so wretchedly good-looking! I'm just enjoying myself a bit, that's all. Besides, you've enjoyed all sorts of men around you at your balls. I haven't!"

Daria made no reply but simply gazed out upon the waters with an aggrieved look on her face.

Later that day, Catarine stared into the looking glass, analyzing herself for the first time in a long while. Her dark, brown curls fell softly across her high forehead, her eyebrows were thick but attractively framed her deep set green eyes. Her high cheekbones and narrow chin gave her whole face a heart-shaped appearance that suggested grace and sophistication. She wondered if Mr. Crosse found her alluring. She chastised herself a little for being like the women she had grown to hate back in Louisiana; women who fussed all day over their appearances and put the highest priority on their attractiveness. Catarine had always felt she was average and that had been good enough for her. She'd always preferred spending her time out riding, overseeing the sugarcane crops or reading from the family library. But today, introspection altering her frame of mind, she was curious about her appearance and just how a man might view her.

She beheld Mr. Crosse with fascination, remembering his dancing eyes and smiling face with wonder and his brown youthful curls that spilled over his ears and around his uniform collar. She wondered what his life at sea was like. To be young and travel upon the waters, stopping at ports all over the world, must be quite a life of adventure. And he had much elegance for a man, being tall and lean and moving with agility and ease. He was such a contrast to Mason who had been stocky, muscle-bound and fairly devoid of grace, despite his riding ability. Comparing the impressions she now had of the two different suitors, if Mason could even be called that, she realized even more now how impolite and passionless Mason had been compared to the dashing Mr. Crosse. She chuckled at herself in the glass fancying that freedom was producing a new confidence in her. And this fact was glorious, she thought, as she smiled with satisfaction at herself in the mirror.

Having the evening appointment before her with Mr. Crosse, Catarine decided to grab her novel and go outside for a few hours of reading and fresh air in the canvas chairs on the deck near her cabin door.

After about an hour of reading <u>Le Comte de Monte Christo</u>, Daria approached her, sitting in the chair adjacent to her.

"Alexander Dumas! I've heard of him. He's a quadroon like me, did you know?" Daria asked, breathlessly excited.

"I didn't know."

"Is that an enjoyable book?"

"It's somewhat depressing."

"Still, I'd like to read it when you are done."

Catarine continued to read without responding. Daria had hoped to make up for their earlier strained exchange about Mr. Crosse. After letting Catarine read on in silence for a few minutes, Daria finally interrupted again.

"Yes, his grandmother was a Haitian. Isn't that interesting? Just like my grammy. I've wondered how white he is."

"What does that matter?"

"I guess it would only matter to someone who isn't white," Daria replied curtly.

As they sat in silence again, Daria watched the noisy birds dive nose first for small fish that danced right below the surface of the water. The gulls argued over the fish caught, bickering amongst themselves and vying for location over the best schools of minnows. As the women sat on, Catarine presently closed her book and the welcomed afternoon breeze began rolling over them and winding through the wooden masts, making the flags snap over and over again in response.

As late afternoon developed, the air grew thick with moisture and the bright rolling clouds, with the blinding sun pouring forth raw heat between them, dominated the entire sky. Catarine shaded her eyes with her book, and squinting, peered out over the sea and noticed for the first time since they departed Havana, that land could be seen. It was still very far away, but she could see the bright blending colors of the shoreline. The entire coast was lined with dark green foliage planted in what looked like pure white sand that mingled into the pale green surf. It quickly became the dark blue gulf that rolled up next to their ship. Between the two liquid colors, she could see the tide rising up and churning, like a gray billowing curtain.

As much as she wanted to stay port side and view the land, she felt virtually driven inside by the stifling heat and the intense need to rest her eyes. It was common for most of the passengers to take afternoon naps in their cabins, enjoying the stillness of the water at that time of day and escaping the heat. Daria, having left her an hour before, was already asleep on her bed when Catarine came in. She opened the porthole, took off her shoes and dress and washed her flushed face with lavender water, then collapsed on top of her spread and shut her tired eyes.

She must have slept quite a while, for when she arose, she noticed instantly the long shadows in her cabin and that the sky out of the window had changed to a softer blue-gray. She woke, alone in the cabin, to the sound of tiny insects buzzing near her ears. Swatting the annoying bugs away, she sat up on her bed, her feet touching the edge of her small chest, the one in which she kept all her money. Normally it was kept well under her bed and she hadn't noticed it sticking out when she had arrived in her room. With her mind on Mr. Crosse, she concluded that the ship must have tilted some during her nap causing it to slide out a bit. She shoved it back under and proceeded to freshen up for what she trusted would be a pleasant evening with Mr. Crosse, together viewing the lovely Florida shoreline.

She didn't see his approach. She was gazing across the dining room from the side bar chair with a somewhat forlorn crease centered on her brow. He watched her a moment and found her profile quite lovely, her brown silky curls flowing in long twists around her shoulders, her hands resting on her pale yellow dress. She had the paradoxical appearance of being capably intelligent and at the same time a damsel in distress needing immediate rescue. And Mr. Seth Crosse wanted to be her rescuer. The unguarded smile that washed over Catarine's face the moment she spotted him pleased him very much indeed.

"So sorry to keep you waiting, my dear. I should have set a time to collect you," he said, taking her hands into his, caressing her smooth soft skin with his thumbs.

"That's all right, Mr. Crosse, I'd rather meet you here anyway," she answered, her thoughts going to the unsettled Daria.

"Please call me Seth," he smiled into her eyes.

They dined together at a private table away from the main hall, much to her relief. They ate in near silence but neither of them found any awkwardness in it at all, rather a tranquility and understanding. They looked at each other, searching each other's face for a familiarity they seemed to share at the table alone and away from the crowd. Their hands touched and it seemed a cloud enveloped them with an alluring timelessness. It was as if they knew each other well and were communicating without words as old friends do.

Time rushed by and supper ended suddenly, the wine bottle empty, so they rose together and went out into the fresh clear night air. Still feeling the cloud of wonder surrounding them, they walked along the deck holding on to each other's arms.

The ship remained in still waters not far off the Florida coast. The shoreline was muted but beautiful under a golden moonlight that illuminated the whole beach line. They stopped to view a group of small wooden boats, barely visible, which were pulled ashore and what looked like brown naked bodies moving around on the beach. Catarine had the sudden urge to cast off her clothes and jump overboard with Seth, swim ashore and become a beach native herself. What a life they would have! The whole place was dreamlike, under the full blazing moon, a place where there was no time and where no one else existed.

Catarine and Seth remained together there with their arms tightly around each other until the moon and everyone else had long gone to bed. Just how long they stayed together that night, touching and holding each other, Catarine wasn't quite sure, but the sky was showing signs that sunrise was near when Seth finally returned her to her cabin. The last thing she remembered as she drifted off to sleep was the wonderful and desperate kissing.

At a luxuriously late morning hour, Catarine awoke alone calm and peaceful. The bright sun could be seen through her window climbing high into the sky. She didn't want to risk the embarrassment of searching late for a breakfast, so she lingered to dress for the afternoon.

By the time she went out, carrying her broad hat and dressed in an autumn green, she expected the bright intense heat but noticed instead a mass of dark gray clouds across the horizon. She couldn't distinguish which way they were moving but trusted the ship's personnel to be watching the sky intently themselves. The shore was no longer in sight and the water churned, listing the ship with dark swells of sea that foamed here and there as it blended and kneaded against the creaking ship. It was still comfortable enough to read but when the dinner bell sounded, Catarine decided she wasn't exactly hungry. Whether it was the tilting ship or last night's excitement that chased away her good appetite, she wasn't sure. She intended on ordering biscuits quickly then returning to the cabin to read when Daria came to her breathlessly, "I despise this ship! The way it tousles one about. I'm feeling horrible now."

"Yes, I am too. Let's just get a few biscuits and go to the cabin."

"And perhaps something to drink," Daria added. "I don't want to wait. Let's go and see what we can find."

Daria slipped her arm through Catarine's and pulled her along. They entered the galley, and looked around while the staff, dressed in white, prepared dinner for hundreds of passengers. No one seemed to care as they stood there in the doorway. Daria, spotting an open bottle of wine nearby, breathing perhaps, as it was almost full, boldly walked over and seized it, and turning directly around, left the galley. Catarine followed her and the two burst into laughter.

"Now for the biscuits." Daria said, no doubt remembering the dessert sidebar, walked to where it was being stocked by the waiters, and snatched up a basket of pastries, spun around and handed the basket to Catarine just as the last waiter left the area. "This will have to do. Let's go."

"You are a delight, my friend," Catarine said then laughed again as they hurried away, their skirts rustling.

By the time they neared their cabin, walking had become a chore as the sea mixed and stirred about with fervor.

They lounged and chatted for several hours eating and drinking as the ship tossed them about more than ever before but it wasn't until the sky darkened that they became concerned and decided to look outside. The sky was black and alarmingly sinister. Several waves loomed up next to the ship as it dipped down and up, down and up. In the wicked distance, small flashes could be seen beneath the heavy blanket of clouds. The whole picture set before them looked like a horrid vengeful argument about to ensue.

They walked around the deck of the ship holding on to get an idea of what everyone else was doing. The whole crew wore serious expressions.

"Get below!" one shouted to them.

Catarine looked about her for Seth but didn't find him anywhere. She realized they were the only women out there. Alarmed, they looked at each other, then lifted their skirts to hurry to their cabin for shelter just as a loud fearful crack split the black cloud and touched the angry water of the horizon.

Hiding in the cabin was not much better, as their ears and nerves were being shattered with each flash of lightning and thunder that rocked the sky all around them. They sat in silence and stark fear for what seemed like hours, until the rains began. The water fell gradually at first together with the wild popping, then increasing to a steady downpour as the white jagged fingers of lightening began to move further away. They sensed a cool feeling of relief wash over them as the rain grew loud and steady, flowing in voluminous sheets and the thunder subsided completed. Their respite from the fearful elements was regrettably short-lived, for as the lightening had moved away to a great distance and the exhaustive rainfall, which indeed was comforting at first, now gave way to winds that began to bear upon their ship with the furry of a snarling animal. Water that once came down in a steady flow commenced to lash across and up against their porthole again and again, thrown there by a gale, vexed and enraged. What had seemed mighty and strong up to that point, their ship now seemed a hapless victim of the immortal sea and sky. The captive women were thrust into terror as they were thrown about their cabin like rag dolls.

Daria was the first to speak. "I'm not staying in here to drown," she said as she painstakingly dragged herself to the cabin door.

"Are you mad?" Catarine yelled to her as Daria exited the room with great effort. "God help us!"

Before Catarine followed her, she crawled over to the chest under her bed and gathered her money up, stuffing it all into her bodice.

"Damn it all!" she said as she made her way out of the room to find Daria.

Water was everywhere and Catarine was completely soaked. Outside, Daria was not anywhere in sight and Catarine cursed aloud for having the double task of saving herself and having to find her impulsive friend in this wickedness. As she made it to the deck, the sky was slate gray and the rain steadily pouring as the sea fought against the ship to topple it. Catarine could see the ship's crew occasionally through the gray blanket of water about her, holding onto the masts, shouting orders and rudely swearing against the elements, as they threw ropes and helplessly manned their ship.

Catarine was frantic as she held fast to both the railing and her bodice of money, her inheritance that, up until then, hadn't been at risk, and while doing so she felt two attacks hit her with equal force. First she felt so terrifyingly alone, without Daria or even Seth, without anyone. After that realization came the other assault. A huge wall of black shiny water clapped down viciously upon her body and would have easily washed her away from the ship and into the tortured sea, but for the fact her foot caught in the rope net hanging over the side of the ship. She dangled perilously on the ship's side, her head harrowingly near the swell of black water, her foot painfully twisted within the meshwork. She swallowed salty gulps of sea water that burned her throat then, grabbing the rope with one hand, then the other, she pulled herself up the side of the ship and held on.

"Help!" she cried but her voice was strangled by the wicked sea.

She held fast to the ropes, fingers fastened, bleeding and stinging and her head going under water with each wave that clapped cruelly against her back. Her focus became surviving each wave and the blowing out of water, and inhaling for the next onslaught. Time was intangible, a mere notion, thus it was unclear how long she hung there fighting the waves. It could have been minutes or possibly hours.

The sea's strength waned and she, dangling by one hand and foot, mumbled something about Bessie as the men approached and stood looking down upon her.

"Give me your hand!"

She heard shouting from above. Who was this? She looked up and saw him. He looked like someone she had seen before.

"Come on now, give me your hand."

She thought for a moment about her mother back at home. She wondered if her mother was missing her. Then Catarine began to cry. She cried for her mother.

It was at that point that she remembered Daria and cried for her. Where could Daria have gone? She must find her! And then her hands began to hurt. They hurt so very much.

"Give me your hand and I'll pull you up!"

It was that man. It was Fuhrmann. He would know about her mother! She must ask him! So Catarine reached up and gave Frederick Fuhrmann her blistered, bleeding hand.

He carried her in his arms to the dining hall, which had quickly been converted into a medical room. He stayed with her as she was recovered by warm broth and bandages along with a draught of bitter medicine to ease her pain.

"Mm, good," she said quietly as Fuhrmann fed her a spoon while an attendant bandaged her hands.

"You're shaking. Are you still cold?" Fuhrmann asked her, setting the broth aside and placing a blanket around her shoulders.

"A little, yes. I don't know why I'm shaking."

"Well, that was an ordeal," said Fuhrmann, shaking his head. He resumed his task with the spoon. Her shaking slowly subsided and she closed her eyes as if to nap in the chair, her wraps being completed.

Mr. Crosse found her being tended to by Fuhrmann and promptly asked him to leave, first with an insolent tone, then one more tolerant, "Many thanks to you for tending to Mademoiselle Dupre," he said finally, seeing Fuhrmann wasn't departing her side immediately.

"I've done a little more than tend to her, you vermin," Fuhrmann replied, raising his voice. "It's you who should leave. If your crew were better skilled at navigation, we'd no doubt have been able to avoid the storm altogether."

"That's nonsense," said Mr. Crosse. He was about to go on but Catarine opened her eyes at the sound of the men's voices and turned her gaze to him.

"Seth, oh Seth," she said trying to sit up. Her unsteady attempt drew assistance from Fuhrmann as well as Seth down on one knee at her side. "It's good to see you. Mr. Fuhrmann here saved me."

She reached out a grateful bandaged hand to Fuhrmann and smiled sweetly at him. Fuhrmann returned her smile then glanced into Seth's hardened face. "Oh, my goodness, I quite forgot. Have you seen Daria?"

"I believe so, er," Seth replied.

"Well, have you or not?" Fuhrmann said, still holding Catarine's hand gently.

"I'm not quite sure," Seth answered. "But I'm sure she is all right."

"How can you be sure?" Fuhrmann said shaking his head. "Useless, you are…"

"I must go find her," Catarine said trying to rise up.

"Oh no, you must rest," Fuhrmann said standing, "I'll so search for her, my dear. Your purser here can stay by your side if you wish since he's not good for much else."

"Mr. Fuhrmann, I'd like to speak with you in private. Very soon," Catarine said quickly.

"Yes, most definitely, my dear."

At that Fuhrmann made a courteous bow and left them in search for Daria.

"I can walk, really, I can. I feel stronger now and I'd like to look for Daria too," Catarine said. "Seth, please take me 'round."

Seth and Catarine made a fairly slow but thorough search around the ship, despite her limping against her injured foot, eventually going down to the galley and the crew's cabins. Seth seemed delighted to tell her that they were at his cabin door and asked her inside for a minute to rest.

"All right, I suppose there is no harm in it," Catarine replied.

As soon as they were inside of the cabin, he took hold of Catarine and gave her a passionate kiss.

"What's that for?" Catarine asked.

"I'm so very glad you are well and here with me, my dear! What else?"

"Yes, it was so very frightening," Catarine said sitting down to rest. She was fatigued by her ordeal. "Oh my, I've gotten your chair wet with my dress. I'm still rather soaked, I'm afraid."

"I'm soaked through still as well. We will never get dry like this. We must remove all our clothes and let them dry a spell."

"Oh?" Catarine asked feigning seriousness. "And what should we do while they dry? Make love to pass the time?"

"That would be splendid!" Seth said as if he had just won a grand prize. He put both hands on her shoulders and pulled her up to him, she smiling warily. He kissed her eagerly then began kissing her on her neck, but Catarine pushed him away with her forearms, careful not to use her bandaged hands. "I'll be very careful. And gentle."

"And I'd be very worried still about Daria!" Catarine said frowning and heading towards the door. Seth grabbed her about the waist and turned her around.

"Please don't go, please," he begged. "I love you, Catarine."

"Love?" she said. "Are you sure?"

"Yes, I'm sure. And when can we ever find a time like this to be alone?" He explained. "The ship is in chaos now. No one knows where anyone is. What better time is there for us to, er, make love than now?"

"While I agree that it would be splendid, as you say. I must go find my friend. She is my concern right now," Catarine said curtly, opening the door and stepping out. But before she closed it on the crestfallen Seth, she added, "And what's more, I don't believe this is love!"

When she entered the dining hall again, she first saw Fuhrmann get up from his chair and then she saw Daria motioning her over. Catarine's exhale of relief was palpable.

"Here's your seat, love," Daria said indicated the chair next to her. Catarine hurried over and Seth dropped away when he saw

Fuhrmann at the table. "They are serving brandy 'round about for all. God knows we need it. No matter that it's too early."

"I'm so happy to see you," Catarine said taking Daria's hand. "You just don't know. I was so worried." Catarine whispered the last part to Daria as they inclined their heads together.

When the frenzy of emotions subsided, the ordeal of keeping alive abated, the remaining souls were left scarcely breathing, collapsed upon their beds weary, nearly all with no thought other than whispered prayers of gratitude for another day of life. Nearby above and around them the crew could be heard moving silently, slowly piecing together the broken and misplaced remnants of their ship. No one spoke.

Presently, through open portholes, the ever developing sky began to be friendly again, the sun having driven away the enraged mass of murderous clouds. The afternoon sunbeams poured into the open porthole as Daria awakened from her nap. Still in her pantaloons, she slipped into bed with Catarine and placed an arm around her waist.

A long while later, after the moon had climbed up into the sky, Catarine finally awakened and turned to face Daria.

"I'm so very glad you are alive," Catarine said. "I was so…"

"I must tell you something," Daria interrupted. "You know that I never want to marry."

"Oh? All right. Is it because of those parties and balls?"

"I suppose that might have something to do with it," Daria admitted but shook her head to the contrary. "I don't wish to marry a man because I love *you*. I love you more than I could love any man." Daria looked into Catarine's eyes believing she would turn away in surprise or anger but instead Catarine's green eyes met hers straight on without blinking. For a moment neither of them spoke.

"I do share the same love for you," Catarine said softly, brushing Daria's hair back away from her brow. "What's more I despise many men, but I know that they cannot all be wicked. My own dear father and brother were not so."

"A hundred or a thousand wonderful men wouldn't make me love you less." Daria explained with tears forming in her eyes, her arm clenching Catarine tighter.

"But, my dear, as much as I love you, and I do," Catarine explained with her hand on Daria's face. "It seems at night, when I lay down upon my bed, it's a man's arms I wish to have around me."

At this, Daria turned away from Catarine and buried her head into the pillow, weeping quietly. "I'm sorry, Daria! I'll love you forever! And I never want us to part. Never! You are a sister to me! If not in the flesh, in my heart of hearts! But, I'm afraid that is all I can give you." Catarine sat up and began crying into her hands.

Daria sat up next to her and the two women embraced. Daria sniffed then said through her tears, "Your heart is a prize beyond measure! My sister you will be, but please, let me hold you close in my arms tonight. The world is so cold and my heart so lonely."

So they slept in each other's embrace the full night through until the sun warmed the air that whispered gently around them and the birds took their morning song.

Conditions returned to normal on the steamship rather quickly, repairs were made, and injuries were healed, as the sky above afforded casual warmth and the tranquil waters below carried them along without any mishap. The Amsterdam, sailing quietly to New York, meandered northward along the beautiful eastern coastline that beguiled and subdued the passengers into easily forgetting their recent ordeal.

Catarine and Daria spent most of their time with the other women their age, Magdalene and Elizabeth. They met them each morning for breakfast and dined each night at the same table. During the day, they spent their leisure in the sun and fresh air discussing all manner of subjects. From time to time, both Seth Crosse and Frederick Fuhrmann would present themselves for conversation or to snag one of them away from the other. Seth always came for Catarine, with whom she agreed to rendezvous almost daily, even if only for a short hour. It was his kisses she craved and less so his conversation. Fuhrmann was friendly with all the women, acting a perfect gentleman, and consequently, seemed not to prefer one to the other. Daria spent time with him and told Catarine that she found him to be genuine and kind.

"I need to speak to him about a private matter," Catarine said to Daria after Mr. Fuhrmann escorted them to their table. "I haven't had an opportunity to ask him about my mother. But I cannot speak of this with the others near."

"Here comes the others. Let's find him after dinner," Daria replied. They dined on boiled mutton with caper sauce, mashed turnips and potatoes. Conversation with their female companions centered on the pleasant weather, the current dress neckline and fabrics of fashionable society, and the politics of the recent elections.

"There's Quakers in New York who have organized and are asking for our right to vote," Magdalene said.

"Imagine that!" Elizabeth exclaimed.

"There are people, especially in the North, who believe all people should have the right to vote. Colored people *and* women," Daria added.

"I'm inclined to agree," Catarine added. "We are really all the same in God's eyes."

They found Fuhrmann returning later from the smoking deck and Catarine asked him if he'd kindly have a word with them. He was delighted and suggested they take a brandy or cordial on the upper deck, which put them at ease.

After a few sips of her sweet drink and settling into conversation initiated by Daria, the expert in small talk, Catarine broached the subject of her mother.

"Mr. Fuhrmann, do you have any news of my mother? It's been four months since I left home and I've wondered many times how she is getting on?" She bit the inside of her lip to prepare herself for bad news and looked at Fuhrmann with wary eyes.

Fuhrmann cleared his throat for a speech, and sitting forward slightly against the table, arms extended and clutching his whiskey, addressed the women in a confidential tone, using his upturned eyes to pluck his thoughts carefully from his head before saying, "I realize the circumstances of your departure were less than ideal. Let's just say this strain left your mother, in her already weakened state even more…anemic. For a time. But then, she rallied quite well, though, so don't despair." Catarine expelled the breath she'd been holding but the look of sadness on her face remained. Daria and Fuhrmann exchanged looks but no one spoke for a few minutes. Catarine seemed lost in another world. "My dear, you know as well as I that your mother is a strong woman. Strong in spirit."

At this Catarine's eyes left the drink in her hand and she looked up at Fuhrmann, holding his gaze for a moment before speaking. "She has much to contend with."

"As did you."

"I'd hoped things would be different now."

"Oh, but they are," he said. "Quite different. One brutal beast removed, a deserving punishment for the other. A double blow in one. It was brilliant, Catarine."

"But, that's not…" Catarine began explaining with her voice raised to a whine, like a little child, but Fuhrmann cut her off.

"Stop! I cannot hear it! I do not need to know what happened that night!" Fuhrmann warned. "That is something you must always keep to yourself. At all costs."

But Catarine was shaking her head and looking at Daria. "You don't understand," she explained.

"Perhaps I don't," he said in a measured tone. "But I'm telling you to never speak of that night to anyone. As far as I'm concerned you left the next morning, running away from home, something you'd had planned for a while. Is this not correct?"

"Yes, I can honestly say that much is true," Catarine brightened.

"Well, then, there we have it."

The next morning Catarine left her cabin early and found Fuhrmann walking the promenade deck at sunrise. "Might I have your thoughts on a few more matters?" she said as she approached him.

Catarine was surprised at his apparent kindness. He was indeed a man of extremes, firm yet gentlemanly, showing deep concern. "By all means, my dear. I'm sure you have many unsettling affairs on your mind. I'm at your disposal."

"How are the others?"

"By others, I'm assuming you are talking about the slaves."

"Yes, the slaves. Are they in health?"

"As far as I know. I don't believe a doctor has been called in for anyone, family or slave."

"Are they being treated any better? Have there been any-more beatings?"

"I have no way of knowing that. But there hasn't been anyone at the tree when I've been on the property, if that's an indication."

"Well, that is something, I suppose."

"Your concern is touching," he said in an even tone.

Catarine looked into his eyes to decipher his sincerity. She'd been told before, by neighbors and friends, that she cared too much for the slaves. She'd been asked too many times why she cared so much. The only answer that she ever had for them was that she cared because she is a *human being*.

She was always perplexed that they didn't care. How could one grow up and play along side with children then turn one's back on them later in life? What did it matter that they had a different skin color?

"I grew up with these people. And when my father was alive, he treated everyone kindly. There was no difference between us," she explained. "But when Koch came along, that all changed. They treated them horribly. If I were back there, if I were running the plantation, I'd give them all their freedom and pay them to work for me if they wished to do so."

"That's very progressive, but not a new idea. It's good that you and your colored friend are heading north, for more reasons than one," Fuhrmann said.

"Yes, we are leaving to get away from the South and its backward ideas. We've both read that people are different elsewhere. Different ideas are talked about anyway," she spoke to him more freely now, remembering Daria's opinion of him. "And, yes, there's the fact that I'm wanted for murder. I certainly haven't forgotten that."

"I'm sure you haven't."

"And that brings me to my other concern," Catarine said, stopping him. "Just what do you suggest I do about that?"

"Well, you have several options," he began explaining but stopped himself short. "First let me ask you a question. Would you like my advice as a friend or solicitor?"

"I, er, I suppose as a solicitor, since we haven't been exactly friends, er, up to this point at least. I want legal advice to be specific."

"Let me be clear," he went on, "I'll give you legal advice but if you ever intend for me to represent you in court then we should establish that possibility now, even if it's a remote one."

"Would you like me to pay you? Is that what you are saying?"

"Only a paltry sum is required by law, but what I'm concerned about is the content of our conversation."

"All right then, let's proceed," Catarine said.

"We have only one day left on this ship before we disembark at New York harbor. We can have a private meeting here at noon or delay until then, which will it be?"

"Why delay? I'd like to know my options right away."

"I expect it to be a lengthy conversation. And we need to keep this completely private, even from our friend Daria. On this ship there's not much privacy as you know."

"All right, I suppose we can wait until New York, but very soon after we arrive please! I must know what to do and I'm relying on you to help me, Mr. Fuhrmann!"

"Yes, indeed!" he said and smiled, watching her as she departed, quite unsatisfied.

That evening Seth came for Catarine to walk in the moonlight one last time before arriving in New York. She was distracted but thought it would be nice to be with him this last time before saying goodbye forever. After a few stolen kisses, which was their routine, they stood at the starboard railing for several long minutes in comfortable silence as she listened to the sound of his breathing near her ear. The moonlight sparkled and flashed gently on the black water before them.

"My dear, I must speak to you about an important matter," Seth startled her with his serious tone. What did he know?

"I regret that I have no token to give you, of what I'm about to say, seeing as we're still on this blasted ship, and I've debated as to waiting until we are at port to ask you this…" he stumbled.

"What is it?" she asked, perplexed.

"Catarine," he said looking nervous, unable to look into her eyes. He held her hands in front of him and spoke to them. "Marry me. Marry me in New York."

"What?"

"Yes, we can stay there awhile," he said looking up into her eyes. "Please say yes, for I can't bear to sail on without you. My orders are to board another ship sailing back to Havana but I cannot live without you! It would be an ugly site to view that same shoreline we've shared together, to see it all alone without you. I cannot leave you in New…"

She stopped him short and said, "But Seth, I cannot marry you!"

"Why? Do you not realize that I love you deeply?"

"Well, actually, no I didn't realize that," she said withdrawing her hands and turning away. "But still it doesn't matter."

"What do you mean? It doesn't matter to you?" Seth grabbed her shoulders and turned her to face him. "I'm so sorry I haven't said it before now. I thought you would know."

"But Seth, it's not that," Catarine began. "I cannot marry now."

"Then later!" he was encouraged and his voice brightened. He took her hands again, and she allowed him to but she wouldn't look at him. "I'll stay in New York with you and quit the ship. We'll have a grand time. You can marry me when you are ready."

Catarine took a deep breath and, holding both his hands in hers, said, "I don't need more time. And I'm so sorry but I simply don't love you."

Seth withdrew his hands and backed away. "Well, then, why all the passionate kisses? You've seemed to enjoy them enough! I thought there was real feeling behind them. Are you an actress?"

"No, I'm no actress," Catarine admitted. "And yes, I have enjoyed all our passion. And I am fond of you but this isn't love. I have found what love is all about and this is not it."

"And you were tempted to stay in my bed with me! I know you were. Isn't that love?"

"Yes, I was very tempted but no that isn't love either. I'm sorry, Seth. Love is something altogether different."

Catarine came close to Seth and put her hands on his face to soothe him but he pushed her away. He turned and hurried away from her, leaving her alone on the deck in the lovely moonlight. Catarine turned to face the water and listened to the sound of the waves lapping against the side of the ship below her. The cold wind penetrated her bones, making her shiver but still she stayed on in the cold alone.

New York

Chapter 6

Catarine and Daria had lived in one of the largest cities in America. New Orleans was a metropolis with world travelers, and a port marketing foreign merchandize of all sorts, yet this had not prepared them for the splendor of New York harbor. Upon entering the mouth of Upper New York bay that morning, with their bags packed up and ready for departure onto dry land, the women were captivated by the vastness of the land on either side of them, the battery, the magazine, and barracks of Fort Gibson, the island of Manhattan before them, and the two rivers that gathered into the bay containing an expansive number of sailing ships and steamers. There must have been twenty or thirty of them in all, of divers proportions, some at anchor while others sailing at various speeds moving in all directions. The strings were out on deck and played for the occasion and their merriment. A violin and viola played a lively duet joined by the cello on the second movement. Women clapped their gloved hands to the beat but looked onward and around them, attempting to take in the entire landscape. No one was deterred by the crisp air, for the sky was as blue as a robin's egg and the sun sent its cozy rays streaming down and around them, as if to welcome them to its winter home. Catarine, although not expecting to see him again, remembered Seth had said that most all immigrants to America from any other country came into the passage through which they were now entering. She relayed this information to Daria who found it equally intriguing.

"I hope we might meet some interesting people while in New York," Daria said smiling to Catarine. "Maybe someone who's just arrived here."

"I hope so," Catarine said quietly, still looking out at the sights that lie ahead.

"Are you thinking of Seth?" Daria asked her. Catarine turned to face Daria. Catarine took Daria's hand in hers and shook her head.

"No, I'm not thinking of him," she explained. "We said our good-byes last night. I'm thinking of our future, you and me. But I must find Mr. Fuhrmann. I need to speak to him after we depart. I'd asked him for advice and he insists on talking with me in privacy. But I wanted you to know what we'd be discussing."

"That sounds like a wise conversation," Daria said.

As they stood there on the approach to the harbor, Catarine turned to look through the hordes of people to find Mr. Fuhrmann. She saw men, dandies, wearing their flat-brimmed top hats and scarf cravats, carrying ebony canes to match. The women passengers were dressed like royals with lace-trimmed pelerines and bonnets decorated with ostrich feathers. The crew appeared relaxed and jubilant, looking forward to time off in the city.

She saw all this in the sea of faces as she scanned the crowd searching for Frederick Fuhrmann.

Then she found him. He was on the deck above them at a distance toward the bow standing with Seth Crosse and the captain of the ship. While this was odd in itself, what was even more unusual was that all three of them were leaning together, looking directly at her, and were wearing serious expressions as they conferred. And they saw her look up at them, Fuhrmann with arms folded across his chest, Seth with his hands pocketed, and the captain balancing himself on the roof bell. Her glance seemed to break up their conversation, with Fuhrmann nodding then heading quickly in her direction. Seth and the captain continued to observe her from above, neither smiling nor acknowledging her gaze. This odd incident sent chills down Catarine's spine. At once, she grabbed Daria's arm and took her along pushing through the crowd away from where Fuhrmann was headed.

"Let's just get off of this ship as quickly as we can," Catarine said as they hurried along. She began forcing her way towards the front of the gangplank awaiting release.

By the time the passengers had all made ready and the crowd was thick with anticipation, they heard both the peal of the great bell followed by the announcement of the steward, "All ashore!" Catarine and Daria, having vied to be nearest the front of the line as possible, jockeyed for position. Many of the others nearby leaned over the railings, waving handkerchiefs to groups of friends on the pier below. Although most everyone was cordial, with a mob so large and compacted, one couldn't help being jostled or bumping into by those in position just adjacent. The two women clasped hands in an attempt to stay together.

Catarine scanned the crowd for Mr. Fuhrmann again, and not seeing him or his co-conspirators, breathed a sigh of relief.

"Daria," Catarine whispered. "Did you see them talking about me?"

"No, who was?"

"Mr. Fuhrmann was speaking to Seth and the Captain. Or they to him. I'm not sure. But I'm sure they were discussing me and it didn't look good."

"Hmmm, that's strange, especially with the Captain involved."

"That's why I think we need to get off this ship without being seen."

"That is impossible!"

"Do you think they are looking for me? I mean for *murder*?" she whispered in Daria's ear so low as to be barely audible.

"Let's hope not, but it's possible. Do you think Fuhrmann gave you up?"

As soon as Daria said this Fuhrmann parted the two gentlemen behind them and stood at Catarine's side.

"You've been found out," he said. "The law wired the shipping company office here in New York when your name was discovered to be on the passenger list." The two women both gasped and turned to him. At the same time the line started moving along and pressing them forward towards the exit ramp. "You'll need to stick with me if you have any hopes of being safe."

"I'm not sure I trust you." Catarine said drawing back from him.

"After all I've done for you? Come with me. We cannot leave from this exit." He took both women by the arms and, turning around, began breaking through the crowd backwards.

Upon seeing them going the other direction, the steward approached them. "What is the problem?"

"This lady has just received terrible news. I'm afraid her husband has died and I had the unlucky task of informing her." Fuhrmann looked at Catarine who then shielded her face and pretended to weep. Daria's arm went about her in comfort. "May we leave another way and avoid this crowd? She almost fainted just now."

"Certainly. Please follow me, sir," the steward replied then walked them to a remote part near the stern to a small gang-plank which he extended. The three of them walked over to the shore alone, Catarine still shielding her face.

"You are wonderful," Catarine said to Fuhrmann. "How can I ever thank you?"

"The job isn't done," he said. "You two get away from the ship. I will fetch your bags and find you later. Meet me at a place called Butter Cake Dick's in an hour."

He gave them brief directions, Daria described their baggage and then he was off. Catarine, still keeping her head down and her eyes shielded began walking away with Daria up

Chambers Street as instructed by Mr. Fuhrmann. Just before they turned the corner, she stopped and relaxed.

"That was frightening," she exclaimed. "I'm so glad that's over."

She turned around to take one last look at the ship, one look to remember the voyage that was full of enjoyment and, yes, adventure, and when she did, she clearly saw Seth Crosse standing on the promenade deck watching her departure.

It was nearly dusk when the next crowd of newsboys swamped the counter again, at least the fourth gang they'd seen. They had come in using foul language, pushing and shoving, these young boys with their leather newspaper bags slung over each of them. And as if by magic, they'd disappear again as the clock struck the hour.

Since the gravity of the situation called for it, Catarine and Daria waited patiently at first, commendably several hours, but then both of them grew weary and dismayed, doubtful even.

"I'm beginning to think we've lost our belongings," Daria said in a woeful tone looking ever toward the door for Fuhrmann. "What could possibly be taking him so damn long?"

"I hope we haven't been duped," Catarine said for the third time that day.

"And there are only so many butter cakes one can eat. I don't believe I'll be eating another for quite a while."

"Here he is!" Catarine exclaimed rising up and waving Fuhrmann over, who came in noticeably void of any baggage. "What took you so long?"

"So sorry," he said breathlessly. "It couldn't be helped. It's a long story but I ended up talking your man Crosse into fetching your baggage for me after they'd been left unclaimed. It was the only way really. With your name registered on the manifest, it must not appear that anyone retrieved them. Officially, he took them as unclaimed baggage to the shipping office." He explained breathlessly while taking off his coat and hat and, turning to Catarine, said, "So, my dear Catarine, you've two men putting themselves out and possibly under suspicion for you. I hope you are grateful."

"I'm absolutely grateful. I don't know what to say," Catarine began.

"Where are they now?" Daria asked. "All our things."

"I took your things to my hotel, the Astor House. Tomorrow perhaps, I'll have them delivered to you. I suggest tomorrow only because I don't want to draw attention."

"What shall we wear until then?" Daria asked. "I suppose that's not our greatest concern but we cannot exactly go about in the same clothing all night."

"I have my money. We can buy something if shops are still open, that is," Catarine answered.

"I strongly suggest that you two get to where you will be staying," Fuhrmann advised. "Have you a plan for that?"

"I'd only hoped to stay in a grand hotel," Daria said.

"Pardon me for saying this, but my advice is that you two should stay either in the Ursuline convent or a boarding house. In the convent, two young women will be protected by the nuns. In the boarding house you could pass possibly as a boy and girl, which I believe is the better choice. I know of a family who takes in women, so Daria, they'll welcome you." Catarine and Daria both looked at each other with surprise, but made no comment to this. "Yes, I'm aware that you dressed the part of a boy while in New Orleans, Catarine. It was a satisfactory disguise. I think you should adopt it again."

"Drat! I suppose I can."

"You must!" Fuhrmann said.

"Do you think we can pass as brother and sister? Half brother and sister?" Daria asked Fuhrmann. "You know how things are in New Orleans. We can explain that we have the same father but different mothers."

"Perhaps, but the least amount of explaining you do, the better. Only explain if pressed or harassed for information. Otherwise mind your own business." He warned them strongly. "And do not use the Dupre name ever!"

"Can we be Daria and Andre Morinay?"

"It would be far better to have different names altogether. Names that wouldn't connect you with New Orleans at all. But those at least are better than Dupre."

Fuhrmann continued with what he called counsel of momentous import. Among other matters, he directed them to stay put in the city until they heard from him again. He promised to get word to them one way or another if the authorities came searching for Catarine.

They finally agreed what their names would be, after a small quarrel, and after that he hailed a carriage and sent them out to what would be their new lodging.

Oh how I wished Catarine hadn't gone 'way. Madam Dupre was wasting away day by day, longing for her baby girl. And I felt like I was doing so right along with her. The warm days had shortened and turned into what use to be days filled with joy but not for us, not on Magnolia Plantation. The holiday season crept by slowly with the black cloud of death hanging overhead. They finally found Mason's body and dug him up. No one suspected me or my brother of having anything to do with it. We was just simple folks. Dumb ones who knew nothing. They all thought Catarine had done it. Done it all by herself. It didn't make no sense but that's what they thought. I just let em all go on thinking that. I didn't know what else to do.

A few things had changed since Catarine had gone. There was no more schooling for me. No more reading after chores in the afternoon like before when I'd come in to the parlor. Perhaps Madam Dupre was afraid of Koch. But I did get to tend to Catarine's gelding Diego. She left him for me. She told me so the night before she left. He was hers and hers alone. But she told me to ride him every day. I rode him bareback all up and down the place and nobody cared. No one told me I couldn't do it. He became mine. My Diego. I finally had something precious of my own.

Chapter 7

1849

The morning fires and burnt coffee insulted Daria's nose after being kept awake hearing the riotous men below their room, drinking into the wee hours. Sitting up and sneezing, she could see Catarine awake, dressed and looking out through their crystalized window, discerning the level of coldness they'd be facing shortly when they went out and away from their tenement house.

"They're getting worse, those two! I hardly slept at all," Daria complained as she threw off her covers and faced the cold winter air.

Their housing arrangement had been made with Germans who had four children they'd squeezed into a small room to allow for renters, needing the money desperately, times being what they were. And as for Germans, they were far better off than the other new arrivals coming into the city. Mrs. Woerner was an excellent cook who could boil cabbage water into a feast if she needed to. But when they took on the two young men, whom they'd known from Wiesbaden, into the downstairs sitting room they converted into a bedroom, the rest and repose of the entire household went awry.

"I'd like breakfast before we go. I cannot work without at least a bite of food. I'm going down," Catarine said as she exited.

Daria, who was equally committed to the work they'd gotten, but also committed to getting adequate amounts of sleep, found it much more difficult to bound directly out of bed upon opening one's eyes in the morning than did Catarine. So she groaned and shivered as she dressed herself quickly and swore they'd leave this horrid house as soon as possible.

Finally arriving for breakfast and feigning friendliness and gratitude, Daria spoke kindly to Mrs. Woerner, asking about her health and her night's sleep, something never reciprocated. Mrs. Woerner gave a neutral answer quickly and put a plate of food in front of Daria as she sat down next to Catarine. Daria reached for the coffee cup close to her and motioned to Catarine to pass the coffee pot. Surprisingly, one of the young rowdy men, Henry, with tousled blond hair, came in, sat down, and greeted them both, looking up with his bloodshot eyes.

"How was your night?" Daria couldn't help saying. Mrs. Woerner turned from the sideboard to glare at her.

"How you say?" Henry struggled for a word. "Just petty, er, no, pretty. My night pretty."

"Pretty good?" Daria helped him.

"Yes! It pretty good!" he said laughing at himself with delight. Daria couldn't help but smile at his enthusiasm. "How your night?"

"Not too bad, I suppose," Daria gave him an answer to which he looked slightly confused then went about starting the breakfast that Mrs. Woerner placed before him.

"We must be off to the orphanage. Thank-you, Mrs. Woerner," Catarine said as she placed her napkin down and pushed her chair back, rising. Daria followed suit. They went to the foyer and began the task of putting on boots, coats, hats, and muffs to brave the weather for their walk to St. Patrick's.

"One thing I do love about this cold weather is how I am quite warmed up by the time we get there!" Daria said gaily as they walked along through the wintry air that seemed to immobilize her lips.

"Yes," was all Catarine said looking straight ahead. Daria looked at her sideways as they walked along.

After they proceeded in silence for a while, Daria took her warm hand out of her muff and slipped her arm into Catarine's arm. Catarine smiled at her slightly but kept up the same walking pace. "Let's stop a moment," Daria said pulling her to slow down.

"No, we don't have time," Catarine said shaking her head.

"I know when something is wrong. What is it? You've hardly spoken for days!"

Catarine sighed and looked down, shaking her head frowning. "Yes, I do have a few things on my mind. Let's discuss them later, all right?"

"Is it anything I've done?" Daria wanted to know.

"It's nothing you've done. But it does concern you very much," Catarine said walking on, leaving Daria standing a moment with a puzzled look on her face. She caught up with

Catarine but knew her well enough that she'd have to wait until later to hear her vexations and that no manner of questioning would bring forth the information any sooner.

In a short time, and after only a few slips on iced mounds they encountered going through muddy streets, they arrived at the orphanage adjacent to St. Patrick's cathedral.

Sister Edith greeted their knock against the huge door, "Ah, here are my two favorite girls! The two southern angels sent by God!"

"Oh, I don't know about that," Daria said.

"If only that were true," Catarine said.

"It *is* true!" Sister Edith said emphatically. "It was God Himself Who brought you here to us. I just know it. Come in now and get warm."

Catarine and Daria looked at each other questioningly, as the Sister began helping them remove their outer garments. She then led them over, as she did each morning to the kitchen fire, to dry out before they'd be ushered into the schoolroom.

They'd started going to mass at St. Patrick's after settling into the city. Both were astounded at the level of poverty, especially the amount of orphans there were about. They were hearing that orphanages were being set up for these poor children, mostly children of immigrants who had died during the voyage over. How sad for them. To be in a new country with nothing at all and one's parents dead after having hopes and dreams of freedom and prosperity. At mass the Bishop had sent out a plea for Catholic women to volunteer at their orphanage. Their circumstance was dire and they needed help. Boys were just recently being admitted, but most were still in the horrid almshouses. There was a great need for Catholic women to help with both the boys and the girls since there wasn't enough sisters to care for all of them. Especially schooled women who could teach these children to read and write. Catarine and Daria couldn't refuse. They both jumped at the request, having no occupation and craving one. So from that point on, they came daily, five or six days a week, having Sundays off and every other Saturday.

Many days they both did, in fact, feel as if they'd been sent there for just such a purpose as Sister Edith expressed. Especially Daria, but Catarine couldn't shake the reason she'd left her home. She was still a fugitive from justice. The troubling fact, too, was that they hadn't heard anything further from Fuhrmann. And it had been several months since he'd sent them to live with the Woerners.

Their day was consumed, as all others with the orphans, with Daria helping groups of boys and girls do their figures on chalk boards and Catarine, sitting on a small stool near the ground, reading and teaching sounds to children hungry to learn to read. The sisters worked hard to keep them fed and clothed with the Bishop tirelessly begging for donations and mounting political calls on their behalf.

The two boys and five girls who were circled around her, with one climbing up into her lap over and over again, called Catarine "Miss Andrea." In fact, since arriving in New York City, everyone called her Andrea. On the buggy ride to the Woerner house, she and Daria had decided upon it, a form of her brother's name. At first it was difficult to be mindful to answer to it, so much so that she had to feign being hard of hearing to the Woerners, perhaps the first of many reasons Mrs. Woerner had since grown suspicious of her and Daria. But now, at the orphanage, with the children repeating the name over and over, and with love and delight affixed to it, she'd grown attached to the label as if it was at least part of who she was.

"We have an errand of upmost importance to do," Catarine explained to Sister Edith in the evening as she and Daria were tidying up the schoolroom preparing to leave. "And tomorrow would be best for us. I'm sorry if this will cause a problem for you, but it must be done on a weekday." Daria understood that this errand must be the concern to which Catarine was referring previously.

"We have no one else," Sister Edith said sighing. "But if you must, please, you are free."

"I believe it can be done in the morning and we can return after completing it. We will be here as soon as possible tomorrow," was Catarine's reply.

After leaving, Catarine suggested a walk to enjoy the evening, as it had warmed up just enough as to not be bone chilling, as most nights had been.

"Let's walk up this way, out of the city a piece," Catarine said. "Besides, I need to talk about something that the Woerners cannot hear."

"All right, what is it?" Daria asked straight away.

"Oh look!" Catarine said pointing at what looked like people gliding around a clearing in the distance. "I wonder if it's a lake."

"It looks like they are ice skating so I suppose you are right." They walked on until they were close enough to see the small lake within the patch of trees, with a group of people watching on the shore and just as many people skating across the ice of the lake, crossing back and forth and circling around. A few benches had been brought near the edge for the express purpose of sitting and attaching skates to one's boots. It was delightful. They watched for quite a while in awe of the activity and the bravery of the ones who dared to go out upon the ice the farthest.

"That looks amazing!" Catarine said with eyes aglow.

"It looks scary but actually quite beautiful. The women look so pretty with their skirts fanning out behind them. It's quite like dancing," Daria said in admiration.

"We should try it sometime," Catarine decided, looking at Daria smiling.

"I do believe you are the brave one," Daria answered.

"Let's sit and talk a while," Catarine said when she spotted an unused bench.

They sat and talked about her concerns. Catarine began discussing the subject of money, which was a huge relief to Daria. Catarine was very concerned that she shouldn't continue to leave her large sum of cash in the Woerner house as they left each day. It was on her mind daily as she left. The money needed to be in a bank and she felt it must be deposited in Daria's name. All of it. Daria started to protest but then realized this was the only way. Catarine couldn't be named on any legal paper. So it was decided that they'd open an account in Daria's name with all of their money. The very next morning.

"Do you still worry about being tracked down?" Daria asked. "I'm not trying to remind you of the past. I just wondered."

"Oh, yes," Catarine answered. "I think of that daily as well. If only I could forget that I'm a fugitive."

"I think you must be safe here. It's so far from home," Daria said softly. She looked into Catarine's eyes and they both knew. They knew what the other was thinking.

"Yes, and that's the other thing," Catarine said back in a whisper. "It's not home, is it?"

When they arrived home that evening, the Woerners had put away dinner and gone to bed. Daria went down to find some food for them and, while looking about in the kitchen pantry, was joined by Henry.

"How you?" he said gaily, smiling at Daria, offering his right hand and holding a beer bottle in the other. She shook his hand awkwardly and resumed looking for food.

"How is it you two can always afford beer?" Daria asked not turning around. "Ah, here is a new loaf of bread. I wonder if she'll…"

"Ja, beer," Henry said and turned, walking away from the pantry. He brought back two beers and poured them into four of Mrs. Woerner's teacups and placed them on the kitchen table with gusto.

He pushed them over in Daria's direction and said, "You drink," he said smiling broadly and then he looked up at the ceiling, indicating Catarine, "you and schwester."

"All right, danke," Daria said. "I'll get my schwester, my sister, Andrea." Leaving the loaf and the beers, she went to fetch Catarine.

Laughing at the odious response she anticipated from Catarine, she set forth the drinking invitation from Henry, and was truly surprised when Catarine sprang up to head for the kitchen without hesitation.

Catarine, who nodded at appropriate times, sat before the two German men with Daria drinking their beer from Mrs. Woerner's teacups well into the night. Daria made attempts at first to communicate, even teach Henry and Karl English phrases, which they repeated fairly well. They were able to have a fairly coherent discussion of their times in New York so far, the voyages over, and their families back home. After a time, with more beer given round again, and with the worrisome tinkling of teacups, they lapsed into hilarity and loud German talk. And even German songs.

"I can't believe Mrs. Woerner hasn't come out here for our heads!" Catarine whispered to Daria. "I suppose they don't know we are down here too. They just allow these two to do as they please."

The men gave up on the small teacups, much to the relief of the women, and went to work on whole pints at a time. Henry offered Daria some of his, which she refused and instead gathered up the teacups to take into the kitchen for a wash. When Catarine was offered some of Karl's pint, she said, "Danke" and took three large gulps before returning it to him. This went on for a while so when Daria came back in, she found Catarine up, dancing about with the men, and gulping down beer.

"Oh mein Gott," Henry shouted when he saw Daria at the door with her mouth and eyes wide opened. "Wir Sind jetzt in Schwierigkeiten."

At this Catarine began laughing and holding her side until she fell down on the parlor couch. Henry, still laughing sat next to her then laid his head in her lap. Daria entered the room, laughing at the sight of them all quite drunk and still wondering where the Woerners were. Karl grabbed her by the waist and twirled her around with his right arm, his left hand still holding his pint, which was held high in the air.

"Lass uns tanzen," Karl said then kissed her on the cheek. Daria blushed and moved over to Catarine who was still laughing.

"Where ever could the Woerners be?" Daria said bending down to Catarine's ear.

Catarine looked surprised and serious for a minute then started laughing again so intense this time that she started crying. "Well, dammit all, give me a pint too then." Daria said to Karl. When he looked confused and shook his head, she yelled to Henry, who was only two feet away, "Beer!" Henry quite understood as he nodded and left to fetch her a pint.

Catarine sat on the couch giggling and Daria sat down next to her after Henry had gotten up. The two women looked at each other and laughed again.

"I'm going to be ever so sick in the morning," Catarine said.

After that night, the days in New York passed agreeably, with teaching at the orphanage, nights at the Woerners, and an occasional evening spent gaily with the German brothers they'd befriended. But for the most part, the highlight of their week became the evenings they went ice skating at the pond on the north side of town. They'd purchased the skates that could attach to their boots and they carried these to work with them on days they planned to skate. It was a great evening activity. Many people went to skate and the sport drew a crowd of watchers as well.

One watcher in particular was a man named Louis Fontaine. He was a handsome man, tall and lean with a pleasant face and flashing blue eyes. His dark, wavy hair contrasted with his eyes and gave him a gentlemanly, elegant look.

Louis always carried his black case containing his most prized possessions. When he arrived at his favorite bench to watch the skaters, carrying his black case, he quickly found his two favorite subjects. He'd been watching them for weeks. They were a unique sight; beauties, both of them. One was as white as the snow that fell from the sky on the coldest winter day. The other was a honeyed brown, as pleasing and mellow as the sweetest ginger snap in a confectioners store window. And the best part was that they were friends. Truly friends. They clung to each other like kindred spirits. It was a beautiful sight.

So Louis watched them. And he sketched them. He arrived sometimes before they would or after, but either way, whenever he spotted them, he opened his black case, chose from his array of pencils, and took out his sketch pad. He smiled each time he'd turn to a new, fresh page of his sketchbook. So much hope. Potential. Then his eyes would find them again. And again he'd see their beauty. When his eyes would glass over with tears, he'd brush them away with his sleeve, careful not to let a tear fall upon his work. From time to time the women would come near him and when they did, he'd hear their voices. Angel voices. They'd laugh or talk with seriousness, their conversation always intense, interrupting each other like sisters. He always paused to hear them. He thought it strange that they'd not noticed him staring. He'd share his drawings with them. One day. But for now he'd just watch and listen.

Catarine was by far the better skater. She had the balance and took to it right away. On her own, unattached from Daria, Catarine could glide back and forth, picking up speed, feeling the cold breeze against her face as she threw her upper body side to side to keep up the momentum. The bumps of ice near the edge didn't topple her; she could regain her balance easily. She could even throw herself into a perfect circle, with her feet turned outward like a ballerina. When she learned this, she felt a rush of pleasure and did the trick over and over as Daria watched her, her mittened hands out to her side in victory.

Daria never minded watching her do a few tricks because Catarine would always help her skate along for as long as she wanted. Daria liked to skate holding Catarine's hand, just in case she lost her balance, which she was prone to do sporadically each time they went. Most of the time, they skated around together and talked of the people around them. They saw lovers there, of course. They enjoyed watching them, especially if they caught an argument or two. A few families came as well. And then there were the watchers, some regulars, who gathered to take in the pleasure of the sport. They discussed how the city seemed to be full of diverse and interesting people, young and old, rich and poor, from all countries. It was a good place in which to get lost. A good place in which to never be found.

Chapter 8

Louis Fontaine, in his small rented room, sorted through his drawings, analyzing each one with a critical eye. He chose the one of the girl with the dark flowing hair, the one in which she was laughing and turning to the side. He'd drawn her from the back and had captured the look of joy on her face. Using the two middle fingers on his left hand, he touched up that noble part of her cheek just so. He deemed her eye to be perfect, so he shaded with his softest pencil to enhance her hair. If only he could talk to her, ask her questions, show her these drawings. He would need to work up the nerve for that. It made him tense to think of it. He put down the drawing so as not to make an error. No blunder could be made on his favorite. He looked through the others. He also adored the drawing of both of them skating hand in hand toward him. He remembered how they'd looked, skating around, carefree and in their own world, oblivious to everyone around them. Several men at the lake that day had stared at them, many actually.

They were a sight. They were both very beautiful and the fact that they were such close friends and of different coloring was unusual indeed. Louis found this perplexing yet utterly refreshing; as refreshing as the cool winter air. Perhaps the drawing of them skating hand-in-hand was the one he'd give to them as a present. Yes, that would be best. They'd like that. And he knew it must be soon, before ice skating season ended.

Sister Edith had been watching them too. They'd been there for months now. Both Daria and Andrea were hard workers and seemed to love the children, but she sensed that something was amiss. First of all, Sister Edith didn't believe these two were sisters for one minute, not even half-sisters as they'd claimed. But she knew most people held secrets for various reasons and she wasn't one to judge, only God could do that. Secondly, the girl Andrea, was so very moody. One day she'd be content, not happy, for she never seemed quite happy, then the next day she would be downright ill-tempered. She contained it well, never losing her temper with the children or with anyone for that matter, but Sister Edith could see it sweltering under the surface. And Andrea seemed so distant. Always. Like she was thinking of something far away. And the days in which she was most ill-tempered, Daria brooded over her and worried so much that it distracted her from her work. Sister Edith had to correct Daria on those days and ask her to pay attention to the children. They were an interesting pair indeed. They were on Sister Edith's mind during her prayers as she wondered constantly just what their secret could possibly be.

"I do hope we will soon be having some warmer weather," Daria declared one morning. Her voice was neutral as she dressed in her winter clothes. Catarine, already clothed and ready, was by their door, lacing her boots up and gathering her bag along with her ice skates.

"Yes," Catarine answered. "But I've so enjoyed skating. Whatever shall we do without it?"

"I know, dear, it's been such a treat. I've loved it!"

"At least it's not over yet, but this might be our last week," Catarine said standing up, brushing her skirts down to straighten them. "I will be so sad to give it up."

"I've enjoyed myself immensely! I'm quite surprised too. If you hadn't pushed me to try it, I never would have."

"I know, sweetheart," Catarine said and turned to leave for downstairs. "Let's be off."

At the orphanage that day, the children were restless and fiddly. Sister Edith assisted them in getting the boys in line, to behave without being yelled at or threatened. They all ended up changing the quiet reading activity into a circle game of singing and going round and turning about which was what the children needed to do to work off their energy. After the rigorous activities, most of the children napped well, which gave each one of the ladies turns at going out for prayer or private reading. While Daria was watching the children, Sister Edith approached Catarine.

"Mademoiselle Andrea, may I have a word with you?" Sister Edith asked Catarine. "Have a seat here with me." They sat together on the bench at the back of the church vestibule.

"Yes, what can I help you with?"

"I'd like to help you with something if I may," the Sister replied.

"But I don't need any help," Catarine began. "Er, unless you are talking about my teaching…"

"No, your teaching is fine. You have been dutiful and good with the children. And you are a smart one. I cannot help you in that respect."

"What is it then?"

"You seem to be carrying a heavy burden," Sister Edith said slowly, emphasizing each word. She studied Catarine's reaction which was sudden, like being slapped or doused with cold water.

"I'm not sure what you mean," was her reply. As she said this, Catarine stood up and walked over to gaze out the window.

"My dear, I wasn't born yesterday, I can see that you are troubled."

Catarine glanced back at Sister Edith's kind but penetrating eyes then turned her face towards the windowpane that shielded the quiet room from the unfriendly air.

"I've seen all kinds of girls in all sorts of trouble. You, my dear, are in trouble of some sort. You have a huge worry on your shoulders. And what's more, it's weighing you down. You can't keep carrying it."

"What do you mean by that?" Catarine spoke to the window pane before her.

Sister Edith was at her side in an instant. She took Catarine's hand inside her two strong ones and said, "You've got to lay your burden down. It'll shatter your soul! You are only going to hurt yourself, nobody else, by trying to carrying it around alone."

"I'm not completely alone."

"I know you have Daria."

"Yes, I have Daria."

"But this might be too big for her also," Sister Edith advised. "You must consider that. You might need to tell someone else. Someone bigger than all of us."

"You mean God?" Catarine asked. "I've confessed everything to Him!"

"That's wonderful! Perhaps you should also tell Father Tom."

Up until that point, Catarine had greatly admired the Sister for her kindness and unprejudiced approach to them and the children, but, whatever spurred her insistence that day, Sister Edith became unrelenting in her campaign to free Catarine from her heavy burden. Before Catarine could get away, Sister Edith had fetched the priest and brought him along to hear her confession. She told Father Tom in her presence that, Andrea has asked to confess "something of grave importance to you and it must be done today."

As the three of them stood in the rear of the church looking grim, Catarine decided to acquiesce to the plan Sister Edith had hatched for her.

"Yes, Father, I have something to confess to you today that cannot wait until Sunday."

"Each day is the same to God," he answered peering into her eyes and clasping her arm warmly. "Let's go to the confessional."

As she seated herself in the wooden structure, a place with which she was not unfamiliar, she envisioned Sister Edith lurking nearby to catch a word or two of her confession.

"Bless me, Father, for I have sinned," Catarine began then she started wondering what Daria was doing. She'd be looking for her at that point. Father Tom shifted in his adjacent seat on the other side of the screen and cleared his throat. "Oh, yes, it's been a month since my last confession."

"Go on, my child," he spoke to her as she sat silent, hunting for words to tell of her burden.

Finally, as Catarine sat knotting the fabric of her skirt in her hands she just blurted out, "Father, the thing is—I killed a man."

"Oh my, dear girl, are you sure?"

"Yes, I'm quite sure, there's no doubt of it."

"Well, that's disappointing," he said slowly. Catarine looked over toward him through the screen between them to see him shaking his head back and forth.

"The thing is," she went on to explain, "I didn't mean to. It was an accident."

"Oh well, that's entirely different from, er, murder, which was what I thought…"

"I know," she responded. "But the problem is that I hated him. I, I suppose I wanted him dead but the act itself was truly an accident. What does that make me?"

"It makes you guilty of hatred, not murder," Father Tom explained. "What were the circumstances?"

"It's the circumstances now that are plaguing me, Father," Catarine said softly. "This one act, this accident…"

"Are you in trouble, dear?"

"Very much so!" Catarine remembered Sister Edith somewhere outside the confessional. How much was she hearing? And if so, did it matter? "I just don't know what to do!"

Sister Edith was indeed nearby, as was Daria. Daria had been searching for Catarine, as they had been planning on leaving and going straight away to the pond to ice skate one more time after work. Daria couldn't imagine what would change Catarine's mind on this. She went looking for her in the rectory and the children's quarters next door, and not finding her, tried the church itself. Sister Edith was rearranging the flowers near the confession booth, which Daria noted to be occupied. Rather than shout out for Catarine, she tiptoed across the stone floor to the other side of the church, not thinking she'd find her in the throes of confession, but stopped short when she heard her voice. When she did, she looked up and noted Sister Edith's guilty look and knew at once she'd been eavesdropping. Daria could only imagine what she'd heard Catarine confess.

Instead of staying to hear the outcome of divine intervention, Daria decided to go on without Catarine to the skating pond.

Father Tom proceeded to question Catarine about the nature of her hatred for the killed man. Catarine explained fully, how he'd been brutal to the slaves at their farm, that he'd bullied Bessie, assaulted her, and finally raped her lifelong friend. The girl raised alongside of her. They'd played together, traded dolls. They saw no difference between each of them. So what if they were two different colors? No one cared in their world.

Not her parents, not Bessie's. Until the Koch's came along and all things changed. Then their world collapsed and the outside world invaded their peaceful one. That's why she hated Mason and his father. And she wasn't too happy with her mother for marrying him either. Not happy at all. In fact, she was very angry with her too, truth be told! Yes, Catarine confessed to Father Tom. Quite loudly. And she was sure Sister Edith could hear or anyone else that happened to be nearby as well. And she didn't care either. Catarine realized that this must be exactly what was meant by laying your heavy burden down.

When Daria reached the pond, she only saw a few ice skaters, although it was still cold. That evening made her shiver as it seemed the moisture in the air went straight through her bones. Sitting down on a bench close to the edge of the pond, she felt lifeless, unmovable. She'd never been to the pond alone before. She wasn't afraid. She wouldn't even be afraid to skate alone, but she felt suddenly paralyzed, as if she couldn't make a decision anymore. This troubled her since she'd once been so independent. What was her problem? Was she so connected to Catarine now that she couldn't make a move without her? Is that what love does to one? Surely not! It wasn't that. It was their inertia, both of them. They must move forward in life. They must settle the past. But how?

Catarine listened as Father Tom responded to her diatribe about the Koch's. He stated that he understood, as did the Lord Jesus, which surprised Catarine. Father Tom also discussed penance and said that since she'd come to them and served the orphans for the past several months, her penance was complete and that the Lord himself had led her to them for just that purpose. But he added that there were several things she must do to be free of this burden. "You must completely forgive!"

"But they are horrible people," she protested.

"Oh, there is no doubt of that, my dear," he agreed. "Those that nailed our Savior to the cross were horrible also, yet he forgave."

"But…" She started to protest but realized every argument that crossed her mind was useless.

"He tells us to forgive seventy time seven. And more. Turn the other cheek. They know not what they do. But you cannot do this in your own strength."

"True, my strength comes and goes."

"But you can have absolution, my dear!" the father said. "Let me pray for you. God the Father of mercies, through the death and resurrection of His Son, has reconciled the world to Himself and sent the Holy Spirit among us for the forgiveness of sins. I absolve you from your sins, in the name of the Father, and of the Son and of the Holy Spirit. May God give you pardon and peace."

"Amen," Catarine said. "Thanks be to God."

"Before you go I have one more question," he said. "Are you wanted for murder? If this is why you came to us, you may stay here as long as you like, but I would advise you to turn yourself in. Face your accusers and find peace."

"How did you know?" Catarine was stunned but imagined Father Tom smiling calmly based on the tone of his voice.

"God has forgiven your sins," he said. "Go in peace."

Daria was so deep in her thoughts that when the man sat down beside her on the bench by the pond, it fairly made her jump out of her skin.

"Bonjour," he said nodding to her as he fiddled with his black case. "Will you be skating?"

"I haven't decided yet," Daria answered. "I'm tired tonight. I just might sit and watch."

"I always sit and watch," the man said.

"Yes?" Daria asked staring ahead although she'd seen him many times.

"Yes, I always do," he said thinking that his reply sounded gauche. But he wasn't sure as it was in English, his second language. He wished to ask about the other girl but wasn't sure how to be polite about it. "You have a friend. On other days."

"Yes, I do," Daria answered, sighing. "She isn't with me today."

"I hope not sick," was his reply, turning to face her. He seemed genuinely concerned.

"No, not sick, just not here," she answered. "I'm not sure if she will come today."

"Ah, you convene here?"

"What? Oh no, we usually come together. Well, we always do. Just today we didn't."

"I watched you before," he started opening his black case which Daria had seen him with on previous occasions. "I will show you."

Louis was thinking that this might be his only chance. He wished the other girl was there. Where could she be? What was wrong? He fumbled with the pictures. The one he had selected was on top, the one of the both of them, but should he show her that one or the one he had drawn of just her?

"Oh my, those drawings are lovely! Let me see? Are they…" Daria looked over at the pictures that the man was searching through. "You've drawn pictures…they're all of *us*?"

"Yes." Louis swallowed hard. He tried to withdraw the one of her, the one of her putting on her skates. He liked that one too, but when he tried to slip that one out, it caught several of the others with a tiny turned up corner, and they all came out, falling to the ground at Daria's feet.

"Oh, my!" Daria exclaimed. She didn't know if she should be honored or distressed.

"Excuse me, I'm sorry," he began. "I didn't mean…"

"What do you mean, you are sorry? You meant to…" she said snatching up several of the pictures as he was putting as many as he could back into his black case.

"Well, no, no accident. I watched you and your friend. I have drawn you because…" he stumbled and blushed.

"They are wonderful!" Daria said looking from one picture to another. "You are very talented!"

"Thank you, mademoiselle. I draw you because you are beautiful." He looked up at Daria and she was about to protest. But she saw in his deep blue eyes the look of earnest, of truth, sincerity and innocence. "I draw beauty."

It was obvious that the man didn't want her to leave. And Daria, she had to admit, was very impressed, even taken with him as much as she could be. But even meeting a handsome French artist couldn't stop her from thinking of Catarine and being troubled about what she'd heard in the church. Daria left the ice skating pond, making excuses to the man, for he'd begged her not to leave until he'd met her friend. She then went by the church in case Catarine was still there, finally going home to the Woerner's.

She found that they were all having supper, Catarine included, and it was she that was the recipient of Mrs. Woerner's wicked scowl. Reluctantly, the older lady put a plate of food before Daria and mumbled something in German as Karl and Henry snickered. When Daria looked up, she was relieved to see Catarine smiling ear-to-ear. So all was well, after all.

After dinner, Karl motioned to Daria and Catarine to come into the parlor by imploring them with the crook of his index finger. "Shhh, we have beer, no?"

"Ya, beer, gut," Catarine was quick to say, then looking at Daria, who looked a little hurt, shrugging her shoulders.

When Karl went out to fetch the beer, Daria said, "I'd hoped we could talk!"

"Yes, we need to talk," Catarine said. "Let's have some beer first. I really like it, don't you?"

The two women contrived, after spending about an hour chatting, dancing and drinking beer with their young German housemates, to take a couple of pints back to their own room for the night. Sitting cross-legged in their pantaloons, they settled into one of their long conversations.

Daria, whose mood had lifted tremendously after arriving home, even before the addition of the ale, set out with an explanation to Catarine, "I heard you in the confessional."

"You did?" Catarine said.

"Just barely. Tell me about it," Daria said excitedly.

"Well, it's not happy news, but, honestly, I was relieved to get it off my mind," Catarine shook her head remembering Sister Edith and how she goaded her into the confession. "Sister Edith had noticed something amiss. At least, that's what she said. She talked with me today about how it is impossible to carry burdens around. You know, secrets."

"Oh, my. I reckon we are not good actors after all."

"I'm not, perhaps you are. You've had more experience than I," Catarine laughed and pushed at Daria's arm good-naturedly. "You've pretended to like those suitors for years."

"Yes, and I was very convincing too!"

"Well, she called for Father Tom and I ended up telling him everything. He is an amiable man."

"Everything?"

"Yes, everything. He is a priest, after all."

The two women talked until the early morning hours. Catarine confessed her growing feelings of doom about running from the law. She felt that one day it would catch up with her. How could she enjoy her life? Daria understood but wondered if they were both to find their calling, if then they'd be transformed, with the past fading into the distance. Catarine wasn't so sure but would consider just what her calling might be. She also confessed feelings of being drawn back to Louisiana, back to her plantation. She kept wondering about how Bessie was, and the others. Maybe that was her calling. To help them have a better life. Back to the way things were before the Koch's came.

"I do have something interesting to tell you. Something strange, possibly," Daria changed the subject as they were lying there having finished their beers and getting sleepy.

"Oh please, don't tell me if it is dismal!"

"Oh, no," Daria said sitting up and smiling down on Catarine. "You'll find this pleasant enough. Remember that man who we saw drawing at the ice skating pond? The one you said was handsome?"

"Yes, I said he looked French."

"Well, you were right."

"Oh, how'd you discover that?"

"He spoke to me."

"How nice."

"That's not all! He sat down next to me and showed me his drawings. Quite by accident really. And they were all of us!"

"What? Really?" Catarine said laughing suddenly.

"Yes, and they are good. Very good."

"Hmmm. So he has been there drawing us all this time?"

"I suppose so."

"That's intriguing," Catarine crossed her legs and put her arms under her head as she did when she pondered something deeply.

"He said it was because we are beautiful to him. Perhaps we should try to find him. We can find out more about him."

"Let's do."

The next morning, Louis took out all his drawings and lined his small room with them as the sun poured into his casement window. He clipped each one on the clothesline he'd strung up against the wall. Bringing each one forth into the light, he appraised them singly from corner to corner, then blew away the graphite dust before clipping the sketches fast, affixing them on the firebrick like mute companions. His next step would be to paint a portrait from the drawings. As much as he loved his drawings, he loved painting even more. He'd work with the paints in the sun drenched daylight hours, when he could best see, mixing and blending each carefully chosen hue on his palette, then he'd go out to look for the women when evenings crept in.

Louis went down to the alehouse for his one daily meal. He spent his money on his art. Rent and art. This was his chance in America. In France, things had been different. For the Fontaines, money had not been a problem. That's not why he had come to this country. He'd come for his art, for freedom. Paris had been a mess, a big smelly mess.

He remembered the campagne des banquets, the political gatherings in which his family was involved. One in particular, more than a year ago, in which he and his father Gerard met with the opposition movement, the citizens revolting against the king. His family had talked night after night about the control the king had on every aspect of daily life, how even his own education at École des Beaux-Arts was clouded by the shadow of government appraisal. Artists had to be approved of and commissioned by the king. It was absurd! "The expression of one's soul should exist in freedom, a God-given right." He heard the words of his father swirling in his head. When they had met with the others in that back alley bistro, the night had turned violent, not at their hands, but by the strength of their oppressors. They'd been found out, and just as they were leaving, several municipal guards had been dispersed to patrol and arrest them as they left. He remembered seeing the gleam of bayonets flash in the moonlight as he stepped out into the gravel path, just ahead of his father. His reaction had been one of protection, as he instantly pushed his father back inside. The next thing he remembered was hearing musket fire outside. They were able to scramble out back with a few others and get safely away. But that night left several uprisers dead, among whom was a family friends' son. The next month, his father paid his passage to America, just before the February 1848 revolution in which King Louis Philippe abdicated and a new government was established. But Louis had no regrets. He was discovering a new beauty in America, especially in the faces of the people.

After work the girls went to the park as usual to see if it was still safe to skate. And they looked for the man Daria had met. The Artist. They didn't see anyone skating, which meant, sadly, the season must have ended. The found that the pond still had ice on it but was melting in spots or people would be out on it. They strolled around the pond instead. After about an hour, they still hadn't spotted the man they were looking for so they headed home somewhat disappointed but wondering if the German men would be available for more dancing again.

When Louis reached the park, he was surprised at how vacant it was. He looked everywhere for his girls, the women he'd lovingly drawn in his pictures. His subjects. But they were more than just subjects to him. He was elated to have met one of them. But he wished he'd asked her name. How very rude of him! He didn't sit on a bench watching passersby this time. Instead, he walked around looking only for the two enchanting women of his drawings.

As darkness overtook the city that night and he still hadn't found them, he grew distressed with apprehension. What if they weren't coming to the park anymore? Ice skating had ended with the turn in season. They likely had stopped coming. What was he to do?

One morning on the way to the orphanage, Catarine stopped to admire a crocus bursting through the hard ground in front of a house at the corner adjacent to where they usually turned north toward their destination. When she did this, she saw a vendor putting paintings into a carriage on the side street they would have normally passed.

"Let's go down here and see what this place is," Catarine suggested. When they approached the house, it looked like a residence, but the man loading the carriage told them it was an artist shop and that they sold paintings and art supplies inside. He suggested that they come back later in the day when they were open if they were interested in the paintings.

"Look, is that our artist?" Daria exclaimed as they were leaving the side street, turning northward toward their orphanage.

"It looks like him. Hard to tell from the back," Catarine answered looking up ahead and seeing his black head bob up and down in the crowd.

"Drat, I don't know his name. And even if I did, I couldn't very well yell to him in the streets."

"That's disappointing. I wonder if he lives nearby."

"I know, let's go back later to that shop and see the art they sell. Maybe they'll know the artists who live around here."

Later that day, when the girls completed their work, they went straight away to the art shop. The scruffy owner was there drinking tea behind the counter. He gave them a growl when they came in, asking them to be careful. Catarine and Daria had a look around, hoping to see themselves featured in a drawing, but didn't.

Daria, approaching the owner, asked politely, "Sir, may I ask you a question about the artists you feature here?"

"No, you may not," he replied rudely. "I'm only lettnya in here cuz ya are wit 'er. I don't let color'd people in. As a rule."

"Is that so?" Daria said at the counter. "Please explain to me why that would be?"

"I find that difficult to believe," Catarine said, who'd quickly presented herself at the counter next to Daria's side.

"Ya do?" the man said and belched what smelled like, to the women, to be tea heavy laden with whiskey. "Something wrong with ya thinker?"

"I'd say yours is the one askew, most obviously," Catarine said. "How is it, a man can be so rude to a woman? Must be the liquor."

"Surely you are pleasant when not drunk off your rocker otherwise," Daria said with a smile.

"Excuse me? I'm not gonna be insulted by the likes a you!" the man said attempting to get up off of his stool without falling by holding on to the wall and the counter.

"I will insult you! You imbecile!" came a shout from the door. They all turned to see the man, the Artist standing just inside the door, black case in hand, face reddened and yelling at the owner. He rushed over to where they were all standing. "How dare you! Excuse toi, man. Apology now."

"Ya ain't from 'er mister," the drunk owner said, turning precariously to walk through a small doorway next to the counter, taking his "tea" with him. With that, Louis grabbed the man from the back and shoved him up against the wall. His cup crashed down on the ground, breaking into tiny shards, as the women gasped.

"Oh yes, you will. Apology now," he said into his ear, flattening the man's face against the brick wall until the drunk man nodded his consent and drooled brown liquid from his large parted lips. Louis then forcefully turned the man to face the women who were both standing there with their gloved hands over their mouths. "Say it!"

"I'm sorry."

"And to the brown one!" He brought the man up closer to Daria, who looked at him with the greatest of distain, while smelling his ghastly breath.

"I'm sorry, miss."

"That's better. You are ashamed! I thought you are an artiste. Can you not see they are beauty?" Still having the man by the cuff of his jacket, he sat him down for a talk. "Can you not see they are beautiful?"

"I see, I see!"

"You don't even know what I talk about!" Louis just shook his head then released his hold on the man. They all stood around looking at each other for a somewhat prolonged time, for the Artist became suddenly bashful when facing the women.

It was Daria who finally spoke. "Well, thank-you good sir. It seems it is always a French man to the rescue!"

Still, no one spoke again for a minute but everyone just smiled at each other politely, Catarine nervously fiddling with her gloves.

"I understand that you are an artist," she ventured.

"Yes, I am," was all he could manage. He remained tongue-tied but gazing at Catarine with eyes of wonder, as if he'd found a treasure. The owner sat, afraid to move an inch, but eyed his bottle of whiskey just out of sight under the counter, wishing for another gulp.

Daria wanted to sit down and looked around the room for anywhere they might have a chat. Seeing that the Artist and Catarine were transfixed, she took a deep breath and said, "I'm Daria Morinay. I'm sorry I didn't introduce myself the other day."

"Oh yes, so sorry. I'm Louis Fontaine," he said, coming alive as if it was a brilliant idea to tell their names.

"And my friend is Catarine Dupre," Daria said and then immediately gasped. The women both looked at each other and then laughed out loud at her error.

"What is funny?" Louis asked. "Did I say an unsuitable word?

"No, *you* didn't. But we just told you my real name," said Catarine.

Chapter 9

"It is abandoned. No one's there," Louis said coming into the barn where the women were hiding.

"How are the animals surviving without someone to feed them?" Daria asked.

"It looks like someone just turned them out. They can graze and there is a water source down the hill," Catarine explained.

"The question remains," Louis said, "why would anyone abandon this place?" They all looked at each other. "The house looks sparse but livable."

"I don't have time to worry about the former occupants. I need to concern myself with that marshal," Catarine replied. "Do you think this is a safe place to stay?"

"Yes, but we need not make a fire or leave any evidence of our being here."

"What about food?" Daria asked.

"And weapons," Catarine said. "Did you see any guns in the house, Louis?"

"No, none of those lying about. But I saw a fruit tree out back and bushes with some sort of berries on them next to the house, Daria."

"That will have to do for our supper," Catarine said. "I'll go fetch them for us."

"No! You stay hidden. I'll go," Daria said. "Louis, stay with her."

Being on the run from a federal marshal would ordinarily make one loathe each day, even the air one breathed each minute, if one's thoughts would even turn in that direction, but Catarine found that since Louis Fontaine was with her, her life had taken an unexplainable upswing. Perhaps it was that he reminded her so much of her brother Andre. He'd been an artist also. And was of the same nature. Andre had concerned himself with beauty in the world and when he saw injustice, he reacted like she'd witnessed Louis react at the art shop in New York. Such passion! Of course, Louis had been defending Daria, which was a noble act, but he was defending all that Catarine stood for as well. And when the federal marshal had come looking for her, Louis didn't bat an eye. He left everything, literally, to flee with them. To protect her. And even though she didn't need a man, at least that's what she felt, she wanted him. Not just any man. Him. Louis Fontaine. She wanted him. She wanted to know him more, his moods, his art, his thoughts. And she loved how he watched her.

Louis thought that coming to America would be about his art. He'd always longed to capture beauty. He'd learned that America was a beautiful country and since Paris was spoiled with turmoil, he was happy to sail away to find beauty and freedom to do his art as he wished. He had not bargained for the unexpected splendor of love he felt in his heart when he looked at Catarine. Such a beauty she was! Inside and out. And he aimed to do anything, anything at all to protect her.

Daria hadn't bargained for this. While, in many ways, she didn't mind doing anything, anything at all to protect Catarine, she wasn't enjoying being on the run nor was she aiming to share her with another. Daria hoped against reason that they'd soon find a remote corner of the world where they could get on with life and forget Catarine's "accident". She'd thought that they'd done that in New York, but apparently someone had turned them into the authorities. She had her ideas about who it was but it didn't really matter.

When Fuhrmann had warned them about the federal marshals coming, he'd simply said to get out of New York quickly. The state. He only had time to explain that word had gotten to them that she was living in New York and that others were helping her. Law enforcement had been alerted by telegraph throughout the state of New York, of that fact he could be certain. Fuhrmann again told Catarine, as he'd done many months before, that he'd catch up with her with word again. Suspiciously, he insisted upon knowing where they were headed. He specifically instructed Catarine not to try to leave the country, as the ports were alerted, something Daria didn't believe and was loathe to agree to, as she wanted to head to Europe, believing that to be their best chance of a clean break and a peaceful life. Catarine promised Fuhrmann that she would go toward Philadelphia. But eventually, they'd all agreed that their best chance of getting away from everyone, whether it be the law looking for Catarine or others who might not be trustworthy, would be to head to a location to which only they were privy.

"Why do we need guns?" Louis asked again.

Catarine had looked through the house and the barn for any firearms that might have been left behind. On her hands and knees, she brushed the hay aside and tried to determine if there was a hidden floor in the barn.

"For protection. And to hunt, of course," she answered still scampering about as Daria came in from the outside.

"I found these," Daria said dropping several items of clothing, including a pair of boots, onto the hay near Catarine, along with a napsack.

"Perfect! I'm sure these will all come in handy!" Catarine said. "We need to gather up all our supplies and be ready to run again if necessary."

"We must leave at some point. How far away from Boston are we?" Daria asked.

"I'm not sure, maybe a day's walk?" Catarine answered. "Maybe more."

"That sounds about right," Louis said. "From what that farmer said yesterday."

"On horseback, it would be much shorter. And easier."

"We can't take those horses," Louis said.

"The abandoned ones?" Catarine asked.

"They are not ours," he reminded her.

"Neither are the clothes. Or the apples. I say we take 'em."

"I'd hate for you to add horse thief to your charges," Daria warned sitting down beside Catarine who'd given up looking for guns. "Besides, I don't know how to ride."

"Not at all?"

"I've never been on a horse. Not ever," Daria said grimly. "What about you Louis?"

"I can ride. What are the penalties for thieving a horse in this country?" Louis asked as Daria and Catarine looked at each other.

"They used to hang people for it," Catarine said quietly. "But I believe it depends on the state. And I don't think it is hanging anymore."

"In France it was flogging," Louis said. The three of them sat quietly contemplating their choices for a few moments.

"I suppose if we were real criminals, we'd not give it a second thought," said Catarine. "But I think we must look to our goal of getting away to a place where we can live in peace. Either that or I should surrender."

"Don't surrender! I don't trust those people hunters," Louis said. "You've made your decision and I have too."

"I'm beside you, too," said Daria. "If we could simply get out of this country. Go abroad. We have Louis here who knows France. What's keeping us from going to Paris?"

"I have thought that too," Louis said.

"Let's sleep on it," was Catarine's answer. "I still wonder about what Fuhrmann said. If he was telling the truth, then I'd be caught boarding ship."

"I'm not sure I believe him," Louis said. "Especially after what you tell of him."

"I don't trust him at all anymore," Daria said. "I used to but not after his long absence and the way he just showed up shooing us away. I'm not sure anyone in New York turned us in. It's possible. But I felt we were safe there."

In the morning, it was decided that they'd head for the city of Boston and gamble with their future by boarding a ship sailing for France. Between them they had enough for steerage tickets, having left with only the money they'd each had with them at the time for daily living. When they reached Boston, they hoped to sell the abandoned horses along with their tack that was left in the barn.

"We did see that federal marshal. He wasn't a figment of our imagination. And he was asking for me," Catarine said as they ambled along slowly in line on their horses through the woods.

She'd given Daria a brief lesson on riding, teaching her how to stay on the horse, as best she could do in the few minutes they had in preparation to depart.

"Yes, but Fuhrmann could have tipped him off to our location," Daria said.

"Why would he have waited so long to do so?" Catarine asked.

"I'm not sure. Maybe he changed his mind about helping you," Daria said.

Louis rode along listening to both the women speculate about who'd turned Catarine into the authorities and also kept a keen ear open to any sound that might indicate the presence of an unwanted person nearby. So far, he felt they were passing in a safe area, woods through which only animals or their pred-ator had trekked.

"Hey, can we slow down? You are going too fast now."

"See if you can go faster by keeping your heels down," Catarine said. "That will keep you in the saddle. Try not to bounce so much."

"That's why I need to slow down!"

"If we are going too fast, or if some reason your horse goes faster than you wish," Louis warned Daria, "just make sure you hold onto his mane and keep your head down. And heels as Catarine said. Whatever you do, stay in the saddle. Don't fall off!"

"I am trying!" Daria said. "That's the last thing I want to do. I will just hang on as best I can."

"If you squeeze him too hard, he will think you want him to go faster," Catarine explained.

"Oh my," Daria said, shutting her eyes tightly. "The things I do for you."

Daria sat firmly in her saddle and opened her eyes enough to peer through her horse's ears to see Louis and Catarine up ahead of her on their horses. They both sat comfortably upon their horses, each barely holding on the reins, as they chatted side by side. She watched them go along, looking about care-fully, but also noticed how easy Catarine took to the ride. She patted her horse on his neck and took her boots out of the stirrups occasionally, dangling them and stretching her legs at his side. Louis appeared to be as comfortable as Catarine on a horse and in the woods. She listened to bits of their conver-sation about guns and the noises in the woods but also about

Louis' drawings and Catarine's dead brother. Here was a man who had, in the few short months they'd known him, changed Catarine more than Daria thought possible.

At first Louis had been shy with them. He'd rescued them at the art shop from the rude man, giving him a taste of his own medicine, but after that he didn't know what to say to them. Just before they were leaving him, he mustered up enough courage to ask them to tea. Soon after that he had them come to his rented room to show them his pictures. They were amazed. After that, he hung about daily, continued to draw them and clung to them, especially Catarine. They established several meeting places since the ice skating was over: the tea shoppe, the river walk, the bakery and the alehouse. At first, Daria thought their time together was excessive, that maybe they were just sharing mutual interests, and then she realized what was happening. Catarine and Louis were falling in love.

Catarine had instantly liked him. He had reminded her of her brother Andre. The way Louis talked about beauty and how he wanted to capture it, was admirable. It was his primary aim in life. He spoke in a low quiet voice when he said these things, like he was telling a deep, dark secret. He'd told them this the first time they'd gone to Odell's tavern. Daria had noticed the warmth in Catarine's eyes. When she asked her later that night what she'd thought of Louis, Catarine had simply said, "He reminds me of my brother."

Louis was an engaging man, in an odd way. A quiet way. He had strong ideas that one had to stop and think about. And he had a presence. His height seemed to dominate the room, even if he just stood there. The thing with Catarine falling in love with him was this: Daria couldn't blame her. If she was inclined to fall for a man, it would be a noble man like Louis. But that still didn't mean she wanted to share Catarine. She didn't *want* to, but it looked like she would *have* to.

It was Louis who looked up first, or rather his horse, who was in the lead. The other geldings halted instantly, ears forward and noses twitching.

"What is it?" Catarine said quickly.

"Not sure," Louis whispered.

"What's that smell?" Daria said as her horse halted behind them.

Louis turned slightly to her and said, "What do you smell?"

"Something foul."

"A lifeless creature?" Louis asked.

"No, not dead. Just…" as Daria was answering they all heard the sound of a snort and a few squeals, then the running of feet through the brush.

"Boar!" Catarine shouted as she turned her horse away from the sound. Daria's horse followed without needing a command. "Daria, stay on!"

All the horses picked up speed at their own volition. The black creatures surrounded them, swiftly coming from their bedding places deep within the heavy brush. The horses kicked out at them as they ran, looking wildly about them with tormented eyes. They dodging the branches the horses took them beneath, as a few slapped their faces and cut into their arms. Catarine knew falling amongst a wild boar family could prove fatal, what's more, she knew pigs of any kind struck fear in a horse's heart, so her only thoughts were to stay on and ride away from the area. She hoped Daria was holding on well.

When the horses were satisfied that they were well away from the smell of boar, they slowed their pace. Daria's heart hammered in her chest but she noticed that it was easier than she thought to stay put on her wide horse leaning back a little as Catarine had instructed her.

They rode along for a while still keeping to the woods bound for Boston as instructed by the farmer Louis had met alone near the farm house where they'd stayed a few nights. He'd told Louis it was about a days journey and they were just southwest of the city. Louis, since meeting him, had reasoned to himself, that if anyone would be accused of horse theft, it would be him, since, as far as he could discern, no one knew that Catarine and Daria were with him.

It was late afternoon, when they came to a clearing that they were forced to enter. A road traversed the far side heading in the direction which they were going, but at the present, no woods were found to conceal them.

"We may as well take the road," Catarine said. They steered their horses for the road bound for Boston, letting them sniff the vegetation nearby.

"It's a good thing we stopped at that rivulet. It doesn't look like any up ahead in the near distance," Louis remarked.

After they'd ridden along for a half hour or so, they noticed a cart coming along against them pulled by two horses. Louis looked hard from a distance to see if the man driving the cart held a gun or looked threatening in any way.

"What should we do?" Daria asked.

"Nothing, there's nowhere to hide," Catarine answered.

As the cart approached, they could all see a little man sitting atop, allowing the horses free rein to pull the empty cart. Not seeing any discernible reason for fear, they all stopped to chat.

"Good day," Louis spoke first, tipping his hat.

"Ah, you're a French man?" the little man asked.

"Oui, monsieur," Louis replied.

"Odd," he remarked.

"Why is that odd?" Catarine asked him.

"Well, I'll be. You're all a strange lot indeed. A French man and two women. One colored!"

For a few moments, they all eyed each other with suspicion. A couple of crows cawed at each other overhead.

"Is she your slave?" he directed his question toward Louis.

Louis seemed to hesitate. Daria was silent, noticing the flush on Catarine's cheeks.

Catarine opened her mouth to speak but wasn't able to reply.

"Oui, monsieur," Louis managed to answer again just as Catarine closed her mouth and exhaled. "And how far is Boston, monsieur?"

"You're a might near it, sir," he said in a friendlier tone still eyeing the three of them up and down.

"Seen anyone else along the way?" Louis asked him.

"Why you asking?" the man answered looking at Louis defensively. The little man sat glaring at them and chewed sideways on a piece of straw.

"What do you have in your cart, sir?" Catarine asked noticing a blanket thrown over contents in the rear. She'd been looking for movement of the contents and hadn't seen any but was curious about his cargo. He'd questioned them directly, so she felt she could ask whatever crossed her mind.

"None uh ya bi'ness," was his answer as his mouth contorted grotesquely, the straw waving about like a flag.

"Va te faire foutre!" Louis said clicking his horse to proceed. "Let's go, fillies!" The women followed, Louis leaving the perplexed man staring after them.

When they were well clear of the man with the cart, Catarine commented, "All right, now that we are near Boston, it's unlikely we'll see any more boar."

"I just want to be off this horse!" Daria said.

"You will be soon, dear!" Catarine said. "I promise! It won't be long."

Chapter 10

There were three men, armed with five rifles, six knives and two handguns, who were concealed behind the mulberry bushes just beyond the fork in the road. They'd left the fourth man with their horses nearly a hundred paces up the road to be sure neither beast nor being could smell nor hear their movement. The men, experienced predators of the unsuspecting but guilty, all waited in gleeful anticipation for their prey to appear before them. The tallest one, the marshal with his hat pulled down low over his eyes, scrutinized the road up ahead for any sign that they were nearing as he ran a dry tongue over his teeth, lips drawn to a snarl and squinting into the afternoon sun. Shorty looked bored, leaning against the small pine, but his rifle was cocked and ready, held fast across his chest in both hands. Booley, hat thrown back and hanging, shifted his weight from boot to boot and frowned at the road.

Shaking his head side to side, he said, "What's taking 'em so damn long?"

The tall one, Meredith, just shifted his eyes in Booley's direction for a half second then looked back to where the road crested. Dust was the sign they were looking for, especially on such a dry day.

When they saw it, Meredith whispered, "Nobody move."

They all saw them coming, the two women and a man riding slowly. It was dead quiet except for a slight breeze disturbing the ground brush and in the distance the strike of hooves against the dirt could barely be heard. Both the man and the woman were being watchful, the man peering down the road and the woman shifting her gaze side to side methodically. Having the sun at their backs gave their prey their only advantage. The woman in the rear, the colored one, rode along unaware, heavily fatigued. When they were about fifty paces away the man stopped cold and held out his right hand to indicate danger. A faint breeze disturbed the sleeping treetops and a lone hawk took flight. Silence prevailed along the road as the horses stopped and the women caught their breath. Meredith exhaled deeply without making a sound and swallowed.

"Louis," the woman whispered but when she did the man held his hand up higher and shook his head quickly from side to side. The man then turned his horse off the road and headed due south. The women followed and then they took their horses into a canter away from the men in the bushes.

Shorty fired his gun first, without a command from Meredith. "You fool!" was all he heard then but knew he'd be in for it later. The three men ran out on the road and up to where the fourth man had mounted his horse and was already heading for the fugitives. By that time, the two women and the man were galloping away from them just out of gunshot range.

"They shot us!" Daria gulped and spit as she yelled out to Catarine.

She gripped her horse with her calves, the toes of her boots buried into his side. As she hovered down, she grabbed his mane hairs and wound them into the reins, the jarring gallop forcing her to condense her effort to the clasps held by her desperate limbs.

Catarine snapped her head back to view Daria behind her, and noted that the distant sky held a menacing mass of clouds. They ran along the open field, Louis's horse in the lead.

"Watch the terrain! For Daria." Catarine couldn't imagine how Daria could stay on her horse if they were to go over anything rough. If they needed to jump.

They heard another shot ring out and then another whistle by them. The horses ran at full speed, and as if sensing the terrain, took them to an incline over which was a creek. At the top of the hill, Louis paused to calculate their distance from the marshals.

"We've made a little progress but not much," Louis said.

"Let's get in the creek and double back," Catarine said. "They won't be expecting that."

They waded in the creek northward, back towards where they come. The cool water splashed up on them with each step their horses made. Traveling upstream, they came to deeper water, brown water nearly to the belly of each horse. Silence fell between them as they listened to the sounds around them, hearing only the swirling water and the breeze disturbing the treetops.

They finally came to a more shallow, rocky tributary and eased their horses out of the water, still attentive to the sounds around them. When they felt they had lost the men, they dismounted, watered their horses and rested for a short while.

"We must move on," Louis said after a short rest.

"I don't know if I can go on," Daria said.

"You'll have to," Catarine said. "Either that or I'll give myself up."

"I reckon we're all guilty now," Daria said.

They rode on until late afternoon, finding the woods they'd left before. They'd talked of camping for the night but decided it would be best to ride on back to the farm from which they'd come, even if they made slow progress. They went along quietly, silently as possible with little to no talk between them.

"Boar," was all Daria said as she lifted her feeble head. She'd caught a whiff of them again, the bitter scent that burned her nose. It was the same smell she'd detected in the woods much earlier that same long day, only this time she had no strength to be afraid. No one answered her. She wasn't sure if they'd heard although they were right up in front of her and weren't talking.

Just as Daria was wondering how far they had to go until she'd be able to lay her body down, she felt her horse gather up its hindquarters and lurch ahead. The next second, his head smacked into Catarine's horse who went into a gallop as Louis' horse reared up before shooting forward ahead of them all.

They all heard the loud squeals and grunts and felt their horses kicking at the running boars beneath them as they ran through the woods. No one spoke. Sounds of the horses' exertion, the frenzied breaths of heaving chests as they ran, could be heard over what sounded like the thudding of a thousand hooves against the scourged earth. Shots rang out over their heads while reason had been suspended for both man and beast in front of the huge black pigs. Gunshots rained around them periodically as they pursued freedom from capture at all costs. They all frantically held on as the horses galloped away from the wild black boars.

Finally, after the gunshots and boars faded into the distance, Catarine ventured a glance backward. Louis was directly behind her but Daria was nowhere to be seen. Climbing a ravine, they could see that the boars had stopped their chase but the marshals were still below them down the hillside that they'd just ascended.

"Where's Daria?" Catarine panicked and pulled her horse to a stop. "She'll be killed!"

"I'll go back," Louis answered. "You can't be caught."

"There's nowhere to hide. I'll go back. I cannot leave her!" Catarine cried, tears streaming down her face as her horse circled around impatiently.

"Don't stay here. They are coming. Run!" Louis commanded.

Catarine hesitated again, but seeing the men looking up in their direction, she turned the other way, sobbing and overwrought. Louis went down the other side of the hill, away from the men who were pursuing their prey.

Louis, after rounding the other side of the hill, found no traces of boar or of Daria. He stopped short when he heard gunshots in the distance, in Catarine's direction, but then went on to check the place where'd he'd last seen Daria.

He saw her horse first. It was standing near a clump of trees at the edge a thicket of bushes. That's when her heard her moan.

"How bad was your fall?" Louis asked as he dismounted his horse and knelt at Daria's side. She was facing the bush, curled up as if sleeping. He stroked her hair and shook her. "Daria." When she didn't answer, he carefully turned her towards him, onto her back and that's when he saw it. The bloody mess. Her mid-section was covered in blood; her arms drawn crossed over in a protective measure. She extended a shaky blood-soaked hand and placed it on Louis' arm. "Were you shot?"

"Boars," she whispered. She smiled up at Louis. It looked as if she were resting, peaceful.

"You were gored?" Louis cried. "Mon Dieu! I will carry you."

"No."

"Yes, I cannot leave you here!"

Daria breathed in and out deeply, slowly. She smiled again and seemed to gather her strength. Then she fixed her eyes on his. "Go to Catarine. Go now before it's too late."

"I cannot just leave you here," Louis said. "You will, you could die!"

Daria closed her eyes slowly and shook her head. "Go to her." Daria slowly lifted her bloody right hand pressed it into Louis' hand. "Give her my love."

Louis stood, shaking and torn. He didn't feel his own tears roll down his cheeks as he stared down at Daria who was a contrast of ruination and odd serenity, her lips pallid and dry.

"Je vous souhaite bonne," Louis said to her, kneeling back down at her side. I wish you well.

"Puissiez-vous vivre cent années," she whispered back to him. May you live one hundred years. He turned and fled on his horse to join Catarine before it was too late.

The rain started in sheets, followed by one lusty thunderclap. It was hard for Catarine to tell whether heaven was angry with her or with the men following her, insomuch as her head felt gashed apart by conflict. Weariness had seeped into her bones. If only she hadn't run. Rain washed the tears away from her eyes as she and her horse slowed to a trot and meandered through small pines and bushes down the hillside, reins slack, directionless. The washing felt good and reminded her of Louisiana afternoons and all those she cared for. Her thoughts turned to Bessie, and when they did, she felt more warm tears join her sopping dirty hair that stuck to her face like unraveled twine. Hanging, that's what they do to murderers. For a few moments, she felt fear once again stab her heart and she kicked her horse to make haste but he only tossed his head in response. Her skin drank in the moisture of the piney rain. She didn't react to the coldness but instead allowed it to pass through her unnoticed and ignored, while her eyes, unfocused, turned her thoughts to days with her father. Days on horseback, even the rainy ones, had seemed intrinsic to her, as deep-rooted as their plantation magnolias. How could they be gone? But they were, gone forever, as her Papa was. As she slumped from her horse and fell to the ground beneath her, a soft fall into the leaves, she would have simply slept there, but instead she gasped as her horse stepped aside and two rifle barrels appeared in her face.

Chapter 11

He hated himself instantly. What lasted perhaps only seconds, seemed like unhurried, sluggardly minutes with his feet sinking in the muddy torrent. Louis saw the marshals easing down the hillside, having abandoned their horses over the knoll. He watched them track her, he studied them as if he were just a curious onlooker, disinterested. He kept to the summit above, the unseen spectator, vacillating between ideas of saving himself or warning Catarine. He watched her slow down, staring ahead as her horse ambled along. The crack of thunder galvanized him away from his stupor as he thrust himself forward against the nearest tree. He opened his mouth to yell to her but instead crouched down and scrambled in her direction as quickly as he could. He stood again as he neared her, only to watch her drop. He heard the metallic clack of the guns being cocked but as he lurched forward in her direction, he lost his footing and slid down a hill into the muddy path. With the taste of revulsion in his mouth, Louis clawed his way to the nearest bush to hide himself from capture.

There were only three of them to retrieve her, and they made a quick work of it. The one they called Booley lifted her up, put her hands together in front of her, and tied a rope around them. The tall one spoke to her but Louis could see she just looked at him and made no reply, blinking into the rain. After she was tied, they walked by the path close to where he was hiding in the mud and bushes. They were so close, Louis could see the moss against the boots of the tall one leading the way, moss he smeared off the path right before Louis' eyes. Booley was next pulling Catarine by the savage rope, her hands thrust out before her unnaturally, slack and open, as if asking for something. Her shoulders followed, tense, but her countenance was absent, missing, as if she'd willed herself to be elsewhere. And the other marshal walked behind her smiling, his gun leveled square at her back. Still, the rain came down in sheets all about them like a monstrous plague.

When they were well out of earshot, Louis slithered out of the bushes but didn't follow them. Instead he sat down in the mud and groaned. He cried out and beat his fists against the glut and lay there in the rain as Catarine was being led away, the fervency of his hopes to save her, and his stupid thoughts of being her champion having drowned dead in the deluge.

Most of the women were just like her. They never wanted to eat and they always slumped into a wordless half-conscious state. Either that or they cried constantly, terror stricken. The way Booley saw it, the way they acted after capture determined their guilt or innocence. He figured the brave ones, the ones who weren't idiot crybabies, were the killers. It made perfect sense to him. He was sure those sniveling, scared-of-their-shadow women that they'd brought in couldn't have even fired a gun or cut off a chicken's head, much less killed anybody. So this woman must be a killer. She was too composed. Silent and determined. He saw it in her eyes. He'd be watching his back.

Meredith's job was to deliver this one alive and well. And he took his job seriously. He tried to entice her to eat but so far she'd refused, even the roasted rabbit he'd held up close to her. He'd hoped she'd be able to smell it and decide to take a bite. She'd only looked away bored. It was the same look she'd had since they captured her, except that one small moment in her tent. As far as he could tell the only substance she'd taken in had been a few sips from his canteen. At least she'd done that. That meant she didn't want to die. Interesting. And that had started on day three so she must have been real thirsty. Maybe it was because all the rains finally stopped and things were drying up.

Meredith's other problem was his men. Booley was a simpleton with a sexual appetite that he'd been known to satisfy with captives a time or two. Shorty's trigger-happy tendency had gotten them into trouble on more than one occasion. Despite Meredith's training, the men he'd been given to straighten out still plagued him with their vices. After Larsen rejoined them, Meredith could finally breathe a sigh of relief, being the only truly competent one he had. The four of them should be able to get this woman back to New Orleans as quick as possible and be paid before the next month.

Shorty slept with his guns around him. Meredith allowed each man to sleep with their personal revolver at their sides and their knives strapped on, but insisted at night they leave their rifles strapped to the horses. That way, if they had to make a quick get-away they'd already be in place. But Shorty took comfort in his firearms and wanted them encircling him as he slept. And for this reason he slept furthest from the fire. And from Meredith's eye.

Upon waking on day seven, Shorty noticed his .54 caliber percussion rifle missing. He feared that Meredith had discovered his disobedience and that he'd be punished straight away. Or, equally possible, foolish Booley, wanting to trick him, had taken his gun away as a joke.

"Bool, you bastard," Shorty snarled and grabbed Booley by the collar as soon as he returned from relieving himself in the bushes. "Where is it?"

"Hey, wha….?"

"Where's ma gun?"

"I dunno nothin bout your gun. Which one?" Booley threw Shorty's arms off him and pushed him down. "Get offa me!"

"Boys, get over here an eat ya something," Larsen commanded from the fire. Shorty got up and went over to the fire kicking up dust into Larsen's plate. "Hey, watch out. You can cook me some more!"

"Where's Meredith?"

"He's in with the prisoner," Larsen replied.

Booley snickered and looked around at them all with a witless expression as he'd done daily when Meredith entered the makeshift tent they'd constructed for Catarine. Meredith had made it clear that he was the only one allowed to enter, which was standard procedure, and something he intended to follow precisely. But this had caused both Booley and Shorty to laugh and guffaw, as if the marshal instead had some immoral reason, and was entering the tent to speak to the prisoner for something other than interrogation and official purposes.

"Twelve lashes if I hear another word about it!" Meredith said emerging from the tent with Catarine. He threatened daily to put a stop to Booley's ridicule by whipping him with a horse crop across his back but had, as yet, not fulfilled his promise.

"What's the problem here, Shorty?" Meredith asked. Shorty began shifting from leg to leg and stammering.

"He can't find his gun," Larsen helped.

"What do you mean, can't find it?" Meredith said stepping forward to Shorty.

It had been a quiet morning, but at that moment, when Meredith grabbed him by the shoulders and lifted him up to eye level, what everyone heard was Shorty releasing his bladder and soaking himself. "I told you to put 'em on the horses. Did ya do that?"

"No sir"

"Of all the damn idiot men, I get you all!" Meredith yelled to no one in particular. "Why?"

"I needed them wif me, sir," Shorty answered.

"No you didn't, fool! *I* tell *you* what *you* need. You sleep sounder than a horse! I know that about you! That's why your guns need to be on them, not you. They'll rouse up!"

"Sir, are you thinking someone else stole it?" Larsen asked. He was still sitting by the fire ring that he had just doused out with coffee.

"Yep, that's what I'm thinking. Some passing thief I guess. Larsen, you get all-a Shorty's guns. 'Cept his Colt. I won't deny a man protection. But that's all you get. And I'll deal with you when we get to Baltimore. And who the hell was on watch last night?"

Catarine remembered hearing them argue about who was on watch the night Shorty's gun was stolen. She figured they'd must have gotten confused and consequently left no one in charge. Or maybe it was Booley's watch and he'd fallen asleep, something she'd watched him do on occasion. They whispered after that incident, which they were prone to do about official matters. She wasn't privy to all their conversations. But she knew where the gun was. Or who had gotten it. He'd made his presence known to her on day three after her capture.

She'd spent all of the first day since being taken prisoner thinking of Louisiana. She was thinking of going back, even if it were to jail and possibly to hang. But before that she would ask to see her mother. And she'd ask her mother to bring Bessie. That kept her going, kept her walking, and alive. If only she could conjure up her father and Andre. But that was just fantasy. She'd see them in heaven. Some would doubt whether she'd make it to heaven but she had absolution from the priest. And she had absolution from God. She knew this to be true. And anyway, she knew in her heart, and Bessie knew, that she, Catarine Dupre was not a murderer.

By day two she'd decided that she'd gamble. She was a risk taker after all. It would be a huge shot in the dark, but she wanted to spite the men who had her, so she refused to take a bite of food. The idea grew naturally from having no appetite, none whatsoever. In fact, she was sure that if she'd put any ration to her mouth she'd retch her guts out and be worse for it. So she just kept her soul, kept her substance and her mind intact and became a survivor. That's what she was, a survivor.

Day three passed pleasantly. Besides the man Booley eyeing her and winking, it was a nice day. She wasn't worried about him for one minute. She could defend herself or simply yell out for Meredith if Booley laid a hand on her. Meredith was an agreeable man. He'd had the others set up a little tent for her to use. It gave her a little privacy and shelter. He'd come inside and whispered questions to her and to try to get her to eat. He always looked at her with kind fatherly eyes. It made her want to talk to him. But instead, she just smiled, which seemed to make him glad or feel like he'd made progress with her. He asked mostly about her companions and she wasn't telling anything about them. It was strange that he wanted to know about "the colored one". Catarine wanted to know if they had found her. Maybe she would ask him but she knew they'd expect an exchange, a deal. She wasn't prepared for that.

Then Louis showed up. They'd pulled up their belongings that morning as usual, and Catarine noticed a fresh sprig of honeysuckle tucked into her bedroll. She thought at first it must have been one of the men, maybe even Meredith, although it was highly doubtful that he'd done that. Perhaps Booley or Shorty but even that seemed unlikely to her. Later that day, after traveling all day and stopping to make camp, they came across a piece of fabric tied to a tree near the stream. Catarine recognized it right away and her heart leapt. It was from the sleeve of Louis' shirt! They all ignored it, as folks typically tie cloth around trees to be felled and as they weren't far from a village, it was commonplace enough.

Much later, after the moon had climbed into the night sky and the men had commenced their snoring, every few minutes Catarine noticed a shifting of leaves so soft that it was barely discernible, yet seemed to grow closer with each development. She froze in her position but kept her eyes wide open and her ears honed-in on the infinitesimal night sounds. When the snoring of the two loudest men eventually reached a pinnacle, Louis was suddenly there, noiselessly lifting the far side of her tent, his face gleaming in the shadows like a divine being. She wanted to cry out in joy. Silently he crawled into her tent and they held each other in muted cries, rocking back and forth. Neither spoke words, for expression was restricted to a few wet kisses. After a few short minutes, with wistfulness, they kissed goodbye and Louis exited the tent, crawling away as quietly as he had come.

Days pressed onward as they traveled south, Catarine riding with Meredith on his grey stallion, she with strength anew from her brief glimpse of Louis. Hunger returned to her but she only allowed herself sips of water from Meredith's canteen. Her thoughts were consumed with Louis and, hour upon hour, she concocted fanciful scenarios of how he'd rescue her, especially after Shorty's gun went missing. She knew then that

Louis had a plan. But then those notions would do battle in the next passage of time with fears for his safety. Four against one was terrible odds. And how was he getting on otherwise? Did he have a horse? And had he, by God, found out what had happened to Daria?

On day twelve, after vomiting yellow bile, Catarine fainted by the creekside. Booley had been watching her and the horses while Larsen and Meredith conferred nearby.

"She's down!" Booley hollered out to them, spit a sizable wad of gob into the dirt and then slowly lifted himself up to fetch her. She looked pale and still, half of her face lying on the small wet pebbles.

"Get 'er up!" Meredith said approaching. "You're one lazy son-of-a-bitch, Booley."

"She just now fell."

"Here, I'll do it."

Meredith kneeled down beside her and gathered Catarine up in his arms and, soaking his handkerchief in the stream, gently washed her face and neck as she stirred and opened her eyes.

"You aint gonna like this but you gotta eat." Catarine blinked into Meredith's eyes and smiled. "Ya hear me?"

Meredith instructed them all that they would be stopping for a while and getting something for the prisoner to eat. Complaints were heard all around.

"I'm fetching her back alive," he explained.

He carried Catarine over to the shade of an oak tree, spread out his blanket and laid her down. He sat there and tried to feed her bits of his tack, which she refused.

"Come on now." He wiped her head again and smiled, something he rarely did. Catarine looked up at him, smiling back.

"Kiss me," she said looking at him with a dazed look in her eyes.

"Naw, I ain't gonna do it, Miss," he replied. Meredith was relieved that his men were not near enough to hear, although he was sure this must be a trick of hers or some such thing. "What you need is food, not a kiss."

"Come on, Louis," she answered.

"Who's Louis?"

"What?" Catarine said confused, then squinting and looking hard at Meredith, sighed and looked away, tears brimming over her eyes.

"Come on now! None of this! I ain't got time!" Meredith forced her to sit up and he shook her, gently but enough to stir her attention. "You got to eat. I ain't beat a woman before and I don't aim to start with you. But I will if I have to. Eat this now."

Frowning, Catarine sighed heavily then obeyed and, taking the hard tack from him, bit off piece by piece slowly, chewing long and swallowing hard, gagging on the first try. He helped her with swigs of water until she had gotten the whole thing down. Then he forced her to her feet. "Now, we'll do that again in an hour. Let's go."

At times, Louis came near enough to hear their conversation. He knew it was risky. He realized they were the professionals, not him. But he couldn't stay away. And when he crept up close to their camp at night, especially on nights that Booley was on guard, Louis could approach from the opposite end, away from Catarine's tent, and if the wind was right, he could catch their voices through the trees, and be privy to just enough of their remarks to know their planned movements for the morrow.

He was aware they were headed to Baltimore. Catarine knew that too; they'd spoken of that openly. What he'd heard was that Meredith was joining another pose, dumping his two morons and heading the remainder of the way in a hired coach. Apparently, for some financial benefit, speed was obligatory; hence they needed to deposit Catarine in New Orleans county seat by July 1st, alive and well. Thank goodness for that. And thankfully Meredith had gotten her to eat again.

They had all closed ranks around her since day fifteen. She had been eating but still ranting on about Louis, still calling Meredith Louis from time to time. It was a bizarre turn of events that was troubling to watch. Louis heard talk that shocked him while watching the men sit around the evening fire late one night after the food had been consumed. He had considered slipping into her tent that night if he got a chance, but when Meredith said, "I 'spose Louis was that man riding with her. I guess they're lovers. That's why she keeps going on 'bout 'im." So that was it. Was she ill?

Catarine hadn't seen Louis in days nor noticed any sign of him. She hoped he hadn't gotten lost or left behind in the distance. She longed for him. She was feeling completely useless, something she hated. She asked Meredith if she could please ride alone but he just laughed at her. She also wanted to groom herself better. Without her hands being tied. She'd indicated to each one of them, whoever was with her at a water source, to please untie her. She'd look longingly at her hands, swollen and bound by the ever-present prickly rope clasp.

It was Booley who finally agreed. One evening when the others were making camp, he took her to a small stream they'd passed a short distance before finding a high and dry spot for the night. In the beginning she'd been wary of him. He ogled her and said filthy things to her when they were alone at first. Catarine figured either Meredith had put the fear of God in him or her own beauty had grown sour, because Booley had regarded her in recent days with a lack of interest, as nothing more than an animal to water or feed.

On that day she decided to speak to him.

"Booley," she shocked him with her voice so that he jumped slightly as he studied the orange westward sky.

"What's wrong with ya?" he asked defensively.

"I just want to be untied," she asked warmly, looking into his eyes. "Please. Just to wash my face better."

"Naw. I caint do that," he said. "We'll both be in trouble."

"I'm not going anywhere. Where would I go?"

"I dunno."

"Please just untie me for a few minutes. I'll sit right here," she said sitting down at the stream. "Come sit here with me if you want."

Booley came over to her and sat down next to her by the water and looked around at the rocks and overhanging branches, as if they'd advise him.

"Oh all right," he said after a while, eyeing her suspiciously. "I'll untie ya. But don't ya go doing nothing stupid."

"I won't," Catarine rubbed her wrists and moaned as Booley removed the rope.

She inched her way down into the water until part of her legs were submerged and, using her hands, splashed water up onto her face. The red abrasions, worse at the boney prominence of her left hand, burnt in the spring water, and although a scab had formed, it had again and again broken lose and bled afresh from days of being yanked about. In the stream it oozed a yellow matter mixed with her torn flesh as she washed it with her skirt. As she worked, Booley eased up closer but she gave him no heed. He watched her work on herself and admired her intensity. He edged over a little closer until they were only inches away, his leg resting next to hers in the cold stream.

In the darkening twilight, she took on a bewitching appeal. Her skin was moist and clean, her hair shiny. As she washed her hands within the folds of her skirts, Booley could not only see a portion of her leg above her boot, the flexed curve of her calf muscle just adjacent to his own leg next to hers at the stream, but also the way she was leaning, gave him a full view of her breasts. They were small but perfect and they too were damp and inviting. He watched the beads of moisture run down between them, only a touch away. She kept working on her skin, cleaning. Surely she was taking her time for him. He looked about them slowly and saw no one. And he knew it was his chance. Their chance. So he took it.

Meredith was never so glad to reach Baltimore and be rid of the most foolhardiness he'd ever encountered on a mission involving a single prisoner. Booley had gotten himself shot, and as far as Meredith was concerned, he wished Booley had died out there. The prisoner was safe but no longer cooperative, and they had damn near lost her. Shorty was missing and was only God knows where. Only Larsen was of any use, but Meredith had to send him off to tend to Booley.

"Lar, get that dead man to a hospital. There's a sister's hospital in town, ask at that bar," Meredith told Larsen who had carried the barely conscious, bleeding Booley across his horse all the way to the outskirts of Baltimore, where they finally parted. Meredith never wanted to see Booley again and didn't care if he died. He'd put their mission in jeopardy and got himself nearly killed.

"We'll have to meet up after I turn her in."

Meredith wanted to cuff her, but he knew she'd get out of them, her hands being so small. He decided on fettering her to him, why not, since they needed to be together until they arrived at their destination. He felt sympathy for her having those awful rope burns but it couldn't be helped at that point. When he arrived in Baltimore, he was loathe to walk into the livery office for his coach with them tethered together such. It was comical, he knew that, and it drew snickers from those inside. He ignored the laughter and did his business anyway. And then they waited outside.

After what had happened, she'd stopped talking again. Only this time, anger blazed in her eyes instead of the sadness he'd seen before. Meredith had tried to cheer her, but to no avail. No matter, he would be adding a charge to her when she was finally booked for murder. Attempted escape.

Booley writhed back and forth against the hay stuffed mattress and twisted the bedsheets with his good arm until they were a knotted rope of sweat and dirt. His bandage lay half open and felt wet. When the nurse came to him, she only shook her head and told him to be still. Instead he sat up and clutched her arm.

"Lay back down," she commanded sternly.

He complied, shaking as he labored to remain motionless, her hands gliding over his abdomen, restoring and taping, refreshing his wounds. His flesh had been torn away with the buckshot he'd received to his left side. His arm had taken a hit or two but it was mostly his belly, being hit like an animal from someone out in the woods. He'd been doing what he did best. He couldn't remember if she'd made any sound. He remembered lifting her skirts. And, of course, he remembered her breasts. He'd seen them first. He'd tore off the top of her dress first. All he could remember was being busy in the middle of things and getting interrupted. And when he stood up, that was it. It wasn't fair. He didn't even know who done it.

The nurse said, "Mister, you've lost an awful lot of blood. I just want you to know you could die from this. You should make your peace with God." And then she left.

Peace with God?

Catarine couldn't stop replaying the incident over and over. The instant she woke up each day, if she were even able to have a few hours of peace, Booley's face appeared in front of her again. That, and feeling him gnaw at her and his hands roughly tearing away her clothes. He had sprung on her suddenly, pulling down the bodice of her dress. She cried out but he had cupped her mouth and slammed her head back against the rocks. Then grinning widely, he opened his mouth to cover hers in a beastly kiss. She couldn't breathe. She kicked and pushed him but he was too strong. Her hand bled freely, she remembered that and was glad she'd soiled him with her blood. As he'd moved down her body ferociously, her impotent fists beat his back. She remembered to take aim with her knee for the vital parts between his legs but he was too quick. He pinned both her legs down with his knees, and sitting up, ripped her clothes away until her found what he wanted. Catarine felt vomit rising to her throat with each recollection. It wasn't the coach ride, as Meredith asked her several times. She always wanted to throw up when she remembered Booley violating her.

She can't remember if she screamed but she did remember that it was Shorty who'd hit Booley in the back of his head with a rifle butt. Catarine had had no time to think. Now, she only remembered images. Shorty's eyes going to her breasts when Booley stood up off of her, and the gunshot that surprised all of them. That spurt of bright red blood. Was it hers? Then her instantaneous flash of comprehension. The next thing she recalled was running, somehow running away from the camp and toward Louis.

His momma taught him about the Lord. The Lord Jesus Christ. Booley, his serum, the color of whey, oozing from under the new bandage, let his mind leave through the dusty window across the room where he lay, and considered if the ill-attempted guidance by his poor momma had any credence. He'd never before reflected on her words, especially not on God or the afterlife. But it seemed to him that since his blood was almost gone out of him, now might be the time to do some thinking on such things. And what would it hurt? To ask forgiveness. She'd told him to pray and he'd never done it. He considered the prayers she had taught him, buried deep inside his memory.

Catarine hated Meredith. He'd caught her before she got to Louis. She was running as fast as she could, down that rocky hill. He caught up with her when she tripped on the rock. It was a stupid thing to do. She knew better and could run better. Now, she had no idea what happened to Louis. All she knew was that Shorty took off after him. Yes, now she hated Meredith with a passion, this awful man to whom she was bound.

Meredith was glad he'd settled for being shackled at the ankles to Catarine. She wasn't going anywhere. It was just the two of them and the coach driver for the ride from Baltimore to New Orleans. He'd left Larsen at the hospital with Booley.

Who knows if he'd recover? Shorty never came back in, even though they waited for days in Baltimore. No telling what had happened to him. Strange. He and Catarine would have to become chummy, even sleep together, no hanky panky though. But he wasn't undoing the shackles for any reason under the sun, he didn't care if she was a lady.

The struggle had been surprisingly equal, due to their unequal stature no doubt, rather than skill. Shorty had kicked the gun out of Louis' hands easily enough. Louis knew not to make a run for it so he took a swing at Shorty's jaw, landing a hit square across his eye socket. This knocked him down, producing blood which shocked him momentarily when he pulled his hand away from his face. But Louis noticed Shorty going for the knife on his belt. When he jumped him, Shorty crumpled and rolled but came up swinging. They stayed at each other, swat after swipe, until Louis saw clear to grab for his gun and point it at Shorty.

Standing, Louis told Shorty that he wasn't a killer so he'd better just run. And he did, away in the opposite direction. After mounting the horse Shorty had left behind, Louis trotted a couple of paces across the top of the ravine then saw a sight he'd not soon forget. A man lying at the bottom of the cliff, his neck twisted awkwardly. It was Shorty. Louis rode the horse down to examine him better. He had to be sure. Upon close inspection, Louis could see that he was dead.

When the nurse came by again, Booley lifted the two middle fingers of his good hand as it sat across his taut stomach, fingering the bandage that covered its swelling contents. He hoped to indicate his wishes to her. He remained still, for to move, even an inch, would cause a fire of pain to shoot through him afresh along with the spillage, the trickle of yet more fluid from his side and onto the sheets. They remained soaked beneath him. He hoped she wouldn't try to change them, because when she did that task, he felt more agony than he'd thought existed this side of hell.

As he moaned, she turned to him and said, "Do you need another shot of Morphine?"

"Yes, ma'am, I do. And I also need to tell ya something."

After days of being latched to the marshal, and having him at her side for everything she did, including bodily movements, even Catarine was relieved when they reached the federal jail in New Orleans. Check in was accomplished in utter shame as she expected but, to her relief, she didn't incur a beating or harassment of any kind. She was only searched by the sheriff, his wife watching, and for some perverse reason they both seemed to find pleasure in it.

Meredith had spoken to her one last time before he departed with a word of advice. "Get you a good lawyer. That's if ya don't want to hang. You had a chance with me. I could've helped ya more."

She watched him walk away, his boots grating against the gritty concrete. "I'm innocent."

He swung around and laughed, hands resting in his pockets, the left holster hanging empty. "Oh now ya tell me. Why'd ya run then?"

Catarine frowned and shook her head side to side. "Thank-you for your help, Meredith." Slowly the marshal walked back over to where Catarine stood. Across the bars, she held her head erect as if to defy her current situation. Meredith smiled. Her bravery was appealing to him.

"Miss Catarine, you are a lady. And I can't see you killing no one. But I ain't no jury. God be with you." And with those words, he touched her face, so small between the big iron bars. He lifted her chin up to his and kissed her tenderly on the lips. He didn't notice the single tear that sprang from Catarine's eyes and ran down her cheek. When Meredith had gone, Catarine wore a desolate look, her face still leaning on the bars, as she gazed down the long hallway where Meredith had departed.

"I'm a bad man and I done some pretty bad things," he started. The nurse had given him his shot and repositioned him. Now she set about to clean his wound again. She smiled as he spoke. "Ah gotta tell ya…Ah killed a man."

"You don't need to tell me anything, son. I can call a priest for you."

"A priest? Well, I dunno. I ain't Catholic."

"It's up to you then," she answered.

"My momma just told me to confess my sins and ask Jesus in my heart."

"You should do what your mother says."

"Yep, I done prayed. But I gotta tell ya. I feel real bad 'bout hurting that young woman. That prisoner. She was nice. I ain't sure she was the killer. But anyhow, I done something bad to her. Really bad. I ain't gone say what, you being a lady and all. But I feel guilty. That's what I feel. Guilty…"

When Booley spoke those last word, his voice went weak and he choked up, sucking back sobs that made his stomach tremble.

"Aw, now, be still if you can. You'll be all right. Be still. Shhh," the nurse said in a gentle voice as she stroked his forehead. She stayed with him as his crying subsided. She watched him a while longer, noticing that his breathing was becoming easier. And when his breaths became slower and more shallow, barely coming at all, she stood and called out, "Clara, call Dr. Henry. This one's dying."

New Orleans

Chapter 12

They kept her alone, no contact with the other prisoners. But this was no consolation for Catarine. She already had had days to consider her plight. She worried about Louis' welfare and thoughts of Daria consumed her. Regret filled her heart as well. She'd left Bessie to deal with the aftermath of their incident all alone. As soon as possible, she planned on requesting a lawyer. But all her money was in a New York City bank, under Daria Morinay's name. How was she to get at it? Another problem was the ever present annoyance of the deputies, who apparently saw very few, if any, female prisoners. She felt in constant danger, and being held apart, in solitary, made her more at risk. Yes, she needed a lawyer right away.

"Hey, you!" the deputy came along down the hallway and stood in front of her cell. She rose up from her bed to hear his request. He had nothing in his hands, which was strange, but she noticed cell keys jingling on his belt. "You up?"

"Yes. What is it?" She feared some new development. Perhaps they were just moving her.

"You got a visitor," The deputy came over to the bars. "Now get back. I have to take you to the arbitration room." He put her one arm behind him and brought her other one across her chest, a secure hold so she couldn't run, which locked them together. She and the deputy walked together down the passageway.

"What? Who?" she cried. Louis must have arrived! Or, God be blessed, Daria! Could it be?

"The lady says she's your mother," the deputy said as he led Catarine down the long hallway.

"My *mother*?" Catarine whispered, astounded, as her mouth fell open in amazement, her eyes wide with surprise.

Although she bore a striking resemblance to her daughter, Marie Dupre Koch had once been an anemic version of Catarine in both soul and body. It had taken excessive amounts of courage for her to make a trip to New Orleans, enter the jail and demand to speak to her daughter, who'd been arrested for murder. Catarine instinctively knew this to be the case but when she saw her mother rise to meet her, who was seated at the table in the consultation room, she was struck by the fortitude she noticed in her mother's countenance. Breaking free of the deputy, Catarine ran weeping, and fell against her mother's embrace like a small child. The deputy locked them inside.

"Oh, my dear, my baby," her mother spoke over her, stroking Catarine's hair as she cried into her mother's arms.

After a time, Catarine lifted her head and gazed into her mother's eyes, searching. "Mother, you must hate me," for her mother hadn't shed any tears.

"No, my dear. I thought you…"

"What?" Catarine asked.

"It doesn't matter. Just tell me what happened. Please!"

"You mean why I left?"

"Yes, what happened that night?"

"Oh, Maman! It was horrible!"

Catarine described what happened the night before she fled her home, the night Mason died. She recounted how she'd come upon them and that he'd raped Bessie. She explained everything to her mother, including the part about the inheritance money she took from the wine cellar and the lie she penned on the night in which Bessie sneaked into her room to say good-bye. To Catarine's surprise, her mother accepted her revelation, about the manner in which Mason had died, and how they'd buried him. Her mother believed every word she said.

"I knew about that money," her mother told her. "Of course I did. I was aware that your father made provisions for you and I was glad of it."

They talked of her father for a while and Catarine reflected at how pleasant it felt to speak of him. After all, they'd both loved him so. Catarine closed her eyes for a few moments, savoring their time, as they sat across from each other at the conference table. When it was time for her mother to go, Catarine asked if she might bring Bessie with her on her next visit, for Marie Dupre Koch promised to visit often. After they held each other tightly once more, her mother turned to go, Catarine being restrained by the deputy once again.

"You know, Koch'll never stand for it," her mother warned.

"Wait!" Catarine cried out as her mother turned to leave. "I have so much more to tell you. I…" Catarine began sobbing again. This time, she saw her mother's hands fly up to her mouth to stifle a cry.

"You'll need to get a lawyer," the sheriff had told her when she was being arraigned the night Meredith brought her in. But who? She didn't trust Frederick Fuhrmann. She must ask her mother on her next visit.

Catarine's cell was perpetually damp from the July humidity, the walls naked except for iron water pipes and a peg for hanging clothes. She'd been surprised to find a small table and chair alongside the low, narrow bed. The cell had high walls which admitted light through a few bars near the ceiling. At least she knew when each morning dawned. She worked out her location, from the side of town which the jail was facing when they arrived the night Meredith deposited her there. She was on the Southwest corner of Esplanade Street. She didn't know if this information would do her any good, most likely not. It was just how her mind worked.

And, despite her racing thoughts of Louis and Daria, namely, her frantic worries that she'd never see them again, she logically weighed her own options, aiming to be fully prepared when she did get to speak to a lawyer. She may not fully understand judicial proceedings, but she was aware of her rights as an American citizen. She had a right to be represented and heard in a court of law and in front of a jury. And she had a right to a speedy trial. But she wasn't sure she wanted speed. That might hasten the inevitable.

"Who are you?" Catarine asked, rising up to greet the stranger that the deputy led down the hallway to her cell.

They stood across the bars scrutinizing each other. The man wore riding boots with spurs that had scraped and tapped against the stone floor, announcing his approach. His riding breeches were stylish but worn and he sported both a vest and a matching green gentleman's jacket. In his hand he carried a satchel, and somewhere, Catarine assumed, was a hat he had temporarily discarded, because the hair above his eyes was plastered down in the shape of a round hat band, giving him the look of having an invisible strap across his reddened forehead. He looked pleasant enough and surprisingly genuine. Catarine guessed, rightly, his occupation.

"Josiah Butler," he thrust a meaty hand through the bars. "Public Defender for the state of Louisiana."

"I never called for a..." she started to answer but realized she better hear him out.

"I'm assigned your case, Mademoiselle."

They spent the next several hours in deep discussion. He asked first about her background, her childhood mostly. He wanted to know all about her life growing up on the plantation. She expected him to ask what had happened on the night Mason had been killed, and she tried to plunge into that several times, only to have him stop her cold. He seemed most interested in her. Her relationship with her parents, how she spent her days. Who was this Bessie girl? Was she only a slave? What had made them friends?

They spoke for about an hour in her cell, he sitting at her desk and she on her bed, leaning against the wall. It was an awkward time. Unprecedented. Why did the deputy leave them there alone? Up to that point, only her mother had entered her cell. Finally, Catarine interrupted his stimulating inquiry into her personal history.

"Mr. Butler," she said, stopping his flow. "I've not yet decided on an attorney. I'd like to consult my mother."

"Er, you…" Josiah wiped the sweat from his brow, which had lost some of its flush, then continued. "Mademoiselle Dupre, pardon me for saying, but your trial is set for July 15th. That is less than two weeks away. Time is of the essence."

"I don't know why!" she complained to her mother and paced her cell. "It's not right that they didn't inform me!"

"But yes, I suppose you should use that man, if you liked him well enough. I don't trust Frederick either."

"That's all I needed to know then. I trust *you*. And if you don't know anyone else. Anyone father would have used."

"Come sit with me. You've worked yourself up," her mother said, motioning her with open arms to sit with her on the cell bed. Catarine climbed up beside her mother and leaned against her breast. She let her mother hold her, stroke her hair, and soothe her as they talked during their visits. "Tell me more about this man Louis."

With tears in her eyes, Catarine again described Louis and how they had met in New York. She told her mother how handsome he was and how kind. Then she lay there thinking, quiet. She couldn't remember a single time between them like this. Tragedy had brought them together. She never really knew that her mother cared so much. Growing up she'd always felt like her mother's huge disappointment. The girl who acted too much like a boy. But now she was lying here in her mother's arms sobbing like a girl and talking of loving a man. And, somewhere along the way, her mother had been transformed into a strong woman.

"Mother, you know," Catarine confessed, sniffing, "I *did* try to be more…womanly. I actually tried to be like you!"

"Oh, heavens, no," her mother replied. "It is I who have, all the while, been trying to be like you!"

He did have the presence of mind to plan ahead. And since Baltimore was a decent sized city, Louis stayed put for a while in the hopes of earning enough money to fund his trip to New Orleans to be with Catarine during her trial. He tried first at the livery, and failing to find employment there, tried a cafe in the center of town which was more than happy to hire a French man to cook. Not that he had much experience with anything but basic fare, he could at least speak French, and replicate the common cuisine, anything for a few dollars. And he could draw on the street corners in his spare time. In America, he had this freedom. But Louis' mind was not on politics; it was on Catarine. He scanned the newspapers for any shred of information, hoping for stories of New Orleans. Trial pamphlets were popular in New York and Philadelphia and growing in popularity in other cities, many murder trials being featured in articles across the country. He hoped her trial wasn't widely known but longed for news himself.

And then there was the question of Daria. He tried to find information about her as well. Poor thing, she'd been left there to die, to bleed to death in the woods. He had noted that there had been four marshals but only three of them arrested Catarine. The fourth man, the one named Larsen, had been busy with another task for a while. He was never able to ascertain what that task had been. Had he simply buried Daria in the woods that day? Finding death notices proved to be a legal matter he was unable to crack without a lawyer.

She heard the rattling and when she did, her first thought was that the deputies had come for her. But it was Louis! He was simply standing at her cell door, fresh and handsome, smiling and trying to wake her. They kissed through the bars, their hands entwining. He tasted of sweet tobacco. She kissed him again, grabbing him closer until she realized he had the keys. He'd gotten them from the guards somehow.

"Shhh," he cautioned. The next thing she knew they were standing outside her cell in an intimate embrace, his lips on her mouth. She leaned in for more but he broke away and led her down a long winding hallway. It went right, then left, then right again. They stopped and kissed again in the pitch black.

She heard the sound of dripping water. She could feel Louis' arms guiding her. How was it he knew where to go? She still heard the dripping. In fact, it was getting louder, deafening! Where were they going? But she trusted him.

"Louis," she said. "Louis!" But her words bounced back into her throat so quickly, he couldn't have possibly heard her.

"Louis!" she yelled, muffled, into her own cell as the drip, drip, drip of the water pipe pounded above her head and she awoke, crying bitterly.

"From what you've told me, I think you should plead guilty to second degree murder."

"But I'm not guilty, Mr. Butler!" Catarine cried out, slamming both hands down in front of her newly hired solicitor. Josiah shifted his large frame at the conference table. It was more from habit than discomfort. Catarine noticed how young he was. At their first meeting, he'd appeared to be middle aged, something expected of a larger man, but sitting across from him in a better lit room, she could see youth in his eyes, along with the freshness and vigor of his skin. This didn't make her feel very optimistic.

"It was an *accident*. I told you all this! Are you an idiot?"

"Catarine, you did *kill* the man. Let's go for manslaughter then." She protested with a groan of anguish, running her hands through her hair, which hung loose about her shoulders.

"I don't want to *go* for anything. I want to be found innocent. Which is what I am! I was defending my friend! Don't you understand?"

"Yes, we will get to that," he explained calmly. "I was hoping to plead you out. I don't want you to hang."

"I don't either," she said quieting down.

The single window across the room admitted more sunlight than Catarine had seen in weeks and she stared blankly at it while Josiah proceeded to write with his pen. Turning, she watched his ornate script. It was meticulous, each line spaced the same distance from the previous one, the letters uniform and pretty. It was an art she'd never truly mastered, another failure as a woman. "So, why are you so calm?"

"Pardon?" he looked up from his penmanship.

"Well, I know you aren't the one on trial," she said leaning forward in an attempt at friendliness. "I am referring to my yelling at your suggestions. And I'm trying to say…I'm sorry."

"Oh, that," he chuckled. "It helps that I have five sisters. They've shrieked and howled at me all my life. It has no affect."

Catarine switched her mind back to that night. Was there something she'd forgotten that could help her? It had started out routine, she'd ridden her horse as usual. And when she returned she heard them. As she walked Diego into the barn, that was first thing she noticed that was amiss. The lamps were not lighted yet. That was unusual. Had they been lit then blown out? Then, of course, she saw them. In her horse's stall. Why Diego's stall? Had Bessie hidden there from him? The more she thought about it, the more questions came up in her mind. Questions she never had the opportunity to ask. They were fully involved in intercourse, or he in raping her. The sounds she heard when she entered the barn were of Bessie's muffled screams. By the time she had gotten hold of the pitch fork, the only tool she could find, Mason was cussing at her and telling her to leave. The first blow was to the back of his head. And she knew it had not been hard enough because she had been afraid of hitting Bessie by mistake. She remembered Bessie screaming loudly and crying at that point. Mason then stood up which, honestly, terrified Catarine. She saw him look to her side in the hay, and she assumed he might be going for his pistol. She then thought the best thing to do would be to knock him out and then they would both have a chance to get away. That was what went through her mind, she was sure of it. But that's not what happened.

"When can I tell you everything?"

"You can tell me now," he said as he put down his pen and leaned back in his chair. He gave her his full attention for over an hour as she related the events of that night. She told Josiah every detail and the questions she had about that night. After all, he wouldn't know which questions to ask. She told him about coming into the barn and seeing Mason on Bessie. She described the blow that killed him, that the pitchfork tine had stuck through his eye socket by mistake, and how Mason had dropped limply to the ground and how she and Bessie had stared in raw horror at him in the hay lifeless before them. She also told about Mason and how he bullied both Bessie and her for the longest time. She told him about how Bessie would feed the horses leftovers at night, that Bessie loved them as much as she did. Before the Kochs came along and ruined all their lives, her Father had allowed

Bessie to ride, a slave girl. But she was more than that to her. She was her best friend. Her father had allowed all of that. Because he was a great man. But everything had changed when her mother married again. And it wasn't long before Mr. Koch started the beatings. No one was spared. If they didn't do as he wished, he'd string them up by the wrists to the big oak tree out front and beat until blood was drawn. Yes, she told Mr. Butler everything she could think of about Magnolia Plantation, her old home. Every single detail. Because she had nothing to hide.

"Do you believe me?" she finally said. She'd stopped trying to read his lovely handwriting upside down.

"It's really not an appropriate question," he answered, still writing. This shocked her. If he didn't believe her, who would? Looking up, he paused in his script. "You see, you must convince the jury."

"I understand that!" She was getting annoyed again. Did he think she was an imbecile? Maybe his sisters were all silly fools. "I'd like to know what *you* think."

"You seem straightforward enough." He went back to his writing.

"You are difficult to read, Josiah. May I call you Josiah?"

"I suppose," was his reply.

"This is just what I mean. You, and another solicitor I've known before, are very noncommittal. I'd like your personal opinion on my guilt or innocence. *Please.*"

"That's a bizarre question," he said, taken aback. "You, yourself know full-well the answer. Why do you care what I think?"

"Because it is most likely what a jury will think! You, you…"
She slammed her fists down on the table, stood up and walked
over to the window. "What's wrong with you?"

"Mademoiselle," he said in a patient tone. "Please understand me. By law you are innocent until proven guilty. And it
is the task of the state prosecutor to prove beyond a shadow of
a doubt that you are guilty. So, at this point in time, I believe
you to be innocent." Catarine looked at her lawyer, sitting up
straight in his chair, explaining things to her as if she was a
child. In fact, he looked so fresh and innocent himself that it
scared her. She turned to look out the window again, something she rarely got to do, her gaze creased with distress. Josiah
returned to his writing with a look of satisfaction.

Catarine returned to the table across from him and cleared
her throat. "I might appear to need a lesson or two on my con-
stitutional rights. But, on the contrary, I have studied history
and government, specifically the judicial system. I trust that
you know much more than I do, but what I do need from you
is your promise that I will win this trial. Because I swear to you,
I *swear* that I am innocent of murder!"

Josiah put down his pen and took Catarine's hands into his
large ones. And looking into her eyes, in a brotherly fashion,
said, "I'm going to do my very best. I can promise you that."

"Mother, I have very little faith in him," she complained as
they faced each other across the conference table. "He seems
to have some good qualities but I don't know…"

"I believe the truth will bear out. Bessie will give testimony for you. That's all you need! Mr. Butler was out speaking to her yesterday. That's what I wanted to tell you."

"That's wonderful!"

"Now tell me about your friend. You never explained much about her."

"She was…*is* a wonderful person. You would love her. I met her in New Orleans. She is a quadroon! And she wanted to be *my* friend!"

"Oh, my! A quadroon? How did that ever occur?" Catarine told her mother about how Daria befriended her the night of the ball. She told her most of the things they did in New Orleans, the errands they ran, the places they went, but kept some of their doings private as she was sure her mother would be scandalized. Her mother's glassy eyes suggested to Catarine that she'd crossed the threshold between understanding her daughter to adopting a dubious skepticism toward her friendship with a quadroon. If only her mother could meet her. If Daria were still alive, that is.

"Mother, I'm so very afraid I've lost them both!" Catarine said with tears in her eyes. She stood up and walked over to the window but there was no sunshine to view. The drizzle of rain could be heard as Catarine rested her head against the window.

"Let's just concentrate on the trial for now," her mother said coming up behind her.

"But I don't want to think only of the trial! How can I?" Catarine's voice rose and she choked back more tears. Her shoulders shook and she cried into her hands. "I'm as worried about them as I am myself! Don't you understand?"

"I'm afraid I didn't realize that they meant that much to you," she replied.

"I love both of them. So very much. As much…as much as I loved…love Bessie."

"My dear girl," her mother said as she turned her daughter to face her. She enveloped the sobbing Catarine in her arms. "Your heart is so big and wide. I've no doubt you can love a number of people. You are just like your father."

And when Catarine stopped crying, she looked up at her mother and smiled. Her mother added, "That's why I never faulted him."

"Faulted who?"

"Your father."

"Faulted him for what?"

"For Bessie. You understand."

"No I don't. What are you talking about?"

"Surely you know. I don't need to tell you! Everyone knew, Catarine!"

"*I* don't know. What happened with Bessie?"

"Nothing *happened* with her. Bessie is your half-sister."

Chapter 13

Catarine tossed and turned upon her bed, thoughts hatching forth based on the new information her mother had given her. She had hoped for a good night's sleep, as she was to appear before the judge for the first time, and, according to Mr. Butler, enter her plea and then jury selection would begin. But, alas, if her mind wasn't stuffed full with fretful concerns already, this revelation swept clear, at least for the time being, her current worries, and enchanted her with one notion and conclusion after the next about Bessie. Bessie, her sister. Her father's daughter. His illegitimate daughter. No wonder he favored her. Was she jealous? No. She didn't feel jealousy. Catarine had to dig deep to conjure up the dim picture of Bessie's mother. For some reason, she'd played a minor role at the plantation. She never worked inside the big house. Was she a cutter? She can't remember women doing that. And was this the reason her mother was sickly? But it couldn't be. Her mother had lost all those babies. Maybe that's why Father had turned to another woman. Catarine's head ached with the new information. Why hadn't anyone told her? Why hadn't Bessie told her?

"All rise," the bailiff announced. Catarine's head still pounded. Behind her stood her mother. She noticed a few strangers in the pews when they brought her into the Casa Curial, the Ecclesiastical House, or so the Courthouse was called in Louisiana.

"The State of Louisiana against Catarine Dupre. The Honorable Xavier Cardena presiding. Thatcher Preleme, District Attorney. Josiah Butler, for the defense."

"Catarine Dupre, you've been charged with second degree murder. How plead you?" the judge spoke directly to her.

Catarine cleared her throat several times before whispering her answer. "Innocent, sir."

"Speak up!"

"I said innocent," she said clearly.

"Do you understand the implications of your plea?"

"Yes, your honor."

"Your honor, we'd like to enter a plea bargain to a lesser charge."

"Please approach the bench." The two lawyers whispered with the judge for a time in which Catarine's heart pounded.

"Do you wish to plead guilty to manslaughter?"

"Yes," Catarine said quietly. Behind her could be heard the word "No" being spoken.

"Excuse me?" the judge asked.

"No, she didn't do it!" her mother said.

"Ma'am, you'll kindly keep your remarks to yourself. Mademoiselle Dupre, how plead you?"

"I am guilty of manslaughter, your honor."

"You'll be charged with both offenses. Along with the others charges. It will be up to the court to decide your guilt."

The gavel cracked the air at the same time a sob clutched Marie Dupre Koch's throat. "Court is adjourned until 8 o'clock tomorrow morning for jury selection."

The evening grew long and bitter and Catarine was about to drift into sleep despite her fits of restless thought when the night deputy came to rattle her door.

"Late visitor," he said grumbling. "And ye only get a few minutes. Come down to the room."

"Who is it this late?" Catarine rubbed her eyes awake and smoothed her hair.

"Says his name is Louis."

When she entered the room, she couldn't believe her eyes. Catarine was so overcome with emotion that she collapsed in a heap on the floor wailing. But she was too late. The guard had slammed the door behind her and locked her in with him.

"Don't be angry! I have an explanation," he said trying to help her up.

"You are a monster! Why? Why?" Catarine beat and slapped the man as he lifted her to a standing position.

"Because I couldn't be seen coming here to talk to you. I had to come under a false name. And I knew you'd see me if you thought I was him."

"I hate you!" Catarine spit her venomous words into the face of Frederick Fuhrmann.

"Listen to me! I have something important to tell you."

"I don't care what you have to say. Get away from me!" She banged with both fists against the thick wooden door for the deputy.

"Catarine, stop. Listen. I'm going to help you."

"How? Nothing you've done has helped me so far."

"Oh, contraire."

"Get out! Guards!" The solid wood absorbed her blows but she still banged all the more.

"Come over to the table and let's talk."

"I'm done talking to you. Ever again." She turned to face the table, approached him and pointing her finger in his face, said, "If you aim to help me at all, go find Louis. And Daria! Do that for me."

"I can't do that for you."

Catarine trembled and flushed, stared squarely at Fuhrmann and then, like a shot, spit into his right eye and ran back to the door to bang again for the deputy.

"I'm sure you think I deserve that," he said. "But I promise in the days to come, you'll see. You will find me to be your greatest friend."

"Go to hell," was all she said to him when the deputy came to fetch her.

What Catarine didn't see were the throngs of people lined up on Chartres Street waiting to be let in. Her mother hadn't told her was how her trial had become the talk of the city.

An ambitious young woman being accused of murdering her fiancé who had recently taken over the family business, was the presumption launched into being. Talk was thick with motives and laced with innuendos and stories of their supposed relationship troubles, all imaginary. People flocked to finally get a glimpse of this woman, to see if she was the beauty she was reported to be. Interviews had been sought out from members of the plantation staff to no avail. Her mother had sent reporters off her property. Thankfully, it was in the middle of cutting season, so Koch was busy in the fields.

Marie Dupre Koch had feared he'd make a fuss about everything. He would have gladly given them an earful about Catarine, all right. Neighbors had supplied the press with comments about both Mason and Catarine. What little they knew was embellished from southern imaginations bred during idle afternoons and from plots of beloved books. They spun story after story of a flamboyant couple, both horse riders each with tempers toward each other, but gentle toward their horses. They'd been seen arguing, shouting from the paddocks as they exercised their geldings. Passersby had noted the voluble Catarine storm off from Mason on many occasion, horse crop in hand, as she headed for the front door of her house. Mason had never displayed an open temper but was widely known to be stubborn and harsh in his dealings with both his slaves and in business matters. He never budged. He could stare anyone down until they gave in to his requests. There were many rumors circulating about his flings with other women.

No, Catarine's mother didn't tell her any of this. She wanted to save her daughter from as much shame as possible. And in retrospect, Marie Dupre Koch was now glad she had been gone all those months. Hopefully this wouldn't be used against her poor daughter.

"All rise. The Circuit Court of Louisiana is now in session. The Honorable Judge Xavier Cardena presiding. You may be seated."

"Mr. Johnson, will you swear in the Jury?" the judge commanded the clerk who was sitting to the front of him.

"The members of the Jury, please rise. Raise your right hands," Mr. Johnson said looking over his spectacles and eyeing the men standing in the jury box. The look on his face was one of disapproval, or near disgust. They looked to be a motley group, as many weren't dressed as handsomely as the clerk himself. Perhaps he viewed all juries this way. "Do you swear as citizens of Louisiana that your decision will be based entirely on what you hear in this courtroom, and that you will not be swayed by any previous knowledge or personal bias concerning this case against the defendant? If so, please state 'I do.'"

"I do," they all stated in one accord, their voices mostly strong and deep with several higher pitched utterances among them.

"Can you honestly swear that you have not formed an opinion as to the guilt or innocence of the accused?"

"Yes," several said, a few looked to the person next to them, bewildered about what to do, and a few others nodded in the affirmative.

"Please state 'yes' if you do so swear."

"Yes," they said precisely together. Catarine looked from face-to-face of each juror, hoping to work out the sense of them, but not one of them returned her gaze.

"You may be seated," the judge said to the jury and clerk.

Louis had no idea when the trial was to begin although he heard Meredith speak of July 1st. The day was July 6th and he was desperate to get to New Orleans. His drawings had fetched him a paltry sum but at least it was something and he had saved a bit from his job cooking. He sat counting his money, covertly in the corner of the bar, on what he hoped was his last night in Baltimore. He had enough for a ticket south to New Orleans. He wished he hadn't needed to sell his horse, but at the time it was that or food. No crying over the past. That's what his father always taught him. Look forward to what lies ahead. And for him, it was New Orleans and Catarine. Tomorrow. He gulped his last swallow of whiskey and exited the building.

He didn't see the men who followed. But he did feel their punches and kicks as they threw him in an alley near his rented room. What hurt the most was the fact they took his bag with his money. All his money to get where he wanted to go.

Thatcher Preleme was a distinguished man, handsome, the women would say. When he rose to speak to the jury and to the entire crowd, he took his time.

"Gentlemen of the jury, I welcome you to the court today. And thank you for giving your time to assist the state with a matter of grave importance." He pranced back and forth, covering the full length of space allotted him, a stage upon which he was born to act.

"As you know, we are here because of the crime of murder. The life was taken from a young man. A young man whose time on earth was cut short. Mason Koch. Who was a contributor, mind you, like yourselves, to his community and to the city of New Orleans." He paused as if to reflect, then went on in a conversational tone, looking from juror to juror, standing at the bar before them. "We all understand that, during the course of living, we endeavor to experience many things, especially when we are young. I'm sure you all can reflect upon your own youth." When he spoke it was jovial, friendly, cordial. He played with his pocket watch in an offhand manner.

"This young man, Mason Koch, encountered a woman. Something all young men do. Only this woman was his step-sister. His father graciously married her widowed mother, so she was in his own home. Catarine Dupre, our defendant, who in the course of time took Mason's life. Hatred formed in Catarine's heart and she chose to murder young Mr. Mason Koch." Catarine, swallowed, horror stricken, astonished at this man's aptitude for telling lies. But who wouldn't believe anything he said? Thatcher Preleme would put any orator to shame. And he swore, right before her, that he'd prove beyond a shadow of a doubt that she "killed Mason Koch with forethought and malice."

Josiah had idolized him at one time. Now he made him sick with his pompous ways. But he'd learned many things from Thatcher Preleme and possibly he'd learn more during this case. But one thing was for certain, Josiah Butler was resolved to win this case. Because he wasn't about to lose to this arrogant rooster again.

"You'll hear medical evidence," he went on, flamboyantly walking across the room, head held high. "And testimony from a trusted family friend." He turned back facing Catarine with a sly smile. "Yes, my friends, this will be a rather simple, but important case. I trust you to reach the honorable conclusions."

And Thatcher Preleme stood smiling to all eyes, smiling as if he were on stage and deserved applause. Catarine felt faint, sick. Josiah slipped his hand over hers on the table to comfort her. He also felt the revulsion that Thatcher had spilled forth into the room and prayed under his breath that the jurors weren't idiots.

The two of them sat at the wooden prison table as they listened to Catarine. Marie Koch, listened partly in prayer, but mostly in growing despair, and Josiah, concerned but not hopeless, planned his next move. Catarine paced and ranted over the speech she'd heard about herself from that lunatic.

"What's more, he didn't graciously marry my mother! That absurd! It was more to the contrary. And who is this other witness they are calling? A close trusted friend? Hmmm." Things were not going well. That self-important, revolting Thatcher

Preleme was portraying her to be a witch and Mason to be someone he was not.

Her mother spoke first, "Mr. Butler, you must do something. He's got it all wrong. Mason Koch was a horrible man, as is his father. Surely you can find someone to testify to that."

"Actually, the character of the deceased shouldn't be an issue," Josiah said.

"The prosecution is making it an issue!" her mother cried. Catarine looked at her mother. She was surprising her daily.

"But, yes, I gathered you here to review the questions I'll be asking Bessie," Josiah spoke. Catarine came to life and sat down expectantly.

"Can I please see her? Bring her here."

"I cannot allow that."

"I want you to know my plans. And please tell me of anyone who could give testimony as to your character, Mademoiselle Dupre."

"Her brother, Moses."

"Did you have any other friends? Other than the, er, the slaves?" She and her mother looked at each other gloomily.

"We kept to ourselves mostly. Catarine was schooled at home. And her brother Andre is dead. There were a few girls who grew up nearby, but not really…No, she didn't really have any other friends," her mother answered. Catarine didn't contradict her.

"Then it will be Bessie and her brother. I've already spoken to Bessie. And I believe strongly that her testimony alone will be enough to acquit you. She was there. Her story matches yours exactly."

"That's because it's the truth."

Louis found that he had reached the end of his rope. He had exhausted all of his means relying on his talents and fortitude. Presently, he found himself bruised, sore, broke, but alive in a room he couldn't afford and in a place he didn't want to be. Desperate times they were, but he had faith that they were temporary. He remembered a place he'd passed a couple of streets away that he never thought he would need use of. But that morning, he hobbled out of bed and made his way to the telegraph office. A new line from Baltimore to New York allowed him to beg for money from his wealthy friend in New York, the one he had rented a room from during his short stay in Manhattan. The man had said when they parted on good terms, "if you ever need anything at all, young man..." He promised to pay him back one day. He'd just need to wait for the funds to arrive by coach.

Catarine was the last one to be seated. When she entered the courtroom, she felt as if she'd walked into an indoor coliseum. Where were the lions? All eyes were on her. She noticed a sea of black faces in the balcony and was disappointed to see only whites in the seats below. She'd been hoping to see some colored faces mixed in. She had counted them her friends during her time with Auntie Rose. The free people of color. Had they not heard of her predicament? Looking nearer to her seat, she spotted Bessie. Her sister, Bessie. They exchanged gratified smiles. Bessie was seated in the opposite set of pews from her mother, who was seated next to Mr. Koch.

To his credit, Josiah objected to nearly all the slurs and innuendos that Thatcher Preleme cunningly slipped into his rhetoric about what he thought happened the night Mason was killed. These were largely sustained by the judge, therefore Thatcher was forced to stick to the facts that they actually had before them.

The court reviewed findings about the body. Mr. Koch & Demetrius had been the ones to dig up Mason's body a full three weeks after his death. That was news to Catarine, and a rather gruesome piece of information. It made her feel sorry for Koch for the first time. And it drew much spectator reaction. "Oohs" and "ahhs" were heard as Demetrius did a fine job of describing the unearthing project done by lantern that night including how things looked and smelled. It had been so bad apparently that not only had they all needed to leave the barn for fresh air, they let the animals out for the night as well. And then there was the detailed description of his hanging eyeball. The court reacted strongly to that information. Maggots had burrowed deep into Mason's brain; the untrained eye could see that clearly when they unearthed him.

"Some-mm big'n sharp had poked him in his head. In his eye ball! That's what kilt him!"

The coroner's report was equally spellbinding. He primarily gave an opinion as to the cause of death: brain herniation due to the angle of a penetrating orbital stab wound. He explained that since Mason was stabbed through the eye socket, the skull's temporal bones being thin and fragile, the weapon went straight through and into his brain. After examining the structures of his brain thoroughly, he concluded that the angle at which the weapon entered the brain caused herniation of the victim's brain stem sufficient to cause instant death. He considered this finding highly unusual and stated that penetrating stab wounds to the brain do not usually cause instant death. Intense rumbling of conversation from the spectators immediately broke out following the coroner's testimony. Judge Cardena rapped his gavel several times.

Thatcher proceeded to question him about the eyeball. Catarine realized he was doing so to heap more condemnation upon her. She ventured a look at Josiah and could see he had a look of disgust across his mouth.

"Sir, could you explain how poor Mason's eye got…dislodged?"

"That would easily happen with the stab wound."

"Wouldn't that have been intentional, to poke a man's eye out?"

"Objection!" Josiah rose to his feet. "We haven't established motive, your honor."

"Sustained. Mr. Thatcher, you are speaking to a medical examiner."

"All right. So you are telling me and this court that Mason's eye ball could…plop out like that from the same blow that killed him?"

"Yes, that's what I'm saying."

"No further questions."

People shifted in their seats. Sighs were heard and papers shuffled at the tables of both lawyers. Bessie and Catarine looked over at each other. It was so good to see her, Catarine thought, no matter what the reason. And she looked good. She was dressed so pretty! She had on a pale yellow frock with rounded sleeves and a high waist that tucked under her discreet bust line perfectly. Her hair had been fixed nicely, twisted up in curls all around. They must have all helped her prepare for this day. It was a real shame that they hadn't laid eyes on each other since that fateful night. But they'd both agreed about what to do.

"Mr. Butler, do you have any questions?" Judge Cardena asked.

"I do," Josiah said, rising to his feet with the energy of a man half his weight. As he approached the coroner, he smiled and turned around to face the audience.

"Thank you, sir, for your expertise. You've assisted us greatly here today."

"I'm pleased to be of service," he responded without emotion.

"I'd like you to give me an opinion. A medical opinion." Josiah looked over to Thatcher who looked primed and ready to object. Josiah smiled at him as Thatcher narrowed his eyes.

"Just how much force would it take to deliver this fatal blow that killed our victim?"

"I couldn't say precisely. It would take some strength."

"Do you believe a woman could do it?"

"Yes, it's possible. A very strong woman," the coroner answered.

"Objection! Your client has already pleaded guilty to manslaughter. She said she delivered the fateful blow!" Thatcher screamed as he stood up waving his arms.

"But did she?" Josiah said.

"What?" Catarine yelled at Josiah. "What are you doing?" The judge's gavel admonished her along with the outbreak of murmurs in the courtroom that morning.

"Mr. Butler! Will there be any other questions?" Judge Cardena spoke to him as if he was a petulant son in need of severe discipline. "If not, court is adjourned until tomorrow!"

"What's wrong with you?" Catarine questioned Josiah as they were being taken back by coach to her cell. "You had me plead guilty to manslaughter."

"I'm just trying to cast some doubt, that's all."

"Well, if you are trying to implicate Bessie, then we are done! I'll get another lawyer."

"No, I'm not trying to do that."

"When will she be testifying?"

"Soon."

Judge Cardena pounded his gavel only seconds after the clock struck eight that next morning. Koch was in the crowd only two seats behind Catarine alongside her mother who was the picture of despondency. Before Catarine could avert her eyes, he gave her a murderous stare and when sitting at the defense table, she felt his nasty eyes boring through her back. Poor Bessie. She'd probably expected to give testimony the day before, only to have it delayed. Catarine wanted to look for her, to exchange happy smiles again, but she was afraid of Koch. He'd be watching her every move. And he'd be watching Bessie too. She probably felt as fearful as she did. More! She had much to lose as well. There would be beatings and no telling what consequences after Bessie took the stand in her defense. Catarine quaked with panic.

"Are you well?" Josiah whispered, noticing her trembling hands.

"No. Mr. Koch is here."

"Hmm." Josiah said, turning around to get a look at him. "He cannot hurt you. You are in state custody."

"I'm not worried about that! I'm concerned for Bessie!"

"Are you saying his presence could affect..." Josiah whispered his question to Catarine as the judge interrupted with his gavel.

"Mr. Butler, the court has come to order. Have you finished conferring with your client?"

"I have a concern I'd like to discuss with you, your honor."

"Please approach the bench." Both lawyers approached the bench and spoke in hushed tones. Josiah turned and pointed to Koch during the discussion. Catarine's sense of dread escalated to the point of feeling both flushed and weak. She broke out in a cold sweat and thought she might faint. When she saw the judge shake his head, she let out an involuntary cry, cupping her hands over her mouth to squelch it from getting louder.

Josiah was back at her side and whispered, "He won't exclude him from the court. He is, after all the victim's father."

"The defense may call your witness."

"We'd like to call Bessie, the slave girl of Jacob Koch."

"Objection!" Thatcher rose with his head held high.

"Mr. Preleme, we've already discussed this in my chambers."

"Your honor, this girl, this slave has no right to testify!" his voice rose a pitch as he shifted his gaze from the judge to the white spectators.

"Mr. Preleme, we are not here to discuss her rights. I'm concerned with justice for our murder victim. And the rights of our accused. And as I just stated, we've been over this matter before!"

"Yes, but pardon my insistence, your honor. We haven't discussed permission from her owner. He doesn't give permission for her to speak."

"Well, pardon *my* insistence, Mr. Butler. She has *my* permission to speak because *she was a witness to the death of Mason Koch*! So now can we proceed?" the judge's face was red and sweaty. He pounded his gavel while giving Thatcher a wicked look for interrupting the trial with his petty objection. "Now, Ms. Bessie, please come to the witness stand and let's get on with it."

Catarine could tell by the way Bessie walked, slow and uneven, that she was nervous. Bessie stumbled and was clumsy getting into the witness box. She started rocking back and forth the minute she was sworn in. She looked from Catarine to the upstairs balcony which held the only friendly faces she could find. They had come to see *her*! They all cared about her but she hoped they cared about Catarine too. Catarine, who had protected her that night against Mason. Now it was her turn to defend Catarine. She must be brave.

Josiah asked Bessie a few preliminary questions, which were simple and designed, no doubt, to put her at ease. He asked her age, her role at the plantation, and some brief questions about her childhood. Then he started asking her about her relationships with the family.

"Do you think anyone in the family considered you a friend?" Josiah asked.

"Yessir."

"Did they all think of you as their friend or just particular ones?"

"No sir, Madam Dupre and Mademoiselle Catarine, dey my friends. And the late Massta Dupre." She looked nervous, as if she'd said too much.

"What about the late brother, Andre?"

"I didn't play with him much. But I do 'member him."

"All right. And how about Mason Koch? Would you say you were his friend?"

"Ahh no sir. I was not. I couldn't be Massta's friend."

"But you just said you were friends with the previous master. And continued to be friends with his daughter." Bessie looked at Catarine with a troubled expression. "I'm only clarifying, Bessie. Is this what you said?"

"Yessir."

"So you were both their slave and friend."

"They was so nice to me. Das why."

"All right. I understand." Josiah smiled and looked at the jury. "Tell me how they treated you. The Dupre family."

"Objection!" Thatcher cried.

"Overruled. I'd like to hear this as I'm sure the jury would. It might have bearing on the case."

"Go ahead, Bessie. Tell us how they treated you."

"Well, they always nice and fair. I played with Catarine when we was little bitty girls. Massta Dupre let me ride de horses. He teach me how. They why I be in the barn with them at night."

"About that night, Miss Bessie. Can you tell me what happened?"

"Yessir, I can."

"Objection!"

"What, pray tell, are you objecting to now, Thatcher?"

"How do we know if this slave girl even knows what telling the truth means?"

"Thatcher Preleme, sit down. She's been sworn in like anyone else. And she claims to be a Christian woman. I'd like not to hear from you again about this matter."

Josiah was the very picture of patience. He smiled sweetly at Bessie and waited until the murmuring had stopped. "Ms. Bessie, now take your time. Close your eyes if you must to help you remember that night. We are in no hurry here. Do you understand?"

"Yessir," Bessie looked at Josiah with enormous eyes. Her rocking stopped when he adopted his calming tone.

"Now, please, tell me what happened the night that Mason died. Can you do that for me?" Josiah leaned down facing her, speaking in his kindest, most gentle voice.

"Yessir, I'll do it," she said looking into Josiah's kind face. The courtroom was completely silent save the sound of the ticking clock against the wall in the very back. Ears strained to hear her quiet but clear testimony. "I took 'em some old carrots that night. De horses. I was almost done feedin' em when he came up to me. The Massta son. Massta Mason. He grabbed me round the waist at first but then he told me to light the inside lamps. Befoe I go. But when I be doing that in the barn, that when he grabbed me again. This time he told me to take my close off. But I say no. The Lawd be watching and I ain't never sinned like that befoe. Then he threw me down in Diego stall, Catarine horse stall. She be gone riding right then. I still said no, please, stop to him, but it angered him. He slap me, he slap me hard cross the face. I don't want to say the things he did to me after that. But it was sin, pure and simple."

"We can get to that later. What happened next?"

"When he was on me, Mademoiselle Catarine came in walking her Diego. She stopped when she saw us. She…she looked surprised. Shocked. Her eyes got big and she cover up her mouth. She hollered at him. She hollered for him to get off me. He hollered back at her and they do that for a while. I dunno. Then he got up. I think he was going after her. I think he was gonna kill us both! The next thing I know, she had got a hay fork and hit him hard in the head. He tried to get her and she hit him again. This time it stuck in him. It stuck so hard she dropped it. And he fell down hard on the hay fork. After that he didn't move."

"What did you and Catarine do after that?" All eyes were on Bessie and her riveting exposition.

"We just stood there. I kicked him to see if he was still alive but he weren't. I didn't know what to do with no dead man with a hay fork sticking outta his head. But Catarine figured it out. She told me to run get Moses, my brother. So I done that."

"How long were you gone?"

"Gone? About as long as it takes you to take a piss, that's all."

"All right. What happened next?"

"Catarine, she told him 'bout what happen. And that we had to hide him. So he said the best place was right there. In the barn. We both surprised. We just do what he say. We didn't know what else to do. He dug the biggest hole you ever saw, and fast too. Under where we keep the grain barrels. He rolled them away and dug that hole. He say that a good place. Ain't nobody ever gonna find him there."

"Anything else about that night?"

"Well, nothing much. 'Cept we said our good-byes. Me 'n Catarine. She wanted to run away from the Koch's anyway," Bessie said looking over longingly to Catarine. "Cuz they awful people."

"Objection! The witness has no idea what was in the mind of the defendant."

"Overruled. Can you please restrict your remarks to what you did, Ms. Bessie?" the judge asked.

"All right, Ms. Bessie. I have a few more questions for you," Josiah said nicely. He was pleased that she had done so well but knew the worse was to come. Bessie, looking up at Josiah with expectant eyes, remained still with her hands folded. "Was this something Mason had done before? Grabbing you?"

"Oh yessir. He done that all the time."

"The grabbing, right? But not the rape?"

"He ain't never before told me to take my clothes off. Or throwed me down in the hay, if that's what you mean. Or the other..."

"Yes, Ms. Bessie, that's exactly what I mean. But he was always touching you."

"Yessir."

"And did you like him touching you."

"No sir!" her voice trembled slightly as she shook her head and began her nervous rocking.

"You've stated that you and Catarine were friends. Do you know if she loved Mason?"

"Objection! This would be speculation, your honor," Thatcher complained.

"Sustained, you'll need to re-word that, Mr. Butler!"

"Bessie, did Catarine ever share with you how she felt about Mason Dupre?"

"Yessir, she did." Bessie looked out at Catarine. They exchanged the sad, intimate stare of two people who knew each other well and had been through hell together.

"From what she's told you, how did she feel about Mason."

Bessie cleared her throat and looked afraid. She looked at Josiah and out over the vast number of people, mostly white faces. Looking back at Catarine, she took a deep breath and mumbled, "She hated him."

"You'll need to speak up, Bessie," Josiah said kindly.

"She hated him!" Bessie said too loudly to Josiah and then began to cry softly into her hands.

The crowd took this as their cue to begin talking. The judge's gavel made Bessie jump and stop crying as Josiah hushed her.

"I'm almost done, Ms. Bessie. Just a few more questions."

"All right."

"Do you know why she hated him? Did he treat her…"

"Objection! This is too much speculation, your honor. Let's just hear from the defendant herself!" Catarine looked at Josiah who didn't return her gaze.

He'd said it wasn't a good idea for her to take the stand. She'd be nervous but she longed to tell her story.

"Overruled, Mr. Butler," the judge had been shifting in his wooden chair and it creaked with the load. Catarine was afraid he'd put off the rest of Bessie's testimony yet another day. "Are you done?"

"I have another question, your honor."

"Please, get on with it."

"Bessie, why did Catarine kill Mason? Was she jealous or protecting you?"

To Bessie's credit she said loudly, over the sound of the gavel and Thatcher objections, "Oh, she was protecting me, sir! That's for sure."

The cross-examination by Thatcher was brutal. He asked poor Bessie several different ways if she had experienced relations with Mason or any man before that night. And despite Josiah's plentiful objections, Thatcher was able to cast doubt upon her alleged virginity as if she were the one on trial. He mocked her relationship with Catarine. He claimed it was all in her head, a slave owner's ploy to get more work out of "poor dumb Negroes". Catarine felt sick to her stomach as she watched her friend wilt before her, the strength she had mustered only minutes before knocked back down at the hands of the arrogant Thatcher Preleme.

"I'm assuming, what you don't want to tell the court, is that you were having relations in the hay that night. Am I correct, Ms. Bessie!" He asked in his most pompous manner as he strutted back and forth between her and the jury.

"No!" she cried desperately.

"No, you didn't? Are you sure?"

"I, er…"

"Speak up! Did you do the act or not that night?" He looked back on her like she was a bug to be squashed.

"No, Catarine stopped us."

"Well, isn't that a pity for you?" Thatcher paraded back and forth smiling. Catarine and Bessie both looked upon him with revulsion. "It's a pity because you would have been able to do what you own momma did." The look of confusion on Bessie's face told Catarine that Bessie hadn't known the truth that her own mother had just revealed to her. Bessie had been just as oblivious as she had been for all these years.

"What?" Bessie asked without thinking.

"You heard me. If Catarine hadn't stopped the two of you that night, you might have been able to have a white man's child. The Master's child. Like yourself." He turned abruptly on Bessie and pointed her out with his outstretched arm, branding her an illegitimate child for all to see.

All hell broke loose. Catarine slumped over, crying uncontrollably into her arms. Her mother, trying to stand up and leave the courtroom, fainted next to Mr. Koch who simply laid her down with a look of rage on his face. Everyone in the lower and upper floors exploded in conversation. No one minded Judge Cardena's gavel.

"I'm not done!" Thatcher yelled. "I have more questions."

"You're done for now!" the judge yelled, red faced and rising from his chair. He was still using his gavel but realized it was useless. "Court adjourned until two o'clock!"

When Catarine reentered the courtroom that afternoon, she thought she was dreaming again. There were the crowds as before, perhaps her mother had even returned after her spell; but the only person Catarine was able to see seated on the bench a few rows behind the defense table was Louis Fontaine. She froze and faced his wistful face, full of happiness and mixed with concern, as he rose in his place. She knew it wasn't a dream though, because of the mustache he'd grown since she saw him last. Catarine tried to break free from the deputy who walked with her, but he wouldn't relinquish his grasp. So, she reached out her arms towards Louis, facing him squarely on, the entire courtroom watching, as he ran up to embrace her over the partition that divided the defendant desk from the crowd.

The trial continued with Bessie on the stand again, her tormentor, Thatcher at her side. The gavel cracked through the thick, July afternoon air and started their afternoon. Judge Cardena simply nodded to Thatcher to start. He began with a review of Bessie's morning testimony, as if anyone could forget, as he pranced around on stage.

"Thatcher, ask your questions of the witness," the judge admonished him.

"I really have just one question, Ms. Bessie," he took a kindly tone but it seemed laced with venom. "Just why did you all need to hide the body?" Folks started talking again quietly. Judge Cardena hammered down his gavel with force.

"The court will come to order! No further chatter will go on in this courtroom, do you hear? Or I'll have you all thrown out! Proceed, Mr. Preleme."

"Ms. Bessie, please tell me, why you didn't call for Master Koch? If this was an accident, if our defendant had been protecting you. Why bury the body? It seems to me you had something to hide. I'm not sure I believe you at all! Sounds like all one big ole lie to me." Thatcher walked over to the jury when he spoke and looked at them face to face as if they were his friends. He snickered and shook his head when he looked back to Bessie. She drew a dry tongue over her parched lips, mouth breathing, then stared at the prosecutor while he berated her to the jury. "I mean, folks, can you all honestly believe anything a Negro says?"

"Objection!" Josiah cried. But Judge Cardena was right on it with his gavel, pounding out justice. Boom, boom, boom!

"Mr. Preleme, you are questioning the witness, not addressing the jury. And I've had just about enough of you."

"All right, your honor," he said to the judge. And turning back to Bessie, said, "Why did you all bury the body?"

"I, I…" she swallowed hard and her breathing continued to be laborious. "I dunno, sir."

"That's all I have then." Thatcher said to everyone in court, arms held up in exasperation.

"You may step down." The judge instructed Bessie who looked like she was about to drop to the floor. She managed to ease herself from the witness box and stumble back to her seat. Catarine watched her sadly and then just stared at the floor. She wondered what Louis was thinking and wished she could tell him all that had occurred so far. She wanted to turn around and look for her mother but even strength to do that seemed tremendous.

"The prosecution would like to call Frederick Fuhrmann to the stand, your honor," Thatcher Preleme said matter of factly. The news sent a shockwave through Catarine. She turned to Josiah and gave him a panicked look.

"You've been a longtime family friend, is this correct?"

"Yes, I've known the Kochs for seven years now. Ever since they married."

"In what capacity?"

"As the family solicitor. However, I've taken many a meal at the family table and have been able to observe interactions between all of them."

"Would you say you are a neutral observer, Mr. Fuhrmann?"

"Absolutely!"

"You have no reward, monetary or otherwise by giving this testimony?"

"That's correct, Mr. Preleme."

"I have a few questions about what you've observed. Would you say that Mason Koch was a polite young man and that he was fair-minded in his dealings with his slaves?"

"Absolutely not. The opposite is true."

"What did you say?" Preleme swung around on him with his mouth hanging open.

"He was a scoundrel. Everyone knew that! And his father is one too!"

"But, but this isn't what we agreed upon! You tricked me!" Thatcher Preleme yelled at Fuhrmann.

"Yes, but I wasn't under oath then. I am now and I'm telling the truth to this court!"

"You, you!" Thatcher approached Fuhrmann with fists clenched about to deliver a punch, but thought better of it while Fuhrmann sat in the witness box as calm and cool as a spring morning. Catarine was delighted in spite of herself. She looked at Josiah hopefully who sat gathering his thoughts.

"Mr. Butler, do you have any questions for the witness?"

"I most certainly do," Josiah said as he sprang up and approached Frederick. Catarine was boundlessly excited. She wanted to question him! She prayed under her breath for Josiah to ask the right questions. Please! "You've stated that you were well acquainted with the family."

"That's correct."

"Were you able to observe interactions between Mason and Catarine?"

"Yes."

"Can you describe those?"

"On many occasions, Mason made inappropriate remarks to her. Remarks about them being a pair, when in fact they weren't. And several times I noted that he grabbed her to kiss her. She always pushed him away."

"But weren't they a couple?" Josiah looked back at Catarine who closed her eyes and frowned.

"Yes, technically. The last month before his death, Mr. Koch told Catarine that she would have to marry Mason or leave the plantation. I believe she agreed just to buy herself some time. Until she decided what she really wanted to do."

"You told Mr. Preleme that Mason was a scoundrel. What do you mean by that?"

"He was an insolent young man. He was unfair to the slaves and beat them for little or no reason, as did his father. He also was a skirt chaser. He had been known to fondle most of the young women of the area. You should get some of them up here under oath. Perhaps they'd tell you." Whispers could be heard about the courtroom.

"Thank-you, Mr. Fuhrmann. You've been very helpful."

As they moved to their seats, Josiah looked at Thatcher who had recoiled down to an insignificant heap of bones and tweed propped up with effort at his table. Josiah smiled and thought that Thatcher did indeed look as if he had had his last cry.

Judge Cardena thanked and dismissed the jury for the day. As they rose to leave the courtroom, Koch suddenly jumped up and yelled at them, red faced "If you don't convict her, I will!" He was subdued and thrown to the ground by deputies as everyone left the courtroom.

Despite Josiah's assurance that Bessie had indeed done very well and that Fuhrmann's surprise testimony had greatly assisted their case, Catarine couldn't help feeling that all was lost and that she'd hang for murder. They were relying on the jury, all men with whom Thatcher had been so friendly, hanging on his even word. She'd watched them. They couldn't take their eyes off of him. And when Josiah spoke, they had looked unconvinced, pondering his words, but only just so. It would take an act of God to release her from the evil noose Thatcher had lain around her neck. And what's more, no one was allowed to visit. Josiah explained that she'd had a rash of requests, Louis among them, to visit. He, Josiah, thought that Koch might have been one of them as well and also reporters begged for interviews for pamphlets. They were being written and in demand. But with Koch trying to see her, the judge being concerned for her safety, had declared that no one could visit. She was alone with her thoughts and prayers. Alone save Josiah, who tried his best to be an encouragement.

Josiah Butler was a praying man. In fact, he not only prayed, he read the Good Book that he kept on his desk. And it was to this Book that he referred for help with this case. He, being raised in the North, was appalled at Thatcher afresh during this trial. What's more, Josiah was astounded at the racial bigotry he saw before him. He knew the subject of slavery was a hotly contested one in the entire country and that in New Orleans, being the center for slave trading, it was an accepted practice. He felt the tradition continued more for economic reasons versus outright hatred and distrust. But what he saw at the trial disturbed him. He wanted to do more than hope that the jury would believe Bessie's testimony. Fuhrmann's would help, no doubt, but he wanted to go a step further. And he felt it to be both his civic, professional, and moral duty to do so. The evening before he was to present his closing argument to the jury was one of the hardest he endured so far in his career. He agonized over his speech for hours on end. And he cried out to God to give him convincing words to say, words that would prick the hearts of the men on the jury to see the truth.

The blasted dreams had come back, and with a vengeance. Catarine tossed and turned each night with dreams of Koch beating the poor dark mare. It was always midnight. She was always awakened by the sound of neighing and the stomping of hooves on the ground beneath her open window. She would see Koch stringing up the poor horse for a beating. Then she'd be instantly down at the tree and helpless to stop him, his eyes wild with fury as he delivered one blow after the next to the beautiful helpless creature. She always woke up shaking and feeling sick to her stomach. When would they ever end?

She didn't even remember walking in. But she did remember her mother's lovely face and the look she gave her as she sat down. Catarine saw Louis too. He was in the background, kind Louis with Bessie at his side. How wonderful that was! They were gathered around her, behind her on this monumental day.

While Thatcher spoke, Catarine willed herself not to listen. She focused straight ahead of her to the broad wood carving upon which the judge sat perched in his place. The eagle of justice. It had been there all along, carved into the wood, watching over them all in this courtroom. The final arguments, as they were called, were to be given on that concluding day. The jury listened as Thatcher, back to his old manner of ridicule, berated her and lied to the jury. And again, he gasped about the very idea of allowing a black slave to give testimony in a court of law. Catarine ventured a quick glance at the jury and noted that several were watching her for the first time.

Josiah rose slowly from his seat to face the jury with a grave expression, stating to them that it was a solemn day. And he urged them to realize the gravity, the weight of their decision that day by listening carefully to his words. He told them they were taking the place of God Himself and as such must seek His guidance and know His wishes in this matter. He spoke of the swearing in of witnesses and how it was an act before the Almighty.

"We all must believe as gospel truth the words of anyone who places their hand on this Bible and swears to tell the truth, because they've then put their eternal soul into God's hands and He, my friends, is the judge on the matter of truthfulness. And as far as the *slave* girl goes, well, that should go without saying. But I will say it, or read it from the Good Book you've all sworn upon. It's time to cast away stones. The matter of the equality of man is covered clearly in the Bible." Several jurors looked at each other and folks shifted in their seats throughout the courtroom.

"'And having put on the new man, which is renewed in the knowledge after the image of him that created him. There is neither Greek nor Jew, slave nor free; but Christ is all, and in all.'" Josiah read from the Bible that he picked up from Judge Cardena's desk. Then shut it softly.

He then looked into the face of each man on the jury. "Neither slave nor free," he repeated. They returned his gaze as if they were in church that morning. "So you see, my friends, we are *all* created in the image of God. Skin color doesn't matter. We've had it all wrong here. Mason Koch wouldn't have died if he'd understood that. And Catarine Dupre wouldn't have needed to protect her friend from being attacked that night."

They allowed her mother in that evening. It was, after all, her last night. The trial was over and the jury was deliberating. The waiting was horrible. They spoke very little. She lay on her bed with her head in her mother's lap. Marie Dupre Koch had grown up herself during the ordeal. She'd faced down her own husband, risking his daily wrath just coming to the trial and most especially coming to see her daughter who had killed his son. She had even taken it upon herself to meet this Louis Fontaine man. And she was protecting Bessie as best she could. But she didn't want to burden her daughter with any of this. She wanted to be strong for her. Her daily prayers for strength were being answered miraculously, and she hoped beyond reason that the jury would see the truth and set Catarine free.

Louis was determined not to miss one more minute in the life of Catarine Dupre. He tried to gain entrance into the jail to visit her only to be turned away. He decided it would be best to stick around near the courthouse until the verdict came in. He had seen the man Fuhrmann in New York City briefly when he came to warn Catarine at the Woerner's. And he'd witnessed Frederick Fuhrmann again on the witness stand himself. Thanks to Bessie, who showed him who Koch was, he knew who to look for walking about town. Louis was nervous but optimistic about the outcome. Everywhere he went, he heard people on the streets and in shops talk of nothing else but the Dupre trial. Everyone seemed to be enraptured with the entire affair, many hopeful for Catarine's acquittal.

Louis wanted to speak to this Frederick Fuhrmann but each time he saw him he had a throng of people around him. Fuhrmann seemed to be hanging about for the verdict like the rest of New Orleans society. If he was annoyed at his instant popularity, it didn't show. He sat calm and collected and spoke to groups of people, anyone who would listen, and repeat his diatribe about the Koch men. The man must have had a vendetta against them from how he went on about them. Louis did what any artist would do. He observed the crowd and he sketched people.

It was late that same afternoon, when tensions were high, that Koch came around the rear of the Le Febre building and saw Fuhrmann casually berating his son to a couple of reporters. Louis had positioned himself nearby in the shade of an oak to sketch the crowd as they gathered in front of a fascinating cast-iron motif.

"You swine!" Koch yelled at him. "I've had enough of you, Fuhrmann!"

"Settle down, Koch! I'm only speaking the truth. You know how bad your son was."

"You are tarnishing his name!"

"He tarnished his own name."

"I'll kill you."

"Is that a threat?"

"It is, you dog."

"I'd really like to shut you up, Koch."

"To the Oaks, Fuhrmann. What's stopping us?"

"You'll be sorry, you miscreant," was Fuhrmann's answer as the crowd rumbled with delight. And with that they began walking away en masse. Louis followed along until they all came to a field nearby with large oak trees spread out, shading a large grassy area. The two men stood back to back adjusting their own pistols as the throng of onlookers took to either side, out of the line of fire.

"Twenty-paces," Koch hollered out as they stood and placed their weapons down at their side. Koch moved first and the crowd counted as the two men marched their allotted length. Fuhrmann was the first to turn and did so with lightning speed. As they faced each other, standing stock still, the crowd hushed except for the cry of a baby being jostled by its mother. Louis noted that they both had an intense barbarous gleam about them but it was Fuhrmann who raised his gun and shot Koch down, with such marvelous dispatch, that Louis jumped in spite of knowing it was coming.

Fuhrmann was standing above him in an instant as he bled in spurts from his upper thigh. "I'd never kill you, Koch, for I'm no fool. But you, sir, are the king of fools."

To her credit, Catarine was able to walk inside the courtroom both strong and in peace. She paused before sitting to see the huge crowd that had gathered in the courtroom that day, both blacks upstairs hugging the balcony, and the whites with a few colored folks mixed in below. She made eye contact with her loved ones. Her mother and Bessie sat next to each other. Louis was farther in the back but she picked him out of the crowd easily. She took a deep breath, turned around to face the judge then sat down when instructed.

She barely remembered anything until Judge Cardena asked for the verdict from the foreman of the jury. Josiah held her hand as the jury foreman stood to answer to the judge.

"Innocent," were his sweet words. She felt warmth surge through her entire body. The crowd broke into merriment, much to her surprise. The judge allowed her mother and Bessie to come forward with embraces. Louis followed them and when he approached, she threw her arms around his neck and wept.

Oh how dreams do come true! We all got our Catarine back. I didn't scarce believe it when they say the word "innocent." And when we all drove home up there together, no one has ever heard such joy come from a bunch of slaves as was heard that day. And to know Koch was shot down too. Oh, glory be! The Good Lord do answer prayers.

Chapter 14

When they left the courtroom that day, she, a free woman, flanked by Louis, her mother and Bessie, Catarine couldn't believe her eyes. People were in the streets cheering. Bessie laughed out loud. Black slaves waved white handkerchiefs over their heads as they walked past.

The carriage awaiting them had Frederick Fuhrmann next to it with news. They all got on for the ride back to Magnolia Plantation. Despite the blessed relief of freedom, Catarine wondered where Koch was and plans stirred in her head to get him away from her mother as soon as possible. Fuhrmann's news proved interesting. He had shot Koch on the dueling grounds. He wasn't dead but had bled out profusely. Koch had been taken to a hospital and was recovering there. Her mother didn't cry for her husband. Fuhrmann offered them his assistance and protection, should Koch regain his strength. They thanked him profusely and then were on their way.

"We've got the plantation to think of," was all Marie said when Louis offered sympathy for her husband's accident.

"And plenty of good help," Catarine said.

Marie said. "Demetrius and Moses are handling things there, and they all want to see you, Catarine!"

"I'm so anxious to see them too! It's been an entire year!"

Work fell in place for all, with Catarine riding out as her father had done each morning, observing the cutting and speaking to all the workers, kindly asking about their families, their health and checking to see if all was well on their farm. She trained Louis straight away to do many things: the ordering, purchasing, and the books. And he immediately took governance of the horses, as he had experience with them and could manage their care.

Catarine and Marie went over the books. Catarine was surprised at how quickly her mother picked up the arithmetic. Koch's system had been different from her father's but at least he had a system and it was in order. They all took to spying out the crannies and crevices of the house, outhouses, and barn only to find a good store of weaponry they had not known about. Abraham Dupre had stored cash in the wine cellar which the women had guarded and brooded over regularly but kept his guns mounted and ready. Koch had a few guns handy but the guns they'd found were thought, Marie said, to be Mason's and not his father's.

It was a cool evening and Louis had prepared a quiet meal. It was something he learned in Baltimore. A simple pate from canned fish they'd spread over the bread freshly baked by the cook that morning. And they'd have a glass of wine. Marie was away at friends for the night. But she knew all about it. In fact, she'd given Louis her blessing and her old ring. They both hoped Catarine would be surprised and pleased.

"Let's dine on the porch tonight," Louis suggested when Catarine came down from washing up. It had been a long day for both of them, she visiting the fields late, riding out on her old horse Diego, whom she had missed tremendously. "The breeze is so refreshing coming off the river."

"I'd like that," Catarine said. "Shall we ask Bessie to join us?"

"No, let's just savor our evening together. Alone."

"All right," Catarine said smiling, looking up from the ledger she'd brought into the parlor where they were sitting. Louis looked over from the window and smiled to her.

"I can't remember the last time we were alone."

"Have we ever really been alone?" Catarine asked.

"Actually, I think not," Louis said coming over to her. He took the ledger out of her hand and pulled her to him. "That's why I intend to make this a notable occasion, my dear."

He kissed her softly at first and she smiled during each pleasurable stroke. Then their kisses became mutual, she kissing him too and pressing herself into him. After a time, he guided her on to the parlor settee where they stayed for a while.

Finally, Louis said, "I need some wine. I've gotten us a bottle."

"But I need more kisses," Catarine laughed and she pulled him back on top of her. Louis encircled his arm around her, and kissed her again. It was Bessie who interrupted them.

"Louis, are you…" she said coming into the parlor. It was Catarine who jumped up the fastest. They all looked at each other embarrassed, then laughed out loud. Bessie said backing away, "No, shoot, I can go back to the kitchen."

"No, Bessie!" Catarine said. "We are just…" And they laughed again.

"Bessie, I think we are ready for supper," Louis said. Then both the women looked at Louis with eyebrows raised and laughed again.

"Tell cook to bring it. You're my sister, remember. We must get you established in the room by me soon. I'll speak to Maman again."

"You think so?" Bessie's laughter changed to a look of confusion. "I'll get your suppa. I don't mind."

"And please, bring another bottle of wine!" Louis begged as he sat down on the settee red-faced. "How distressing!"

"I need some fresh air!" Catarine let herself out the parlor door and onto the front porch. Louis joined her and they sat in the swing until Bessie arrived with the wine, placing it carefully on the small table. Oaks lined the passageway between the front porch and the Mississippi River levee creating a tunnel through which a pleasant gentle wind passed.

After a time, Louis spoke as he poured them wine at the small dining table. "Catarine, I have something for you."

"What is it? I love surprises!"

"Your mother said you did. I'm quite happy about that. You've seen this surprise before. Only it wasn't yours. Now it will be."

"What? Whatever could it be?"

"Well, first I must ask you a question," Louis said getting down on one knee in front of her at the table. She narrowed her eyes at him curiously.

"Louis! What are you doing?"

"Catarine, will you be my wife?"

"When?"

"I, I, I don't know when. What kind of question is that?"

"It's cutting season."

"I'm well aware of that!" he said annoyed. "Do you want to marry me or not?"

"Well, yes, of course I do! Who else would I marry?"

"How romantic."

"That's not what I meant."

"Do you love me?"

"Yes."

"Good! Thank God!"

"I'm sorry, I'm not very good at this sort of thing. Shall we start over?"

"No," Louis sat back on the porch chair looking dejected. "I love you, Catarine and I long to make you my wife. Don't you feel the same way?"

"I love you too, Louis. Truly I do. But I don't want to marry straight away. Can we wait awhile?"

"I'll wait for you forever. If you'll promise to be my wife."

"All right then! I just don't want to marry yet."

"It's settled then. We are engaged to be married."

"Yes, I agree," Catarine said smiling. "What is my surprise?"

"If you don't care for it, you must tell me. I'll remedy it," Louis said withdrawing her mother's old diamond ring from his breast pocket and put it on her ring finger. "Do you remember this?"

"Barely, but yes. And there is no need for remedy. How wonderful! I see now, you've spoken to my mother about our engagement." Catarine hugged Louis so very tightly. "I do truly love you, Louis. And everything is perfect!"

Jacob Koch rose from the hospital bed with vengeance on his mind. In his mind, he vowed retaliation for sins against him, or what he perceived had been done to him. When released from his stay, notification was made, as requested by the authorities. Fuhrmann was made aware. There had been no point in talking to Koch as he recovered from his deadly wound. But it was critical to stop him now, before he reached the objects of his revenge. Fuhrmann knew just how to get rid of him. For good.

"Maman, are you happy?" Catarine asked Marie at her dressing table early the next morning. "I was so surprised."

"Yes, I'm so pleased! It will be a delight to plan a wedding, after all the horror of that trial."

"Oh, I do want to wait a while though."

"Whatever for?"

"I don't know," Catarine looked at her mother sadly. "I can't explain it really. So much has happened."

"Too much."

"And there are still things I don't know."

Marie sat wondering about her wounded husband. She knew she would have to see him again. Things at the farm had changed back to how they were when her first husband had been alive. Catarine was running everything with the same fair-mindedness that Abraham had done. The slaves were happy. Things were going well. She prayed Jacob wouldn't return and ruin it all. He and Catarine would sorely disagree.

Catarine hadn't planned on marrying yet, the notion had taken her by surprise. She was still grieving the loss of Daria. Everything else had been restored to her. Her mother and the farm. Her sister Bessie. Her sister! She was riding again and that was wonderful. But no Daria. A bitter pill indeed. And if Koch returned, she was planning on sending him away. She wasn't going to put up with any nonsense. She'd call the law if he caused any trouble. She'd call Fuhrmann. She now realized she could trust him.

Koch made his way around New Orleans looking for and asking about Fuhrmann. He ran into dead ends at each bar and tavern along with each solicitor's office in which he entered. Odd. Suddenly, no one knew anything about the man that everyone knew. Koch didn't understand that. And he didn't notice the odd man followed him everywhere he went.

When Catarine returned from riding out that morning, she untacked and released Diego to the paddock and went around by the slave quarters to see the state of their affairs. She usually did this every few days but hadn't yet that week. As she made her way around house to house, she stopped to play with the children that ran about in the yard. Several of the mothers were at the cane pots, stirring and keeping the kids away.

"Good morning, Lisette," she greeted one of the mothers. "How are y'all doing?"

"We're fine, Mz. Cat'rine."

"How are the children?"

"They be fine too."

"Do you need anything?"

"My husband's shoes be coming apart. His feet be blistered at night."

"All right. We'll see about that." As they spoke, they all heard the sound of a gun firing from down the road. "What's that?" Catarine ran around to see but couldn't find the source of the noise.

Entering the house, she saw her mother had returned from her errand in the city.

"Mother, did you hear that?"

"Hear what?"

"The gun fire?"

"No," Marie answered confused, rising up from her desk in the parlor. "Catarine, I have wonderful news!" Catarine stood looking out the front window through the curtains.

"You'll never guess what…" her mother started.

"It's Koch!" Catarine yelled. "Get the guns. Where's Louis?" Marie ran to the window that Catarine had just left. She looked pale and terrified. Catarine ran to retrieve the mounted gun.

"Koch," Catarine confronted him at gunpoint from the front porch. "What are you doing here?"

"I'm here to get what belongs to me," Koch said to Catarine bitterly.

"And what might that be?"

"Move aside." Koch said coming up on the porch and entering the house. He paused for a moment and looked at Marie who just stood staring at him from the parlor door. He went upstairs to their bedroom. Catarine followed him still holding the gun on him.

"What do you want, you better tell me now, Koch!" Catarine yelled at him.

She watched him as he began looking around the room, holding a saddle bag. He unlatched it and proceeded to load his clothes inside. He then stormed out of the room, ignoring her. She followed him downstairs.

"I want my horse," he said in a kinder tone to Marie as she stood frozen at the door. "That's all." She nodded her head. Then he turned to face Catarine. "And as far as you go, missy, you get outta my way. You haven't seen the last of me! I'm getting my revenge. You mark my words!"

"Get outta here, Koch. And don't ever come back. You aren't welcomed here. This is the Dupre home."

"Yes, it is," Marie spoke up. "I didn't think you were coming back here, Jacob. But go. And take your horse." And with that

Koch marched off to the barn, saddled up his own gelding and rode away.

"That was easier than I thought," Catarine said to her mother who had a somber look on her face.

Louis had returned from out back during the discourse between Koch and Catarine. He had pulled out his own pistol when he saw that Catarine was holding a rifle on Koch. He wasn't taking any chances. They all went up on the porch to cool off and relax after Koch left. "I wonder why he left without a fight?"

"I know. And that's what I was about to tell you," Marie said snapping to attention.

"What do you mean, mother?"

"That business I had in New Orleans. A woman stepped forward to buy the plantation."

"But we didn't want to sell it! Mother! How could you?"

"Two women, actually. We did sell it, Catarine," her mother said matter-of-factly, looking satisfied between Louis and her daughter. "They bought it with the stipulation that Koch would leave for good. And he agreed to leave town."

"What?" Catarine sat blinking at her mother. "So, he knew about the sale? They paid him to go?"

"Yes, they paid him off."

"That means he will never come back."

"Yes," Marie spoke as if to convince herself.

"He agreed to that?

"Yes. And all the slaves. They bought their freedom."

"Who, who would do that?"

"It was a free colored woman named Rochon. Rose Rochon."

Catarine's face went white and she felt suddenly faint.

"Auntie Rose! That's Auntie Rose!" Catarine got up, disoriented and trying to steady herself, holding her hands up to her heart.

"You know her?" Marie was aghast.

"Yes, I know her! Who was the other woman? You said there were two women."

"I don't remember the other one's name. But it's on the papers, if you want to examine them."

Catarine nearly fell over herself getting into the parlor, to the desk where the newly signed papers lay. Her mother and Louis followed her in, all in a frenzy of excitement. There at the bottom of the legal document were two signatures: Rose Rochon and Daria Morinay.

"It's Daria! She's alive! Oh, Louis!"